Restart Again
Volume 1

Written By: Adam Ladner

Art By: @TsukiZuramaru

Table of Contents

1. REINTEGRATION
2. FIRST ENCOUNTERS
3. JOG MY MEMORY
4. LESSONS OF THE PAST
5. NEW HORIZONS
6. CHANGE OF PLANS
7. UNITY
8. A PLAN IN MOTION
9. REUNIONS
10. THE LONG ROAD HOME
11. HOME
12. HONESTY
13. PREPARATION
14. PRACTICE
15. WHAT THE FUTURE HOLDS
16. ON COMBAT AND MAGIC
17. WHO YOU REALLY ARE
18. THE FRUITS OF OUR LABORS
19. FINAL EXAM

1. REINTEGRATION

The terribly familiar feeling of weightlessness whipped at my stomach as the darkness around me flashed away, replaced instantly with swirling, disorienting colors and shapes. I clenched my eyes shut, which only worsened the sickness I felt in my gut but offered a small relief from the assault of multi-colored lights. My ears were ringing as the sound of a howling wind raged past, adding to the feeling that I was falling down into an unending void.

Anything is better than that darkness...that void.

I shouted something angrily, shaking my head back and forth, but the words were whisked away into the storm. I fought desperately against the assault on my senses as I tumbled headfirst through nothingness.

I'm almost through. Just a few more seconds...

My knees braced instinctively to catch myself from a drop I knew was coming. Even through my eyelids, I could tell the flashing was getting brighter, and the screaming storm around me reached a fevered pitch.

With a final blinding flash and a small *pop,* everything changed. I landed on my feet with practiced grace as if I had only fallen a few inches. Opening my eyes, I found myself standing before a massive cobblestone wall. It stood at least two stories high, casting an imposing shadow as it stretched out into the distance on either side of me, curving off out of sight. Merlons stood atop the wall with arrow slits dotting their faces. Immediately to my right stood a large wooden gate guarded by two men holding spears, clad in dull iron armor. A queue, starting at the guards and following a well-worn road out behind me, bustled anxiously.

The people in line were as varied as I had ever seen: a pair of tanned, burly men with dark hair and roughspun clothes tapped their feet impatiently behind a hunched, grey-bearded man who seemed to be showing the guards a crystal ball which swirled with smoke and a pulsing purple light. Next in line was a wagon filled with casks, driven by a slim, pale man and pulled by what looked to be a pair of oxen, only with one large, straight horn on the front of their heads. After them came a half dozen women wearing aprons and plain dresses, all carrying baskets of apples on their shoulders; they were followed by a man with furry, vulpine ears pointed up above his head and a bushy grey tail behind him. He pushed a wheelbarrow filled with a strange lavender colored hay.

I sighed heavily, furrowing my brow as I looked up at the bright blue sky above me. *Medieval era. Demihumans. Magical items. Temperate climate. Overall, typical high-fantasy fare.*

"FUCK!" I cursed, too loudly. The group of women nearby jumped and looked concernedly in my direction. One of the guards looked up from the old man, cocking an eyebrow as he observed me.

"Oi! Get to the back of the line, or I'll give you something to yell about!" He shared a laugh with the guard beside him.

I rolled my eyes at him. "Get stuffed, loser," I muttered, not particularly quietly. With an exaggerated turn, I paced towards the back of the line. Many of the people gave me suspicious looks as I passed, though I couldn't tell if it was due to my outburst or something about me physically. As I reached the back of the line, a few dozen people deep from the main gate, I realized I hadn't physically taken stock of myself. A quick glance at my vestments confirmed my theory; I definitely did not fit in with the local fashion here.

Still dressed the same. At least the rules are consistent, so far. The thought was comforting in a way, though it was still tinged with bitterness. Reflexively, I reached back and pulled the hood of my cloak up over my head. Made from a soft and supple fabric, colored a rich, deep black, and hemmed with quicksilver embroidery, the garment flowed down my back to my calves. Although it was a bright summer-feeling day, I nestled deeper into the cloak, feeling comfortably cool. *Enchantments carried over, too. Good to know. If magic is as common as I think it is in this world, I should probably try and stack those as much as possible before I...*

I shuddered and let the thought fade without completing it. *Focus. Take stock. Wallow in your self-pity later,* I chided myself. Looking down briefly, I was pleased to find the rest of my effects were also intact. A boiled leather chestpiece, dyed a dark blue and chased with the same quicksilver pattern as my cloak. A black bandolier with four silver globes, each about the size of a chicken's egg, which clinked softly as I ran my hand across them. Slung in the opposite direction across my back, a blue and silver scabbard for a hand-and-a-half sword, currently empty. A black and silver belt with a rather heavy coin purse attached at my hip. I quickly pulled it off my belt to peek inside and was satisfied by the gold and silver coins flashing back at me. My boots, comfortable and broken in with clear signs of use, still seemed—

"Oi!" A voice cut through my meandering thoughts of personal inventory. I had apparently been moving forward unconsciously with the rest of the line and was now face to face with the guards at the gate. The man on the left, standing almost equal height with me at over six feet tall, scoffed as I came to my senses. Beneath his helmet I saw he had a badly crooked nose, most likely from being broken too many times. Blonde, greasy hair fell down over his eyes. "Now, what's a fancy lad like yourself doing out here with the common folk?"

I shrugged half-heartedly. "Doesn't really matter, right? I'm just trying to enter with everybody else."

"Oh, well you see, that's where you're wrong, friend." The guard had a devious twinkle in his eye and sarcasm laced his words. "This gate here's the Trader's Gate. Imperial Law says, to pass through the Trader's Gate, you gotta be a trader." He looked me up and down with comically overblown movements. "He doesn't look like much of a trader, does he?"

"No, can't say he does." Chortled the other guard. He was a short, fat man with a bristling moustache and a vacant expression. "Can't say he does at all."

I sighed deeply, sensing where the conversation would be headed next. "Gentlemen, I'm sure we can come to some agreement." I reached down and slowly pulled the coin purse from my belt, fishing through it carefully. "Maybe we can all agree I've gone out for a stroll, and my goods have already been delivered inside?" My fingers felt the familiar coins within the pouch, but a realization froze my hand. *This isn't the currency of this world. I don't even know what an appropriate bribe would be.* I settled on two silver coins, drawing them slowly from the bag and handing them to the tall guard.

A grin quickly flashed across his face, and I knew I had guessed correctly. He turned the coins in his hand, and after a moment of observation, the grin disappeared as his brow furrowed. "This isn't Imperial currency..." Squinting, he eyed me more closely. "Where you from, boy?"

I smiled pleasantly, hiding my growing disdain as best I could. "Far away from here, friend. Though, I have to say, silver is silver, no? I'm sure a discerning man such as yourself would know where to spend it."

"Aye..." The guard leaned down close to his companion to share a series of whispered words and facial expressions I couldn't quite read. He handed a coin to the short man, who admired it eagerly with a large, toothy smile. Eventually, the tall guard straightened, a wry grin on his face. "Aye, we could do that. But it would be well out of our way to do so, and losing valuable time...Well, I'm sure you understand our predicament."

I stood a moment in silence, choking back the bile I felt rising in my throat. *Not five minutes in this damned world and I'm already being gouged!* "Of course, of course." I reached into the purse and withdrew two more silver coins, handing one to each of them. "It's been a pleasure chatting with you, but I really must be going. I have trade affairs to attend to, and people to meet."

The short man laughed stupidly. "Right, right. 'Spose it's time for you to head in." He reached back with the butt of his spear and banged the gate twice. After a short pause, the wicket gate creaked open. "Nice meeting ya."

I nodded silently as I pushed between the two men and headed to the entrance. *I will not forget your faces, assholes.* "Enjoy yer stay in Yoria!" The tall guard called after me, laughing. I grimaced. *Your face, especially.*

Past the gate, a cramped street extended out in three directions. To my left and right, a narrow road with dozens of stable stalls followed the curve of the wall. Ahead, the main road through the gate ran only forty or fifty feet before making a sharp turn and disappearing behind a slightly askew three-story building. The rough cobblestone road was uneven and broken in multiple places. Though I heard the sounds of a large crowd of people, I seemed to be alone at the entrance aside from a young boy sweeping a nearby stall and a single guard sitting disinterestedly on gate duty. Curious, I slowly began to follow the main road towards the noises ahead of me.

The buildings that lined the road on either side were crammed together in a haphazard manner, as if they had been constructed on top of one another whenever the need arose. Many were in a state of disrepair with broken windows, tattered shutters, and extremely faded paint. *It would seem the city of Yoria is not the bustling metropolis I had hoped it was,* I thought to myself in disappointment. *I guess I'll just find a place to sleep, get information on where the real capitol of this place is and leave as soon as-*

As I rounded the corner, I was taken aback by the source of the noise: An enormous open-air market sprawled out in front of me, filled with thousands of people. Stalls of all shapes and sizes were aligned on what looked like a rough grid made of dark blue marble tiles. Small pop-up stands comprised of a single counter and an awning, wagons unhitched from horses and used as storefronts, and more permanent half-building like fixtures with display cases and lock boxes all commingled together, continuing on as far as I could see into the distance. The market spread all the way up to the city wall to my left, and to my right...

My breath hitched in my chest in surprise. As I exited the alleyway into the market proper, I was finally able to see what the tall line of buildings had hidden from me until now. The city expanded for miles in an enormous circle, all seeming to surround an imposing fortress on top of a distant hill. From where I was standing, I could make out lush areas of greenery, sections of lovely multi-colored houses, and even a decently sized lake. More of the city was, I assumed, hidden behind the keep at the center. The sight was truly beautiful and not at all what the ramshackle buildings at the entrance had implied. *Huh. Never judge a book by its cover, I suppose.*

***

2. FIRST ENCOUNTERS

As I wandered through the crowd, I was impressed by the total diversity of the market. The foods for sale had a rich, smoky aroma, with plants and animals I couldn't recognize prepared over roasting spits or chopped up for stews. Random trinkets, clearly imbued with some sort of low magic, flashed and buzzed and zapped with a dazzling array of color. However, it was the people that truly caught my eye.

The crowd was made up mostly of humans, with skin colors ranging from the palest whites to the deepest blacks. Then there were the demihumans. The most common of them among the throngs of people were extremely similar to humans with small animal characteristics: The ears of a cat, dog, or rabbit with a matching tail, short tusks below the nose like a boar, or plumed wings sprouting out where the shoulder blades would be. Beyond that, I caught a glimpse of what looked like a lizardman, standing like a human would, but fully covered in scales with a large tail dragging behind him. I thought I saw a hulking bear-man at one point, but as I approached, it turned out to be a large human man wearing a bear pelt cloak.

Every discovery as I passed through the market left me feeling...nothing. It was all new to me, but I felt no sense of wonder, no thrill of discovery. *This place might be new, but the experience isn't.* I scowled at the thought. How many times had I found myself in this exact situation? Wandering a world I know nothing about, taking in the sights like some sort of vacationer, like it's some sort of amazing adventure?

Three. Three times. Three, god damned, wretched fucking times. I stopped to lean against the post of a fruit stand and rubbed the bridge of my nose in agitation. Why should I wonder at what an amazing world I'm in, when it's just going to be taken away, and replaced with a shiny, brand-fucking-new world to wonder at again? What does it matter what I do, if I'm going to be reset back to square one in the end?

I sighed deeply and took a moment to center myself. *No. Not square one. I've still gained...something, through all this.* I shook my head and kicked off the post as I began my trek through the market again. *I have my gear. I still have my enchantments. Once I have a room, I can see to thoroughly checking over the rest of my kit. Most importantly though, I have knowledge. I know what to do now that I'm here, and I know what NOT to do.*

I noticed the crowd around me had begun to shrink, and I realized I had reached the edge of the giant market square. *I've spent long enough moping, at least for now. Time to take care of the essentials: food, drink, and shelter.* At this end of the pavilion the tiling transitioned into a more commonplace cobbled road leading off towards the center of the city. Various signs hung at the transition, but the writing was completely foreign to me. *Great. Another alphabet to learn.*

Picking a random person out of the crowd, I approached a slight wolf-eared woman in a red dress doing my best to smile pleasantly. "Excuse me, miss? Perhaps you could help me out, I seem to be a bit lost. Is there an inn nearby?" She eyed me suspiciously, no doubt off-put by my out-of-place attire.

"Uhmm, yes. Right up the road, the second corner on your right." She gestured towards a sign hanging right next to me. "That one. Trader's Pavilion Inn. You're...not from around here, are you?"

I chuckled amiably. "You caught me. What gave it away? The clothes, or the illiteracy?"

"Actually, it was the inquiry about where to rent a room. Most people from Yoria don't need to rent rooms, because they...live here?" She grinned wryly, her playful sarcasm plainly written on her face. Her eyes were a bright green, blazing and alive in the late afternoon sun.

Oh, I like this one. I scratched the back of my head and laughed. "I hadn't considered that, but I suppose that's a better tell." I turned to leave and waved over my shoulder. "Thanks for the help, miss!"

"Uhmm, sir?" Her voice called out from behind me. I turned, eyebrow cocked slightly from curiosity. "Tell the innkeeper that you're a friend of Melrose. That'll probably save you a copper or two on ale."

Taken off guard, I stammered an awkward response. "Oh, uh, thanks for that...Melrose? I presume?"

"That's right." She smiled sweetly, then turned and headed towards the pavilion. "Enjoy your stay in Yoria!" Her slim silver tail wagged in what I assumed was a happy motion as she left.

I'm glad to see that not everyone in this world is like the gate guards. With directions to guide me I started down the road towards the inn, a small smile on my face. As I walked, enjoying the warm clear weather, I eventually realized I was grinning like a fool and shook my head to reset my face to its default expression: scowling. *I know what NOT to do.*

I began to worry as time passed that I had somehow missed the turn to the inn. The instructions had been so simple that I expected to find a row of buildings just over the first hill, but after walking for fifteen minutes I was instead entering a beautifully manicured garden. The flora I passed as I continued onwards was fascinating. Slender stalked flowers with dual bulbs at the end, each a different vibrant color. Fruit bearing bushes weighed down with perfectly spherical, glossy green fruits. Trees with trunks so intricately curved and twisted that they were almost certainly designed artistically.

As wonderful as the garden was, I breathed a sigh of relief when it gave way to a wide paved street leading to a city block. Buildings totally unlike those at the trader's gate were aligned neatly along the main road in the distance, with well crafted, intricately shingled houses and boldly lettered signs. Foot traffic increased dramatically as I reached the first intersection and I began to find it difficult to proceed at the leisurely pace I had grown accustomed to in the gardens. Crossing the first intersection, I scanned ahead to find a sign that would hopefully match the one Melrose pointed out to me earlier. *Mental note: Make learning the local alphabet a higher priority.*

On my way towards the second intersection I was distracted by some curious trinkets in a shop window; Glowing crystals of all shapes and colors, a small rack of what I assumed were wands, and various bits of jewelry. Each item had a small tag affixed to it with a few small lines of text, presumably the price or the purpose of the item. I looked up to the shop sign, doing my best to memorize the series of characters. *If magic is as prevalent here as it seems, maybe I should put learning the basics of the system higher on the to-do list as well.*

Soon after the magic shop I came upon the second intersection. Luckily, the sign for the inn was easy to spot, with two universal pictograms displayed prominently on the sign: an overflowing stein and a bed. I pushed through the heavy wooden door, eager to finally find a moment to relax. My senses were completely assaulted by what I had come to know as classic tavern fare. The smell of old ale layered lightly over fresh pipe smoke. Chatter was surprisingly high; as my eyes adjusted to the relatively dark interior, I realized this building extended much further back than I had initially anticipated, and it was filled with at least two dozen people.

    I approached the bar, which appeared to be unattended. There was no visible bell to ring for service, so I took a seat on one of the barstools to wait. Leaning against the counter, I took a moment to scan the room. Immediately apparent to me was the fact that a large majority of the patrons were demihuman. None of them seemed particularly interested in me, which gave me some relief. *So far, the racism in this country seems to be minimal. That's a welcome improvement.*

    The rest of the room appeared standard as far as taverns go. Lots of round tables with stools, a rather cozy fireplace with a large stew pot set over it, and plenty of shady corners for illicit meetings, two of which were currently occupied by solitary, hooded figures. In the center of the room, some of the tables had been pulled back to make room for a small stage area, sitting about a foot above the floor. It was empty except for two stools which currently were unoccupied.

    "What can I get for ya, stranger?" A chipper voice asked from behind the bar, startling me. I spun around quickly and was confused to find the area behind the bar still empty. I heard the clinking of glasses from further down the bar, so I stood up to peer behind the counter. A man, standing not four feet high, was rummaging through a shelf beneath the bar. Running along the baseboard of the bar was a series of step stools, each directly across the bar from a patron's chair. I sat back quickly in my seat, hoping the man didn't see me staring at him.

    "I'm actually looking to get a room here for a couple of nights. A friend of mine recommended I come here; said you'd know her. Melrose?" I said her name, almost as a question. *I hope this isn't some prank to make me look stupid. Should I really be asking for a discount from this stranger, on the word of another stranger?*

    The man's head popped up in front of me suddenly with a wide grin across his face. "Oh, a friend of Melrose's! Any friend of hers is a friend of mine." He held out a small hand. "The name's Sherman, nice to meet ya!"

"The pleasure is all mine, Sherman." I shook his hand and smiled. "So, if I were looking to get a room for...three nights, and maybe some simple meals to eat, how much would I owe you?"

"Ah, straight to business. You really are a friend of Melrose." Sherman chuckled. "We don't have much in the way of food, aside from the stew on the fire that is. Yer welcome to a bowl if you've got a room. Three nights, that'd put ya around...25 crowns, courtesy of Melrose."

I met his stare blankly. After a long pause, I chuckled nervously, pulling out my coin purse. "25 crowns...that would be...about..." I stalled, fishing through the various coins in my bag, none of which had a crown on them. "Well, Sherman, you see..."

"Are ya broke, lad?"

"Well, not technically speaking." I pulled out a copper coin and a silver coin, placed them down gently on the bar, and slid them over to Sherman quietly. He looked from the coins, up to me, and back down to the coins with a wrinkle in his brow. Picking up the silver coin he flipped it in his palm to observe both faces, and then followed suit with the copper.

"Yer REALLY not from around here, are ya?"

"No sir."

Sherman stared me down for a moment, and then burst into laughter. I looked away and pursed my lips as my face darkened. "Oh my, that really tickles me." He tried to regain his composure, wiping a tear from his eye, but another round of laughter caught him unprepared. "I don't mean to make fun of ya lad, but it's a funny situation, right? How far away can ya be from where you don't know what a crown's worth?"

I weighed my options momentarily, settling on a shrug. "Very far away."

"Right, course ya are." He grinned a toothy grin, though it was lacking quite a few teeth. "Listen, seeing as yer a friend of Melrose, I'll help ya out. But in the future, it might not be a great idea to let on you don't know how the world works around here." Sherman nodded towards the patrons behind me. "Some people...they may not play fair with ya, if ya catch my drift."

Damn it, he's right. I should know better than this by now. "I appreciate your help, and your honesty." I gathered my money and placed my coin purse back on my belt. "I didn't realize how difficult it could be to...adjust to a new city."

"Of course, lad, of course." Sherman hopped down from his step stool and rustled through another cabinet, returning with a palmful of coins. He dropped them down on the bar in front of me. I noticed the familiar pattern of copper and silver coinage I had become acquainted with in the past, although the size, shape and imprinting was different.

"So. Yer small coin, that's the crown." He held up one of the copper coins. "We call it that because...well, that's easy to figure out." Indeed, a crown was depicted plainly on both sides of the small coin. "That's mostly what yer gonna be spending around here. Some call 'em coppers, some call 'em crowns, it's all the same."

He moved on to the silver coin, of which there were only a few present. "Yer silver coin is called a stein. Most people, they call 'em 'silver steins'. Guess it just rolls off the tongue, ya know?" He handed me the coin to examine. It actually showed three vessels: A stein, a jeweled goblet, and a small cup. Both sides were, again, the same image. "Now, one of these silvers steins is worth 50 crowns. A bit steep, perhaps, but silver is a lot rarer than copper now isn't it?" I handed the coin back to him, nodding silently.

Sherman leaned in a bit closer and lowered his voice. "Now, I shouldn't really be showin' ya this, but..." He produced a golden coin from his back pocket. "A gold imperium." He didn't offer this coin out to me to take, but instead kept it in his upturned palm. This coin was noticeably more intricate than the others; It was roughly the same size as the other two, but the artwork was much more detailed. It showed what looked to be a massive castle, with an impressive spire in the center. At the top of this spire, a window was punched out through the coin, leaving just a sliver of a hole.

"Impressive, ain't it?" He withdrew the coin and placed it back in his pocket, patting it lightly. "They say the picture is harder to copy this way, 'specially that little window bit. Keeps the counterfeiters away, I 'spose." Carefully, he began to pick up his other coins, silvers first. "One imperium is worth 20 silvers. That one coin in my back pocket could rent a room here for a whole season." He scooped up the remaining coppers and gave me a wink. "Needless to say, let's keep my finances a secret from the other guests, hmm?"

I nodded quickly. "Of course. Your secret is safe with me."

"That's good to hear, lad." Sherman hopped back down to return his coins to their proper location. "Now," he said from somewhere under the bar, "about yer payment."

"Right." I fished a silver coin out from my purse. "If you can find a place to exchange this for a stein, maybe we could call it even?"

"Aye, that could work." Sherman's head popped back up in front of me, a semi-toothed smile stretched across his face. He reached out and snatched the coin from my hand with alarming speed. "I'd recommend ya find a place to make some exchanges yerself. Maybe somewhere more...official than the place I'll be going." He gave me a knowing raise of his eyebrows. "Maybe the Imperial Bank? I'm sure they'd be interested in the fascinatin' coins ya got in that pouch."

Anything to avoid a third encounter like this one. "I'll do that. Hopefully, this Imperial Bank is in the city?"

"Indeed it is. Further in towards the keep, in the Noble's District. I suppose you'll be needin' directions?" He laughed at his own joke. "That'll hafta wait I'm afraid. Bank would be closed by the time ya got there." Sherman disappeared momentarily and returned with a key attached to a small block of wood. "This'll be for yer room. If you go up those stairs," he motioned down the bar to a small staircase set in the corner, "and follow the hallway right, should be the last door on yer left."

I took the key and bowed my head gratefully. "I truly appreciate the help you've given me today, Sherman. I hope I can repay the favor, somehow."

"I've got half a dozen ideas already, lad." Sherman chuckled. "You look like someone who can handle himself, aside from a lack of street smarts o'course. Anybody who can get things done is a valuable asset 'round these parts." He motioned me away towards the stairs. "We can talk about that tomorrow. I'm sure yer tired from yer...long trip here."

"That I am." I sighed deeply, only now realizing how tired I really was. Before I could stand up to go, however, my stomach gave a rather audible grumble. "I suppose I might be a bit hungry, as well."

"As I said before, I don't keep much in the way of food. I can get ya a heel of bread and some ale, or a bowl for some stew."

"Ale and bread would be great." I pulled my coin purse out once again. "How much will it run me?"

Sherman held up a hand and shook his head. "Consider it part of yer room charge." He hopped off his stool and clattered around under the bar. I could just barely make out the wisps of thin white hair on his head bobbing down the length of the bar, so I stood and followed him down. "Though, there is one thing I could use from ya."

I paused, uncertain. "What would that be?"

A mug of ale, foaming and running over, appeared atop the bar. "Yer name, lad." His hair bobbed back down a ways to a small cabinet where he pulled out a loaf of dark bread. "If we're to be helpin' each other out, I might need to call ya something, someday." He reappeared before me and handed me my bread and ale.

"How rude of me, missing introductions." I smiled pleasantly. "You can call me Lux. Happy to be of service to you, Sherman."

"Lux. Lux." He tested the name out loud a few times. "Alright, Lux. When yer all prepared, head on down here tomorrow and we'll have a chat."

"I look forward to it." I held up my stein in thanks and headed to the staircase. I ate the bread, just a nibble at first, but growing in voracity as I climbed the stairs. *It's certainly not the best thing I've ever eaten,* I thought to myself, *but something about that...journey leaves you hungry.* At the top of the stairs I found a single hallway running straight ahead with doors lining both sides. Four doors down, the hallway turned 90 degrees to the right and ran down to a dead end.

As I reached the end of the hallway, I pulled out the wooden block Sherman had given me. A badly faded symbol on the block matched the small metal engraving hammered into the door. The lock was simple: A single hole for a key and a small metal latch below it to lift. The key turned hard, and the door seemed to stick after the latch had given way. I put my shoulder to it, opening the door at the cost of some spilled ale. I grimaced, now short on drink and slightly sticky.

The room was unimpressive, but standard as far as my experience with inns had been in the past. One small chest of drawers. A single, long bed with a well-worn mattress and sheets. Wooden, unadorned walls save for a single small window at the back of the room. A nightstand with a candle, almost completely melted to the base. Overall, a passable room for the price.

After locking the door behind me I crossed the room, set my ale down on the nightstand, and flopped down on the bed in relief. I sighed, more of an exasperated yell from the volume, and rubbed my face. "Again, again, again...again." I allowed myself a minute to wallow in my depression. *Get it out now. Feel pitiful, you deserve it.* I stretched out, eyes closed, every breath another deep sigh. Minutes passed as I slowly began to destress, my sighs becoming less comically loud and the rubbing of my face less aggressive. *Alright, time to get to work.*

***

3. JOG MY MEMORY

I sat up, stretched my arms out above my head, and hopped to my feet. *Time for an in-depth analysis. Up first....magic systems.* Running my hand across my bandolier, I pulled a silver globe from its resting place and turned it slowly in observation. *Still intact. Honestly, surprising for a mana construct.* From the top of the bandolier I withdrew a well-hidden silver pin. The bottom was a slender hollow shaft, leading up to an intricately ornamented mechanism on top. Thin silver filigree wove around delicately to create what looked like a rose bulb, in the center of which sat a small button.

Taking the globe in one hand and pin in the other, I quickly punctured the surface. Although it looked and felt like a solid silver sphere, aside from its near weightlessness, the pin passed through with almost no resistance. *Alright, moment of truth.* I pressed the button in the device's center and immediately determined it was working at full efficiency; the dull tugging at the edge of my mind and draw on my stamina was an unmistakable feeling. It stopped after only a moment as I released the button and removed the needle, but I couldn't stop a smile from coming to my face, feeling relieved. *Mana still works the same as it has before. Excellent.*

The globe began to warm in my hand and glowed a faint orange against the growing shadows in my room. It swelled quickly, growing to about the size of a softball. The matte silver exterior became translucent and I could see a shining orange liquid under the surface. I spun it lazily, admiring the pleasant glow. *Time for an efficacy test.* Setting the orb down on the bed next to me, I held the silver needle to my palm and pricked the skin. Blood slowly began to well up where the tip had pierced my flesh. *Ouch.*

I returned the needle to its secure location at the top of my bandolier and retrieved the orange globe. Balancing it on my bleeding palm I clenched my fingers closed around it, bursting it like a water balloon. The liquid spilled out over my hand, sending a tingling rush up through my arm. The excess fluid ran between my fingers, misting away in moments where it landed on the wooden floorboards beneath my feet. In just a few moments my hand was dry, and the room looked exactly as it had before with no signs of orange liquid anywhere. I poked at my palm gently and was pleased to find the flesh perfectly repaired with no hint of an injury.

"Complete success, alright!" I jumped up from the bed, pumping my fist in victory. After the moment passed, I felt rather silly standing and celebrating by myself, and sat back down quickly. Through absent minded muscle memory, I ran my hand along the bandolier and found the empty slot from which I had taken the silver orb. On the opposite side of the clasp, I depressed a small switch. I felt the slight drain of mana use as a new silver orb grew out from the bandolier, replenishing my stock to the max of four.

No need to test the other three now. The concept is proven...and I'm getting tired. As if to punctuate the thought I yawned, bringing a tear to my eye. "Aaaalright, one more test, and then sleep." I wiped my eyes and stood up again, unslinging the empty scabbard from my back. *Nothing flashy, proof of concept, and that's it.* I held the scabbard out horizontally in front of me with my left hand and reached out to where the grip of the sword would be with my right. Closing my eyes and exhaling, I curled my fingers slowly until I felt the familiar worn leather grip I had spent so long making. As the mana drain tingled in my fingers a grin curled my lips. With a swift pull, the room was filled with a beautiful ringing of metal on metal.

The setting sun shone gloriously off the bastard sword's blade. It was personally hand forged manasteel and engraved with a set of Old-world runes. Looking over the weapon filled me with a satisfaction and happiness I hadn't felt in a long time. "Hey beautiful. I've missed you." I tossed the scabbard down onto the bed and traced my finger along the runes with a loving tenderness. My hand slid down the length of the blade, over the ornate guard, and came to rest against the small golden band wrapped just under the pommel. The joy I felt moments before became tinged with sadness and longing. I spent a long time wrestling with the emotions as they rose and fell: nostalgia, wistfulness, joy, sorrow, anger, regret.

The room falling into darkness finally snapped me out of my sentimental self-reflection. Looking out the window, I noticed the sun was now completely set, replaced by a beautiful full moon. *How long was I sitting here?* Slumping back down to the bed, I gingerly placed the weapon back into the scabbard and leaned it against the bedpost. Running my hand across the pommel I expended a small amount of mana and the blade flashed away, leaving an empty scabbard once more.

I yawned more violently than before, reflexively stretching until both my shoulders popped. I rolled my neck around until it yielded a similar pop, then stood slowly and began the process of preparing for a good night's rest. I removed my coin purse from my belt and set it on the bedside table. The chest of drawers across the room was just large enough for my bandolier, cloak, shirt and leathers. Slipping out of my boots, I took a moment to be thankful for anti-fouling enchantments placed on my socks and undergarments. "I get the feeling that I won't be..." A yawn interrupted my muttering, "...I won't be finding much deodorant around here."

With my preparations completed I crawled underneath the single blanket on the small mattress. The fabric was a bit scratchy but provided some warmth against the chilly room. *I take my cloak for granted too often.* Curling up to combat a small shiver, I closed my eyes and rested my head on the straw pillow. Sleep came almost instantly as the weight of my world finally crashed down on me in full.

The sky overhead was bright blue and completely clear of clouds. I was sweating from exhaustion, and the sun beating down from above made the day uncomfortably hot. The rhythmic chopping of my woodsman's axe was the only sound in the clearing save for a slight rustling of leaves in the weak breeze. My shoulders ached from a day of exertion, but it was a sweet pain. It felt good to be strong, and to use that strength to achieve a tangible goal.

I leaned on the axe for a moment, wiping my brow and letting out a satisfied sigh. For my entire life, I had never felt like I knew what my purpose was. Bouncing from job to job with a half-finished computer science degree, renting a small one-room apartment barely big enough for a bed, a shower and some choice kitchen appliances, and random one night stands that never resulted in a second date...It left a hole I could never figure out how to fill. I was about to be in my thirties and felt like my life to that point had been completely wasted.

Until the day when everything changed. I furrowed my brow, doing my best to think back to what happened, but as usual I came up empty. I was watching TV from my bed, half drunk and dozing off, and then...blackness. Blackness, and pain. With a shiver, I put that particular memory aside and reflected on my life after arriving here.

It took a while to adapt to the strange new world, but I found myself oddly suited for it in the end. Technology was nowhere to be found: Horses pulled carts of farm goods, smiths forged weapons and armor for knights, and a printing press was considered advanced machinery. I quickly found a job in the village I appeared in as a smith's apprentice and lived in a small addition behind his forge.

Two and a half years had passed since I first appeared here. I smiled, proud of how far I had come. Initially I was a weak, pale, lanky stick of a man who would rather stay inside drinking and watching anime than go out and interact with somebody in public. Through the hard work at Ashedown's forge, I was now fit, tanned, and pleasantly adept at interacting with people. I could care for farm animals, forge a variety of high-quality items, and even wield a sword with a middling level of expertise.

Satisfied with the amount of wood that was chopped before me, I lodged the axe head down into the chopping stump and began loading the afternoon's work into a wheelbarrow. It would take at least four trips with the wheelbarrow to move all the wood from the clearing back to the forge, so I filled it as high as possible without the threat of tipping and began the short walk back. It was a nice winding path through the thicket behind the forge, and I took my time on the trip to appreciate the respite of the shady trees.

A faint melody began to drift through the trees ahead of me. It was a lilting soprano voice, softly singing of times gone by and glories won. This song was one I knew by memory, and the voice stirred my heart at its first word. I doubled my pace, a large smile rising to my face. The wheelbarrow bounced loudly off the uneven roots of the forest path, and the voice ahead stopped.

Rounding the last corner, I burst from the tree line at a near sprint. The wood jostled violently as I came to a sudden stop and sent the top layer spilling to the ground. I hardly *noticed; my attention was fully drawn to the clothesline directly ahead of me. Standing before it was Amaya, the most beautiful woman I had ever seen. Her face was beaming with a wide smile and softly closed eyes. A deep purple sundress complemented her free flowing, shoulder-length golden hair. From the top of her head, two rabbit-like ears folded down lazily, further amplifying her adorable aura.*

"Done already, love?" She asked sweetly, skipping over to meet me.

I took her hands in mine and pulled her close, leaning down to plant a quick peck on her forehead. "More or less. The hard part's done, anyhow." Looking over her shoulder I noticed the basket of linens was only half emptied onto the drying lines. I cocked my eyebrow and gave her a smirk. "Those clothes giving you a hard time today?"

Amaya rolled her eyes and pushed me away playfully. "I thought you would be gone for another half hour or so, and I figured…" She looked up to the sky and smiled. "Well, it's such a nice day outside, and I got distracted." Suddenly, she flopped down into the grass, giving a soft squeak as she stretched out in the sun.

I laughed, marveling for the thousandth time at her perfection. Following suit, I landed lying down next to her, our faces just mere inches apart. "You know…" I put on my best over-the-top sultry voice, "If you wanted some help being distracted, I've got some ideas of what we could do." I ran my hand softly down the side of her face, twirling her hair in my fingers.

Her eyebrows shot up as her eyes widened in exaggerated shock. "Sir, how unchivalrous of you!" Amaya turned her head away, her nose up in pretend indignation. "A lady would never even consider such a thought."

"Oh, of course, of course, how rude of me!" I sprang up to a kneeling position. "I beg your pardon, m'lady. I'll leave you to your purity and your laundry. I have some wood to stack, after all."

I turned to go, but Amaya caught my hand and yanked me back to the ground. "Not so fast." She pulled me into an embrace, then brought her lips to mine for a kiss. I closed my eyes, doing my very best to memorize everything about this one perfect moment in time. The ground beneath us was comfortable, but slightly uneven. The sun was relentlessly beaming down on us, but a breeze blew by and tempered it nicely. Amaya's lips were soft and warm with a faint taste of raspberry. I could smell her perfume, a mix of lavender and berries, layered atop her natural earthy musk.

As she pulled away, I opened my eyes and drank in Amaya's beauty. Her eyes, a light purple, were wide and loving. Her skin was lightly tanned from days spent in the summer sun, flawless in its complexion. A button nose sat cutely in the center of her face, just barely crooked to the right. Although I had seen her nearly every day of my new life, I always managed to find a new aspect of her to love whenever we were together.

At that moment, I realized that Amaya was the one thing I had been looking for my whole life, the solution to my emptiness. I grinned, dumb in love, and brushed the hair from her face. "I love you, Amaya."

She smiled, the most beautiful smile I had ever seen. "I love you, Elden. Forever."

A clatter across the room woke me in a panic. My head spun wildly looking for the source of the noise. In the center of the room where the moonlight pooled in from the window, a small silver globe was rolling in a lazy circle. I scanned through the darkness towards the chest of drawers where I had left my bandolier. A familiar figure materialized in the light of the moon. I stared on, incredulous. "Melrose?"

Her features unmistakable now in the light, Melrose smiled and tilted her head to the side. "Nice to see you again, Lux." She approached the bed slowly. "I came to see how you settled in. I'm glad to see you found the place! Sherman told me which room you were in, and the door was unlocked, so I just...let myself in." Her hand moved up to one of the straps of her dress, which she slowly pushed from her shoulder. "I hope you don't mind."

Alarm klaxons were firing in my head. *You know this isn't right. Put the pieces together.* I scooted to the opposite side of the bed from her, still fighting off the last remnants of sleep as I tried to make sense of my situation. "What are...what are you doing?"

Melrose grinned. "Well, after we first met, I was worried you might not get here in one piece."

I never told her my name was Lux.

"After all, you couldn't read any of the street signs." She laughed, beginning to kneel onto the bed next to me.

I definitely locked the door behind me when I came in.

"From first glance, you didn't look very imposing, and there are some...unsavory characters in this part of the city." The red strap of her dress fell down her shoulder.

My bandolier was in the drawer, and the drawer was closed. I tried to scoot further away, but I had reached the edge of the mattress.

Melrose ran her hand across my bare chest. "But now, I guess I feel sort of silly having thought that. You can *definitely* take care of yourself."

All at once, the pieces fit together in my mind. *Identify the threat.*

"So, I was thinking...maybe you could help take care of me as well?" Melrose pushed me back against the headboard and hopped up quickly to straddle my waist. She reached behind her back to grab her dress, beginning to pull it up over her head.

There! Just for a moment, I spotted a garter belt on her upper left thigh. A sound I had been expecting finally reached my ears: a small click and the rush of metal against leather. Her dress had begun to fall back down, but I was already taking action. Before her dagger could appear from behind her back, I bucked my hips hard, launching her towards the headboard. I brought my elbow up, connecting hard with the bridge of her nose. Now unseated, her weight no longer pinned my legs, allowing me to ball them up and extend at full force into her chest.

Melrose spun backwards, bouncing off the bedpost and landing on the floor with a yelp. As she struggled to recover, I sprang from the bed and retrieved my scabbard, taking a defensive stance. She leapt up from the foot of the bed, her face now a mess of blood. The fire in her eyes I had noticed when we first met was still there, but it was changed now. A cold, ruthless flame stared me down from across the bed.

"You just had to put up a fight, didn't you? You know how much it'll cost to get my nose repaired?!" She spat out a glob of blood. "I guess it'll be on your dime." From behind her back, she produced my coin purse. "Sherman said you were loaded, and this certainly feels full enough for a nice vacation. Maybe a few vacations." Gloating, she pulled the drawstring, opening the purse and glancing inside.

I couldn't help but grin as her expression changed. Frantically, she upended the purse and shook it violently, but nothing came out. Melrose growled angrily. "What sort of trick is this? How are you doing this?!" I stared her down, saying nothing, but continuing to grin. She flourished her dagger, pointing the tip at me. "Nothing to say? I guess I'll have to cut the information out of you, one little piece at a time." She cackled. "Unless, I suppose, you think you can take me down without a weapon."

"I figured you would say something like that." I grimaced, feeling justified in taking counter action, but not looking forward to the results. For a brief moment I closed my eyes, looking inwards to begin the process of opening up my mana reserves. Feeling the surge of energy tingle down my spine, I held up my scabbard and withdrew my sword from the ether. The grip was cool and comfortable in my palm, and the familiar metallic ring put a determined calm over my mind. Gently, I tossed the scabbard back down onto the bed next to me, taking a more aggressive stance.

Melrose took a step back, her face a mix of shock and...was that fear? "How...how is that possible? Without incantation, without a catalyst? What sort of magic is that?" She was speaking frantically, clearly re-examining the choices that had led her to where she was at this moment. Her grip readjusted on her dagger repeatedly, her indecision clearly breaking through her overconfident demeanor. "Where did you learn that? Magic like that shouldn't be possible without…"

Don't give her time to recover! I tuned out her babbling, setting to work on combat preparations. *Combat acceleration.* The runes on the end of my sword burned with white light, sending a quick pulse down the blade and into my sword arm. I felt my mind quickening, and Melrose seemed to slow down. The nervous fidgeting of her blade, the backpedaling step she took in reaction to the flash, it was so sluggish and predictable. *Windstep.* A green flash came from the runes, and my limbs surged with pent up energy. *Greater sharpening.* Red light now, covering the edges of my sword in an angry crimson. *Heighten senses.* A blue glow, and the room sharpened into extreme focus.

With every evocation, the mana flowed faster through my body, the channels widening in response to my adrenaline levels. It had only taken a moment to prepare, and my body was burning with stored power. Melrose had begun to recover, seemingly done with her questioning. Her dagger thrust out awkwardly as she began an off-balance charge from the opposite side of the bed. I quickly analyzed my tactical options. *The room is too small for full swings. She's fighting with fear and instinct, not practice. I'm still curious about her motives in all this, so a non-lethal response...for now.*

I took two strides forward, completely closing the distance between us. Her dagger was slow and clumsy, and I easily dodged the stab. Gripping my sword in both hands, I twisted sideways and dropped to one knee, using the extra acceleration in a crescent slash aimed at her dagger hand. If I hadn't been watching, I would never have known the blade connected; it sliced through her wrist without resistance. My blade continued, traveling easily through the straw mattress and shattering the wooden bedframe below.

Melrose recoiled, screaming in pain as her hand separated from her arm and fell to the floor with a dull thud. Blood gushed from the stump at the end of her arm, which she tried in vain to staunch with her free hand. She fell backwards, writhing in agony as she screamed incoherently. Beyond Melrose, I heard more commotion. Through the door, I could hear patrons of the inn had started to fill the hallway and were now running away in fear from the screams. One set of footsteps was moving in the opposite direction, coming towards the room, a very telling gait in my ears. Casually, I reached down and pulled the dagger from the severed hand.

I stood facing the door at the ready, weighing the dagger in my hand. *Non-lethal.* The wooden door burst open, revealing Sherman charging into the room with a crossbow leveled at my chest. He hollered a battle cry and loosed a bolt downrange. I easily sidestepped the shot, returning fire with the dagger. It flipped end over end in a graceful, deadly arc, impacting blade-first into his dominant shoulder. Roaring in pain he dropped the crossbow, grasping at the dagger with his non-dominant hand.

Before he had a chance to react, I charged across the room, swinging my sword flat side first at the side of Sherman's head. It connected with a satisfying *thunk* and he stopped yelling, knocked to the floor unconscious. I kicked the crossbow into the corner of the room, well out of usable range, and closed the door. Kneeling down I retrieved the dagger, withdrawing it with a soft squish, and then checked his back pocket. I was satisfied to find the golden coin he had shown me earlier still there.

From behind me, I heard Melrose was crying now. Turning, I found her crawling towards me, her face awash with fear and pain behind the blood. "P-please, please don't kill meee!" She wailed, most likely beginning to feel lightheaded from loss of blood. I stepped past her, crossing to the chest of drawers. Rummaging through my belongings I withdrew a tonic orb and the hollow needle, quickly activating the mana process. I placed the needle back into the bandolier and returned to Melrose, kneeling in front of her. Placing my sword behind me, well out of reach of her remaining hand, I reached forward and grabbed her damaged arm. "Please, no more! It huuuuurts..." She cried out in pain.

Insistently, I pulled up the stump in front of me and crushed the tonic in my fist directly above the wound. Initially, Melrose screamed, most likely a gut reaction, but I could see the relief flood over her bloody face. The healing liquid almost immediately staunched the wound, knitting together flesh to leave the stump closed flat. She let out a labored breath in relief and slumped backwards. "Now, you have some explaining to do," I growled down to her.

She looked up at me, broken and helpless. "I don't know what you want me to say."

"Try starting with why you broke into my room and pulled a knife on me."

"That's never the plan!" Melrose insisted. "Usually, nobody has to get hurt, and they never even know I was here." She sat quietly on the floor for a moment before motioning to the pile that was Sherman. "We have a deal. I pick a mark, butter them up, and send them his way. He gives them this room, and then I come in with a key at night. He gets a cut of whatever I can find." Another pause. "It's never gone this wrong before."

I sighed deeply, pinching the bridge of my nose. "Out of all the people in this damn world, I picked you. That sounds about right." Sherman began to stir behind me, a low groan coming from his crumpled form. I stood up and addressed Melrose coldly, levering my sword towards her broken face. "You're going to take your little man, and you're going to leave this room, and we're never going to see each other again. Then, you're going to..." I trailed off, alerted to loud footsteps on the floor below. Four sets of heavy boots thundered towards the stairs. *Guards. The other patrons must have found someone to investigate the commotion.*

As they approached, Melrose picked up on the sound as well. Suddenly, with an energy I thought was long gone from her, she sprang across the room back towards the bed. She rolled through the blood that had pooled from her severed hand and began to scream, a convincing replication of her legitimate cries from moments before. *No...she wouldn't.*

The wooden door was smashed open and four men in matching iron armor charged in. Melrose was sobbing now, holding her removed hand in a pitiful display. *You know how this ends. Don't fight now.* Wordlessly, I dropped my sword and fell to my knees. The guards were shouting, one commanding me to surrender, another trying to assess Melrose's condition, and a third calling for backup down the hall. The cacophony of noise and the rage of being played like a fool was too much to bear. I let my battle evocations fade, and my world shrunk back to its normal, dull semi-clarity.

A guard was in my face now, I realized foggily, and he was yelling loudly and pointing at something. I couldn't understand what he was saying, but I had the undeniable urge to break his nose with my forehead. Two guards ran past me, and soon after returned carrying Melrose between them. Our eyes met momentarily, and I saw an immense smugness in her face. *I will not forget this. I will not forget you.*

My arms were yanked roughly behind my back, and irons locked around my wrists. A second guard was clearing the room, collecting my belongings into a small pile; sword, scabbard, coin purse, cloak, bandolier, clothes, armor, and Melrose's dagger. *Everything I have left, my entire history...reduced to a single pile.* My head was starting to clear from the post battle withdrawal, and the guards' voices finally came into focus. "...down to the dungeons for now. Sick bastard wasn't satisfied with her services and wanted to 'teach her a lesson', she says. Damn scum."

A shove knocked me forward, and I was led out of the room and through the inn. I followed the guard in front of me silently, knowing that anything I said would only make the situation worse. As I walked through the street, shirtless and shoeless, passers-by eyed me with disgust. *I'm just another criminal now,* I thought bitterly. *A lone stranger with no connections to anyone in the world, thrown in the dungeon to be forgotten. Though, I suppose I earned it. I trusted a stranger with a pretty face. You'd think I would've learned by now.*

***

4. LESSONS OF THE PAST

My cell was damp. It had been damp since the ceiling started to drip after I first arrived five days ago. Or, at least, what I assumed was five days. There were no windows in the prison; five sides of my small box were made up of grey cobbled stone, and the sixth was wrought iron bars. Furnishing was sparse, consisting of only a small cot and a raised seat with a hole meant to be some sort of toilet. I had been pleased to find that this world had at least some concept of sanitation: The "toilet" hole traveled down into the darkness, where I could hear constantly running water, most likely a sewer.

Surprisingly, I had taken quite well to prison life. I received two meals a day, comprised of a stale chunk of bread, a thin stew of questionable makeup, and a cup of water. The guard who delivered my food was the only human contact I had throughout my stay so far; The three cells I could see looking through the bars were empty, and I never noticed any patrols walking by. The hallway outside was lit by torches ensconced between each cell, which kept the interior of the cells relatively dark.

I performed body weight exercises and calisthenics at least three times a day. With the meals lacking any sort of real nutrition, physical atrophy was a real concern. Otherwise, most of my time was spent in meditation. I had a lot of information to sort through and a lot of emotions to deal with. I was still furious with Melrose and Sherman, but as time passed, I became more disappointed with myself. *I should know better by now. Even after she betrayed me, I still had some sort of unconscious trust in her. Another lesson learned.* I knew that making internal peace, even one based mostly on anger and resentment, was important to making it through a period of isolation like this. *A lesson already learned...fortunately, I suppose.*

Being completely unsupervised between meals left me time for more interesting trains of thought. I found it was a simple enough task to draw my sword from the ether around me. The mana draw was more pronounced as my scabbard was much farther away than usual, but I had been working on expanding my mana pool for decades, so it was a non-issue. *Apparently, this isn't a prison usually used for magically inclined inmates. That might prove useful, should I find the need to...leave unannounced.*

Some of the things Melrose said during our second encounter had also piqued my interest, and I was finally ready to begin looking into them in earnest. *"Without incantation, without a catalyst? What sort of magic is that?"* The memory was crystal clear in my mind. She had obviously been taken by surprise, which told me that magic was not a common occurrence among the general population of this world. *Incantations and catalysts...seems like a typical 'wand and chant' method of spellcasting.* I had been working on a theory for the true nature of mana in my previous life, but now I felt like I had all the pieces to prove it. I shuddered momentarily. *Thinking about living multiple lives still feels so...unnatural. And that transition between them, that void. It's...*I let the thought die, choosing not to remember.

I had always believed that magic, in the classical sense, was possible. As far back as my first life in 21st century New York, it was a thought I often pondered. A power, lying dormant within humanity, just waiting for someone to crack the code of how to access it; It was a nice dream to get me through the listlessness of my mundane life. However, that dream started to become a reality when I found myself in a new world.

On first glance, one could be forgiven for thinking that the world of Alderea was the same as my own, with nothing particularly magical to be seen. However, when I finally began to train in sword combat with a knight passing through our town, I realized there were more subtle powers at play. Any fighter worth his salt knew about "Combat Enhancement Techniques", which, through intense focus and grueling practice, allowed the combatant to heighten their battle prowess in a multitude of ways. For the week that I practiced with the knight, I was only able to begin to use the most basic enhancement he knew, "Lesser Agility".

"Alright, kid, like we practiced. Wide stance. Deep breaths. Picture a—"

"Yeah, Brusch, I know. Picture a river flowing through me." I cut the knight off, frustrated. "You keep saying that, but it doesn't get me any closer to actually understanding what that means." I was standing with my eyes closed, holding a dull *sparring sword out in front of me in both hands. My body ached in multiple places from where Brusch had smacked me with a similarly blunted blade.*

The knight sighed with an almost audible eye roll. "I told ya, kid. Ya got the energy inside ya, but ya don't know how to get it out." I felt a finger poke me roughly in the middle of my spine. He traced it up my back, across my shoulder, and down my arm to my sword hand. "Ya don't move the energy by yourself. Just let it go. If ya stop holding it in so hard, it'll flow all on its own." He paused for a moment. "Once ya know what it feels like, you'll understand what I mean."

"That's great, except to know what it feels like I would've had to have done it already! And I can't do it if I don't know what you mean!" I opened my eyes and turned to glare at him. He was pudgy for a knight, barely fitting into the rough chainmail and boiled leather he wore. He was bald, with small sunken eyes and a long wispy moustache that seemed to constantly be tickling his wide nose.

Brusch shrugged. "That's just what I know, kid. Ya paid me to teach ya, and this is how I was taught. Not my fault if ya just don't have it in ya."

I bristled at the challenge. There was a tight knot of resentment in my gut, which had been slowly starting to burn with shame over the course of the week I had been training with him. I didn't want to believe I just didn't have the ability to master something so seemingly simple. "Oh, shut it. I paid you good coin for these lessons, which I'm now regretting." I turned back and shut my eyes once more, starting back in on the breathing techniques he had taught me.

"Good, breathe. Focus on the energy inside ya, down in your core." He walked around me in a slow circle, observing. "Once ya feel it there, say the words, and let it all go. It'll flow where it needs to go."

I desperately tried to look inward and find the "energy". However, all I found was the self-doubt and anger I was trying to lock away. Exasperated, I gave up and let it overwhelm me, ready to give Brusch the full extent of how I was feeling and try to get my money back. Before I could even open my mouth, the energy exploded out from my core like a bolt of lightning through every inch of my body. I was so shocked at feeling "the river" that I nearly forgot the words.

"Oh!...Lesser Agility!" All at once, the energy rushed down my arms and into my sword. My eyes snapped open, and everything seemed sharper, somehow, glowing with a faint green buzz. "Brusch, I did it! I...I did..." The clarity faded immediately, replaced with the encroaching blackness of tunnel vision. I heard a thumping sound, and lazily realized it was my own body hitting the ground.

According to Brusch, I woke up five minutes later. He was red in the face from laughter, saying something about my graceful dive into a heap. "Oh man, that was the best one I've seen in a long time, kid!" He slapped his knee and started laughing again.

"This is something that happens often? And you didn't think to warn me about it?" I yelled as my face darkened, scowling at his laughter at my expense.

"Rite of passage, kid." Brusch took a few seconds to get the last chuckles out. "The first time ya tap into that energy, the body doesn't really know how to control it. It sort of just goes all out, and leaves ya with nothing left in reserves. Hence the nap." He smirked, but my angry expression kept him from another laughing fit. "Now that ya did it once, it'll be a whole lot easier to do it again. And next time, ya probably won't pass out. Keep practicin', and you'll be able to do it four or five times in a row before ya run out of gas."

My eyes widened as I suddenly realized the new world of opportunities opened to me. "And after that, I'll learn better techniques?"

Brusch shrugged. "Maybe. Not from me, though. I'm outta town at daybreak tomorrow."

"Awwww. And I was just starting to get it." I looked down, now disappointed. "Could you at least tell me about some of the other techniques, so I can try practicing those too?"

He looked me up and down with a measured look, then nodded. "Alright kid. But promise me ya won't try something way out of your league. If ya overexert yourself too much, it could cause some permanent damage."

I bounced up, running over to him, the roller coaster of my emotions cresting high again. "Thanks, Brusch! You're the best! If you're ever in town again, I'll give you a great deal at the forge!"

Brusch smiled. "I'll hold ya to that, kid."

It should have been obvious that "Combat Enhancement Techniques" were just magic evocations with a different name. Back then the true gravity of my situation hadn't set in yet, and I was still living under the impression that I was in some sort of anime style video game world. Everything was new and exciting, and I was finally feeling at peace with myself after so many years of restlessness. Nowadays, I was all too familiar with how things really worked in these "life in a new world" scenarios. The dampness of the stone cell I was currently sitting in punctuated that thought a little too perfectly.

I shouldn't even be in here, I thought sullenly to myself. *It won't be long now. I'll be dragged up out of this cell into the presence of some noble, and they'll tell me about some growing threat, and how I'm supposed to be the one to go stop it.* My expression darkened, and I scowled at the empty cell. *That's how it always goes. Someone telling me my life isn't mine to decide, and instead I have to sacrifice everything I have for some kingdom I've barely heard of.*

That's how it had happened in Alderea, and the same thing had happened again in Hedaat. As soon as word started to circulate of a new, mysterious stranger in town, it was only a matter of time until the ruling party became involved and ruined everything. In Alderea, I had years to start a new life before I was discovered. A random man appearing in town wasn't exactly uncommon: There were a lot of towns in Alderea and a lot of people in those towns. It wasn't until I had truly distinguished myself that anybody cared about the random stranger.

Hedaat had been a different story. It had barely been six months before I was summoned before the court and told of my "epic destiny".

I shouldered the door open aggressively, sending it flying open and bouncing against the wall with a loud crack. Snow blew in from behind me on biting winds, spinning wildly for a moment before settling down on the plush red carpet at my feet.

The room was dark, with only two small gas lamps lighting the barren grey metal walls. Slamming the door shut, I pulled off my heavy coat and threw it across the room, followed by my gloves and hat. They landed in a pile on the floor, next to the chair which was the intended target.

From the next room, I heard a small shriek and the shattering of glass, followed by quick footsteps leading towards the door across from me. I ignored the approach, instead going about the task of setting a kettle of water to boil with a heating coil on the countertop in the kitchen area. There was a timid knock as the door creaked open slowly. A small, high voice called out to me. "S-sir? You didn't return on time from your meeting with the Council, I was worried...is everything alright?"

I slammed the kettle down on the coil and turned towards the voice. "I don't know, Alda, does everything seem ALRIGHT to you?!" I flipped the switch on the burner and small sparks crackled from the base to the iron kettle. After a moment, it set into its usual hum, and the coil began to heat. I paced over to my pile of clothes on the floor, picked up the coat, brushed some dirt from the collar, then turned and threw it across the room again. "Fuck!"

Alda recoiled at the outburst. "I-I-I'm sorry!" She ran after my jacket, apologizing the whole way. "It was a stupid question, I'm sorry. What can I do to help, sir?" Her small frame disappeared from view for a moment, completely enveloped in my thick coat, then reappeared at the coat rack. Her demure figure was clothed in a traditional maid's outfit, slightly disheveled from rushing around after me. Her eyes were wide and worried, a pale icy blue, and her young face was flushed. Silver hair flowed down and covered most of the right half of her face as she moved.

"Nothing. You can't do anything to help." The kettle had started to whistle, and I crossed to remove it from the heat. Through habit I unconsciously went through the motions of making tea as I stewed in my anger. "The Council, in their infinite wisdom, have decided that I am the 'Chosen One' and must travel south at once to stop the rise of the 'Devil Worshippers of Bahruut.' What a bunch of fucking nonsense." I sipped on my tea, burning my tongue.

"No, you can't leave! If you're gone, the lab will close down, and then I'll..." She trailed off, looking down at her awkwardly fidgeting hands.

My rage left me all at once. Though she was trying her best to hide it, the pitiful sniffling sounds told me Alda had started to cry. Oh, now you've done it, asshole, I cursed myself silently, realizing too late that I was taking my anger at the Council out on her. I set down the tea and put a hand on top of her head, lightly fixing her hair. "Hey now. You don't have to worry about that, Alda. I promised you, right?"

She tilted back and looked up at me, her head only just high enough to reach my sternum. Tears were welled up in her eyes, and the adjustment of her head sent them streaming down her cheeks. "But, the C-Council said—"

You put her through this too often. "Since when have I ever cared what the Council says?" I laughed, scratching her head playfully. "Besides, our work here is way more important than some southern cultists, right?"

Alda smiled, her face now awash with happiness and relief. "Right!" She leapt forward and hugged me around the waist for just a moment, before stepping back. Though her face was flushed from crying, I saw her blush even further. "Sorry, sir, I got carried away." She wiped the streaks from her cheeks with the back of her sleeve. "I'm glad that you'll be staying...but won't the Council force you to go?"

I tilted my head to the side, thinking for a moment. "Well, I suppose they can try." I looked down at her after a pause and returned her smile. "Are you going to let them take me away?"

Her laugh was infectious. "They won't make it past the doorway!"

"Great! Well, with that settled, we should probably get back to work. Jaren didn't leave his lab to me so I could sit around whining in it, right?" I clapped my hands and looked around, now reinvigorated in my work. "Were there any developments while I was gone?"

Memories from Hedaat were still open wounds for me, and I did my best to clear it from my mind as quickly as I could. Dwelling on that will not make my stay in this cell better. I clapped my face lightly in my hands and shook my head, vocalizing random noises in an effort to reset my mental state. *Okay. Tonight is the night.*

    I sat cross-legged in the center of my cell, motionless aside from the rhythmic rise and fall of my chest. There was no way to measure the passage of time in the dungeon, but I found the quiet to be soothing and didn't mind the waiting. Eventually, the silence was broken by the echo of footsteps and clinking metal from the hallway. A metal tray appeared, carried by the usual city guard. "Mealtime, prisoner." His gruff voice barked out, same as always. He shoved the tray through the slot at the bottom of the cell and retrieved the empty one I had pushed into the hallway after my previous meal. Without another word, he turned on his heel and left, footfalls fading away into silence once again.

    The meal, as always, was unappetizing. After the third day of exactly the same food, morning and night, I had stopped tasting it altogether and ate only out of necessity. With such a lack of substance to the meal, every bite was important. When the tray was clean of every speck of food and the cup was empty, I shoved them back out into the hallway. It would be a stretch to say I felt full, but having adapted to the new diet plan, my hunger was sated for the time being. Assuming I was correct in my estimation of how much time had passed since I was originally imprisoned, I had about twelve hours of solitary confinement before my next meal.

    "Alright. It's time." I spoke out loud as I began a brief calisthenics routine. I found speaking aloud to myself awkward and uncomfortable, but from prior experience I knew that it would help keep me sane in the long run. My stretches were a welcomed change of pace after sitting in the same position for an entire afternoon. With my blood pumping and my mind focused after the quick stretching regimen, I reached out and drew my sword from the air in front of me. The hilt was comfortable in my hand, a welcome extension of my arm. "It's good to see you again, beautiful."

    As I examined the weapon in the dim torch light, my eyes paused on the runes inscribed down the length of the blade. It was an elegant improvement I had made to the Combat Enhancement system back in Alderea. After my initial training with Brusch, I sought out every knight and freerider I could find passing through our village and paid them everything I had for lessons. I learned with an insatiable voracity, and soon found that my random teachers could no longer present me with new problems. We would spar, and sometimes I would pick up a new sword technique or stance, but the Combat Enhancements stagnated quickly.

I inevitably found myself training through random trial and error. Some things were a natural progression; moving from Lesser Agility to Agility was a simple enough idea, though it was much more energy intensive. Evoking those enhancements until I could barely stand, day in and day out, slowly but surely increased the maximum amount of mana I held within me. I had started to wonder about the actual process of evocation as well.

Why would a knight stand across the battlefield from his opponent and loudly tell him exactly which enhancements he chose to use? The beginning of real combat was an embarrassing display in my eyes, with men trying to speak as fast as possible to gain a slight edge over their foe. I tried for weeks, in vain, to evoke even a basic enhancement with only my mind. Without fail, I could tap into the energy down in my core, but I could never activate it in a meaningful way without saying the words.

It was Amaya who solved the problem for me with an innocent and unrelated comment while watching me train. *"How can you remember all those different enhancements? I would have to write them down and read them off a list during combat. I guess it's good I'm not a fighter, isn't it?"* I had run off wordlessly, too excited to speak. At the forge, I found an engraving tool, and carved the simplified rune for agility into the end of my sparring sword.

With intense focus, I channeled my energy down the length of the blade to the rune. It flashed with a bright green light, and the enhancement activated instantly. I was so overwhelmed with excitement that I sprinted back at accelerated speed to the field I had left Amaya in and tackled her in a loving embrace. Finally, the door to advancement had opened to me.

It was a simple enough process after that to carve as many runes into my weapon as possible and start practicing. My skills grew rapidly: It only took a week to be able to activate any rune on the sword individually, without activating them all at once. Next, after memorizing their placements, the runes could be evoked while holding the blade facedown, the characters out of sight. Soon after that, just through manipulating the amount of energy I expended, I could cast Lesser Agility, Agility, and Greater Agility through a single simplified agility rune.

My advancements had slowed after that. My techniques were so far ahead compared to those of the knights I had met so far in Alderea that I shifted my focus to increasing my energy reserves, confident I could outperform any opponent in a one-on-one combat. Now, sitting in my cell with over a lifetime's worth of extra experience, I saw how limited my scope had been. Why should I be limited to runes depicting the standard combat enhancements? How could I be limited to runes carved onto a weapon, and not another surface? My opportunities seemed endless...aside from the small issue of being locked in a cell.

***

5. NEW HORIZONS

"Alright, time to get my thoughts in order. Make a list of tasks, evaluate the potential, and execute. Current ideas to test: Unconventional Enhancements, Incanting Spells, Unconventional Implements, maybe, oh! Maybe it doesn't need to be an implement at all? Could a piece of paper work? The wall? My hand? My mind, maybe? What if..." I muttered to myself for quite some time, interrupting my own thoughts in a stream of consciousness sequence of ideas all firing off in my brain at once.

"Wait. Just slow down a minute. Start with something simple." I chided myself, realizing how much time I had wasted thinking of plans well beyond my current capabilities. "The easiest thing to start with would be adding a new rune, but something more abstract. Fire, maybe? Inscribing a rune, though..." I took a moment to weigh my extremely limited options. Holding my blade out in front of me, I ran my non-dominant thumb across the edge, hissing at the pain.

Carefully, I traced out the basic rune for fire on the flat of the blade in blood. It certainly wasn't elegant, but the rune was unmistakable. Drawing on my mana reserves I cautiously began to channel energy through my body. "Keep it low, nice and easy," I whispered to myself. With measured precision, energy slowly entered the manasteel and flowed towards the blood rune. All of my focus was trained on the symbol, echoing the word in my mind over and over again.

To my amazement, the blood began to bubble and steam, and a dark crimson flicker sprouted from the center. It rippled out slowly across the face of the blade, creeping down towards the hilt. "Holy shit!" I exclaimed in pure shock. "There is no way I figured this out on the first try! I can't believe it's working as well as—" My excitement was dashed as a sharp pain burned into my fingers. In my premature celebration, I had failed to notice the flames hadn't stopped at the hilt and had spread down to my sword hand.

"Fuck!" Cursing, I threw down the sword and shook my hand rapidly to kill the flames. As soon as the grip left my hand, the fire flickered out, and the blade returned to its normal light blue color. Unfortunately, the pain didn't subside as quickly, and I spent the next five minutes blowing on my first-degree burns.

"Well," I hissed out through clenched teeth, "I suppose this is still a victory. A small victory."

While cradling my burned hand, I pondered on how to proceed. "I'm sure the wizards of this world don't have to constantly worry about setting their hands on fire every time they cast a spell. Although, they're incanting something, which implies a greater degree of specificity than just 'fire'. All of my enhancements apply to my entire being, so I guess it makes sense the fire was trying to spread..." I shuddered. "No more single rune tests."

Wincing, I pressed on my cut thumb, drawing a fresh well of blood. I drew a new fire rune in the same place as the first, which had mostly bubbled away after my first evocation. Afterwards, I paused for a moment to consider my next move. "How do I make magic more specific? I could just...focus harder, I suppose, but I've never had to keep enhancements contained before." Dragging my thumb down below the fire rune, I made the symbol for "blade". I smiled, satisfied with myself. "This can't possibly go wrong," I mocked at myself.

With my new runes in place, I moved my mana down the length of the sword again, this time attempting to activate both runes at once. The drain on my energy told me I had succeeded, which both exhilarated and scared me. The two runes flashed as expected, but this time, the fire rippled out from the entire blade at once. Gritting my teeth, I held the blade as far from myself as possible, ready to drop it at the first sign of the fire spreading too far.

However, the fire never passed the hilt of the sword. It glowed a deep crimson, setting shadows to dance on the wall behind me as the flames licked up and down the blade's face. Even with the weapon held at arm's length, the heat was impressive on my hand and face. "Oh yeah. Yeah, this is what I'm talking about!" I swung the blade in a quick arc, the blistered skin of my sword hand forgotten in my excitement. It hissed and crackled as it cut through the air, but the blaze didn't waver for an instant.

"Okay, let's open it up and see what we can do!" I increased the flow of mana down my arm, adding fuel to the crimson flame. It swelled substantially, now leaping in bright arcs from the sharp edges. The light now completely illuminated the cell, and a red glow spilled out into the hallway past the iron bars. An unstoppable grin curled my lips as I moved the sword up and down before me. The heat was beginning to hurt my hand, but I couldn't stop now.

"Final test! Fifty percent throttle for two seconds, then cut power!" I extended the blade out straight, pointing through the bars of my cell towards the empty one across from me. "Three...two...one...GO!" Power surged all over my body, tingling my extremities with an energy I hadn't felt in years. When the mana reached the blade, it roared to life with a snarling crack. Scarlet flame burst out in all directions before me, sending me staggering backwards. I closed my eyes against the flash as I struggled to maintain the constant stream of vicious flames.

When the heat became too much, I cut off my mana reserves to the sword. Although the fire had been much more intense this time around, it blinked out just as quickly. Surprisingly, I found the manasteel blade still cool to the touch, as if I hadn't been burning my hand only moments before. The same couldn't be said for the iron bars of my cell, however. They were glowing a dim orange where the sword had been pointed, steaming angrily in the damp atmosphere of the prison.

"That...was incredible." I fell back onto my cot with my hands shaking, whether from exertion or excitement I couldn't tell. It had been years since my mana had been drawn on this heavily, and I certainly had never used so much at one time before. The feeling in my body was electric; it was like a runner's high, but for my mana channels instead of my muscles. With the code seemingly cracked, I could see the possibilities multiplying in my mind; magic was finally a viable option, and the only limitations were my imagination and my vocabulary.

"So, where do I go from here?" I asked myself aloud, lying down on the lumpy old mattress. "If I can channel magic through my sword with a rune, there's no reason to believe it wouldn't work for any element I can think of. It might be beneficial at some point to make a list and start testing them eventually, but maybe I should switch gears and explore new ground." Lying my sword down next to me, I held out my hands above me to observe them. My right was an angry, blistered red from the fire, and my left was a smudgy, sticky red from the large cut on my thumb. "Maybe...I can do something about this."

I gently picked at the freshly clotted wound on my thumb, opening it once more with a grunt of pain. Blood dripped down onto my face, drawing a sputter and an exasperated sigh as I sat up to prevent a further mess. Onto the upturned palm of my right hand, I carefully drew the rune for healing. I took a moment to calm myself, closing my eyes and taking deep breaths as I settled my legs into a comfortable cross-legged meditation stance. Once I felt centered, I opened my eyes and concentrated on the healing rune.

Mana flowed down my arm, surging into my upturned hand. It began to circulate around my palm, a result of my focusing, but to my dismay, there was no reaction from the rune. I scrunched up my brow and closed my eyes, redoubling my efforts. I could feel the mana pooling in my hand but, try as I might, I couldn't force it up through my palm to the rune. The absence of my sword was overly apparent in this moment; I had never channeled mana outside of my body without an implement before, and it was clear that it would take more practice than a single attempt to master it.

"Just...go already!" I yelled in frustration. Energy cascaded down my arm, and the overabundance of mana in the extremity started to feel uncomfortable. Pressure was building all throughout my arm and the usual tingling sensation of channeling mana had changed to a burning that was growing at an alarming rate. "Gah!" I let my focus go, and the energy rocketed back through my body, overflowing into my other limbs until it slowly pooled back into my core. I flopped back down onto the mattress feeling winded and let down. After the instant success of the first test, I thought I'd be able to figure out anything.

I sighed deeply. "Well...that sucks." Laying in silence for a moment I couldn't help but laugh at myself. I was tired, bloody and burned from what I realized was less than a minute of testing and experimentation, and even though I had accessed a new form of magic on my first try, I was disappointed in myself. "I guess I have plenty of time to work on this. No reason to expect it all on the first try."

Absentmindedly, I ran my hand around the pommel of my sword, tracing the golden band embedded at the bottom. "I never really thought about it before, but I am using an implement to cast my magic like most classical wizards. I never thought it was useful in Alderea to use Combat Enhancements when I wasn't holding a blade, and in Hedaat..." I trailed off, staring off through the wall of my cell at an unseen memory. "I had other things on my mind back then. Casting magic without it might be harder than I had anticipated." A new thought crossed my mind, and I sat up with a small grin. "There is one more thing I can test today."

When I had first made the rune enhancements to my sword in Alderea, I had never gone back to openly chanting my combat enhancements; it seemed like such a step backwards to waste time speaking the words. Now, though, I realized it had clouded my judgement in regard to my advancement in mana manipulation. My left thumb, now a terrible mess of swollen skin and blood, was a testament to that. I swung my legs off the edge of the bed and took my sword in a two-handed grip. I was tempted to start my testing right away, but I stopped when I remembered the continuously spreading fire from earlier.

"Which words do I need to use when casting magic? Does magic care about grammar? How specific do I need to be?" I pondered the questions for a while. The realization was finally setting in now that, without having seen how magic worked in this world, I was at an extreme disadvantage in figuring it out by myself. "Without a guide, I guess I should just...start somewhere." I took a moment to prepare my incantation and adopted a ready stance.

"Lesser Sustained Self-Healing!" I felt the drain of mana, and a moment later, a sudden wave of relief over my entire body. Both my blade and my skin seemed to sparkle with a green, otherworldly light as the spell continued to work. Removing my left hand from the sword's grip, I saw the large slice on my thumb slowly begin to weave back together, skin joining separated skin in an uncomfortable display. After a few seconds of holding the spell, I felt satisfied with the test's results and stopped channeling the energy before the cut was fully healed.

"Onto test number two." I cleared my throat and regripped my sword with two hands. "Lesser Self-Healing!" As expected, the dim green shimmer returned, but only with a single pulse. The mana drain was more pronounced with this spell, yet it faded immediately after activation. "Alright! Sustained spells exist." The discovery was exciting, and I took a moment to feel proud of the accomplishment. "Now, just one more test, then I'll break for brainstorming and sleep."

"Lesser Sustained Self-Healing, Wounds!" A new sensation coursed through my body upon the spell's activation. Cold, tingling energy sped across my extremities, seeming to stop and linger only on my damaged hands. After a moment, the feeling was replaced with the relief I had felt before, and the green shimmer appeared again, focused around my wounds. This time, I let the spell linger until the puffy red burns on my right hand had completely healed, about ten seconds of channeling in total.

I breathed a sigh of relief and ended the channeling. Cautiously, I flexed my right hand, and was happy to find that the visuals matched the reality: My hand was completely healed of my burns. "This is definitely the best discovery so far." Even though I had started to understand some of the rules of magic I had created even more questions for myself. Could I use this magic on someone else? How specific of instructions can my mana...understand? Is it based on my intentions, and the words are just a catalyst as well?

The continuous stream of thought was giving me a headache. I sat down on the cot and leaned against the cell wall as I rubbed my face. "It's too much for today. Sleeping on it will do more good than anything else I could try tonight." Yawning, my exhaustion finally caught up with me. Flipping my sword casually in my grip, I held it up over my shoulder and went through the motions of sheathing it. The weight of the weapon lessened in my hand as I moved, and by the time it was fully "sheathed" the blade had disappeared into the ether, transported safely back to the scabbard in whatever storeroom it was kept in.

I sprawled out on the mattress, laying my head on the pillow and dangling my feet off the bottom of the bed. Standing around six foot three with a slim runner's build, I ran into the issue of ill-fitting accommodations quite often, and this world had been no different. After a satisfying pop from my hips, I curled into a ball under the single threadbare sheet I had been provided. The temperature in the prison stayed at a consistent cool-but-comfortable level, for which I was very grateful. "Finally," I muttered to myself, "a night where I'll be worn out enough to fall asleep." It was difficult to keep a sleep schedule without any view of the sun, but it was important in maintaining a positive mental state.

A smile spread across my face as I closed my eyes. From the moment I woke up in the morning, I looked forward to going to sleep every night. It gave me the chance, small as it was, to see her again. "See you soon, beautiful." It wasn't long until I had drifted off, searching for Amaya in my dreams.

Rain was pouring off the small enclosure around Ashedown's forge, falling heavily enough to rival the crackling of the fire within. I wiped my brow, looking off into the storm for a moment, and then returned to hammering the thin strip of metal before me. After weeks of secret tests and practice runs, I was finally making a real attempt at forging a gift for Amaya. The precious metal was much more difficult to work with than my training material had been, and it was costly to come by, so I was moving with slow precise movements today. Careful, well-placed hammer blows wrapped the long strip of annealed gold around a thin iron rod, the delicate metal finally approaching a connected loop.

Once the strip of gold was completely wrapped around the rod, I set down my hammer and tapped the iron against the anvil to dislodge the loop. I studied the gleaming band, rolling it back and forth in the palm of my hand. It was still a crude thing, mostly made up of dents and smudges, but it could technically be called a ring. I smiled with extreme satisfaction at the work so far. Now, I had to heat and reshape it, smooth the dents, sand away the scratches, and polish the metal to a glossy finish. It would take a lot of work, but it would be worth it.

I slipped the ring into my chest pocket and walked to the edge of the forge enclosure, washing my hands in the rain runoff. I took a deep breath and let out a content sigh. The smell of rain always made me happy.

"I love the smell of rain." I jumped at the sound of Amaya's voice. She was leaning against a support in the center of the room, laughing now at how startled I was. Her hair was dripping and stuck to her face, and her dress was soaked from her trip through the downpour. "I'm sorry, did I interrupt your...staring into the distance time?"

"You did! It's a very important part of the smithing process, and I'll thank you to be more mindful of that in the future." I circled the small shack and hugged her from behind, resting my chin between the long fuzzy ears on the top of her head. "I was thinking the same thing when you walked in. I find the smell of rain so soothing."

"Petrichor." She placed her hands over mine and squeezed them lightly. "That's what they call the smell that comes with rain."

"Huh. The more you know." I spun her around and placed a quick kiss on her forehead. "I'm sure you didn't head all the way out here in this weather to teach me a new word, right? Did you need something?"

Amaya blushed slightly, perfect white teeth flashing in a shy smile. "No, not really. I just wanted to see what you were working on today."

I looked around the forge for an excuse, not ready to show off the project I had been working on. Doing my best to not show it on my face I turned to a nearby table and picked up an old practice sword. "Just a bit of this and that, today. There aren't any big orders in right now so I've just been practicing some random techniques in the small forge." I pointed out some nicks in the old blade. "I'm trying to get better at weapon repairs so I can take more of the smaller jobs off of your father's plate."

"Oh, you don't have to worry about him. He might not say it, but he likes you, and appreciates everything you do to help with his business." Amaya came over to the table next to me and tried to pick up the forge hammer, giving a laughing grunt as it slowly dragged off the table. She struggled against its weight for a moment, but gave up the fight, dropping it to the ground. "Dad never wanted me to help him with his work, and I wouldn't be very good at it anyways." She took one of my hands in hers, her skin soft and warm. "We're lucky you showed up."

My face flushed as my heart swelled, and I looked away. "Nah, I'm sure you would've gotten along fine without me."

She looked up at me, her face suddenly serious. "I wouldn't want to get along without you, Elden."

I had to bite at my lip to keep from tearing up as my emotions surged. Dropping the sword, I took both her hands in mine and pulled her close. "You'll never have to. I'm here for the long haul, love." We stood for a moment in silence, basking in *each other's presence. Her eyes were closed as she brushed a tear away, but she had a smile on her face.*

"Good!" Amaya hopped up and kissed me on the cheek, then spun away from me towards the door. "I've got to go get things ready for dinner. Don't be late, love." She paused for a moment at the exit, looking me over, then smiled and ducked back out into the rain. I watched her as she left until I couldn't see her through gloomy weather. My hand raised to my breast pocket, feeling the rough metal ring inside. A small grin came to my face.

"Soon." I whispered under my breath, heading out into the rain after her.

***

6. CHANGE OF PLANS

I woke to the sound of footsteps in the hallway outside of my cell. In my groggy, still half-asleep state, it took me a few seconds to realize that there was more than one person heading towards me. One set of footfalls was familiar; heavy, even echoes of military boots, belonging to the prison guard. This time, though, it was accompanied by a light, stuttered scuffing of soft shoes, as if someone was being dragged along with him. As if to punctuate my thought, I heard the voice of my usual guard yell, "The more you resist, the worse your stay here is going to be!"

Another prisoner! The footsteps stopped for a moment, then resumed in unison, all sounds of resistance now quiet. I quietly got up from my cot and moved to sit at the back of my cell, giving myself the best view of the approaching scene without seeming overly interested. When the footsteps finally reached my field of view I was surprised to see that the prisoner being escorted by my usual guard was a small, frightened looking young woman. The pair stopped in front of my cell as the jailer worked through a ring of keys, eventually settling on one to open the door directly across from mine. He pushed her through roughly, knocking her to her knees, and without another word, locked the door and left.

The girl looked around her cell in a panic, frantically scanning her accommodations as if she would find something that would make everything alright. Unfortunately for her, the cell contained the same utilities as my own, and she soon slumped down further onto the floor in defeat. She stayed in that position for quite a while, and as time went on, I began to hear light sobbing sounds from across the hallway. *This certainly is not what I was expecting from my new neighbor.*

Any preconceived notions I had about what a prisoner would look like were completely wrong in this case. Her hair, a deep black like my own, was braided neatly down to the small of her back. She was dressed in a makeshift roughspun gown, similar in composition and quality to the pants I had been given when I arrived. Her skin was a fair white, much lighter than mine, giving the impression that she didn't often spend time in the sun. Though she was currently facing away from me, curled into a ball, the glimpse I had of her face had seemed to be of someone in their mid-twenties.

A thought suddenly shocked me. Almost in a panic, I looked down over my hands and felt the sides of my face. *How...how old am I?* My new companion completely forgotten, I recalled my sword to my hand and began attempting to polish it. Frustratingly, the fabric of my pants was difficult to leverage and did a poor job, and I hadn't been given a shirt, so the idea quickly failed. Without stopping to think about it, I channeled mana to the blade and muttered, "Mirrored Reflective Blade." The full length of the metal shimmered for a moment, and then resolved itself into a perfectly mirrored surface.

Holding my breath in anticipation I put the blade up to my face. The person looking back at me was a complete stranger. His jet-black hair was disheveled and shaggy, hanging down past his ears. Piercing grey eyes scowled under thick, defined eyebrows. He had lightly tanned skin, free of blemishes and wrinkles, and the scruff of a beard left to grow too long along his jaw. *I'm...young again.*

I slouched back against the stone wall, unsure of how to feel about the revelation. When I started my first new life in Alderea, I had been 27. My life in Hedaat had started five years after that, and I had never once stopped to think that my age had been changed in any way. Now, though, I knew that it had. There was a creeping sense of dread building in the back of my mind, making the hair on the back of my neck stand straight. The implications of the knowledge I had just gained were far reaching, and potentially terrifying.

No. Stop it. I shook my head and squeezed my eyes shut. *Just...not now. Later. Be productive now, shut down later.* After a moment, I peeked my eyes open. The same, young face from before was still looking back at me. Shutting the mana off to my sword made the image ripple away, replacing it with the cool blue-tinged manasteel I was used to. *Hey, I just used magic to do exactly what I wanted without even thinking about it. Making something mirrored was definitely outside my wheelhouse. That's a great step forward, right?* I put the sword away behind me, sending it back to its scabbard, and tried to keep my mind focused on other things. *The girl. Talk to her. Find out why she's here, what she did...anything.*

"Hey." I called out, standing up unsteadily. I walked to the edge of my cell and leaned on the bars as I observed the girl opposite me. "Are you alright?" She bolted upright, seemingly startled by the fact that the world still existed around her. Slowly, she turned her head, and a look of shock took over her face when she saw me in the cell across from her. *She thought she was alone down here.* She did her best to right herself, standing to fix her hair and dress as she backed away from the bars to the wall behind her.

"Yes. I'm f-fine." She replied, sniffling. Her eyes were downcast, looking anywhere but directly at me.

I cocked an eyebrow, staring at her for a few seconds in silence. "Alright then." I turned and walked to my cot, stretching out with an exaggerated yawn. Flat on my back with my feet hanging over the edge of the cot I closed my eyes and waited. From across the hall I heard the light shuffling of feet and the creak of a long unused cot. It was only a minute until I heard her crying again, more heavily than before.

"You know, you don't really sound fine." I spoke out to the ceiling, still lying with my eyes closed. "What did a girl like you do to get locked up down here?" Letting the statement sit for a while, I was surprised that I heard nothing in response. The crying was a bit quieter now, but the girl stayed silent otherwise. *Well, she's certainly a stubborn one. Though I guess she probably doesn't realize the full severity of her situation.*

"If they've put you down in the dungeon with me, that means they plan to keep you here for a while. They don't just throw you down here for stealing a loaf of bread or cutting a purse." I had gathered as much on my trip into the prison. There were multiple holding cells on the ground floor that had been occupied with a large number of people: Drunkards, simple thieves and the like, by my estimation. But here, multiple levels underground, I hadn't seen a single prisoner in my hallway. This was where the dangerous ones were held. *And her...*

"But I didn't do anything..." Her reply was so soft I barely heard it, even through the silence.

I did my best to suppress a small smile. *Now we're getting somewhere.* "Well, somebody thinks you did, obviously."

"I didn't do anything!" She repeated, much louder this time. I heard the cot squeak again as she stood and took a few steps. "I was at home sewing with Mother, and they came and started arguing with Father outside." There was a fire in her voice, her fear and anger clear.

I could hear her breath was ragged and hard from across the hall. Clearly, she was beyond crying at this point. *Anger is better than hopelessness.* "So, tell me, what did your father do to make these men angry? Cheated at dice at the tavern one too many times?"

"No!" the girl shouted at me. "My father is a good man! They always come to our house and make trouble for him, like breaking his wagon or trying to take his money, and we didn't do anything wrong!"

Things were starting to add up in my head, and a knot began to twist in my gut. I sat up and spun to look at her. The girl's face was flushed from yelling and she no longer avoided my eyes. "Who is 'they?' Bandits?"

"The city guards! It's always the same ones, every time! The fat stupid one, and the tall one, and the twins!" A tear rolled down her cheek. "My father is a good man..."

My blood turned to ice in my veins. *It can't just be a coincidence. The two guards from the gate...those conniving fucks.* "The tall man with the crooked nose, and the fat man with the mustache, right?"

Her eyes widened, and I knew I was right. "You know them?" She paused a moment for an answer, but then leaned toward me intently as she continued. "That means that you believe me, right? If you know those two, you must know how awful they are!"

I scowled. "Yeah, I know them. I had the displeasure to meet them at the Trader's Gate last week when I arrived in the city." As I watched her expression change, I took a moment to reflect on her situation. *She's obviously terrified after the day she's had. If she can keep her spirits up in a place like this, she has a stronger resolve than I thought.* "So, how do you fit into all of this? Why did the guards arrest you?"

"I don't really know." Her brow furrowed. "Father told them he was done paying their 'protection tax' after they ruined Mother's garden again a few days ago. They came back this morning with their friends, but Mother told me not to listen, and after that..." She trailed off, uncertain. "I'm not sure what it has to do with me, though."

I'm sure Dad is already back to paying them by now. Probably double. And if he toes the line, maybe his daughter will come back home. Although, if these scumbags are low enough to kidnap someone for leverage, they won't miss out on the opportunity to take advantage of a beautiful woman like her. My fists and jaw clenched at the thought. *How long are they going to keep her down here? Locked away, obviously without any just cause...*

"It's not your fault. And it's not your father's fault, either." I didn't know what she was thinking, but my first impulse in a situation like this was always to blame myself. *That's not something you want to carry with you.* "There's always someone out there looking to take advantage of good, honest people. And there's not always someone to stop them."

The girl's face flushed as she looked away. "Thanks for saying that...and for believing me." She laughed softly. "You know, when I first saw you down here, I thought you looked scary. Your face is kinda...angry."

I chuckled as I gave a forced smile, scratching the back of my head. "Yeah, so I've been told." I motioned around my cell. "Well, I know it's not home, but as far as prisons go, it's not the worst one I've been in. The cot isn't bad, it's got a toilet, and I've had two mediocre meals a day. I'm sure you won't be here long, so you'll be fine down here." I forced another smile, doing my best not to show my worry for her potentially dangerous situation.

She laughed again. "I've never had people bring me meals before." The girl paused for a moment and cocked her head to the side. "What's your name? I hope you don't think it's too presumptuous of me, but we'll probably be stuck down here together for a while, so I'll need to call you...something."

Careful now. "You can call me...Lux." I gave a curt nod. "It's nice to make your acquaintance, miss...?"

"Lia. Well, it's Marlia, but everyone calls me Lia." She walked to the cot and sat down, her legs hanging off the side. "So, you really think I'll be out soon?"

I caught a grimace before it reached my face. "Well, you and your family haven't done anything wrong, right? They can't just keep you here forever for no reason." *They probably can.* "Someone will figure it out soon and send you back to your parents." *They probably won't.* "You think you can deal with bland food and a small bed for a day or two?" *Those are the least of your worries.*

Lia nodded. "I can do it! Thanks, Lux. You're making it...not so bad down here." She looked away again, swinging her feet. We sat in silence for a while, until it was broken by a rather loud yawn from across the hall. "Wow. I guess I forgot it was the middle of the night."

I nodded. "Kidnapping and adrenaline will do that. You might want to get some sleep; you have a long day of nothing ahead of you tomorrow."

"Right!" She slid back up the cot and wrapped up under the thin sheet. "Goodnight, Lux!" Lia called out as she settled down to sleep.

"Oh, uh, goodnight Lia." I responded awkwardly. *Don't hold it against her; her life's been turned upside down and I'm the only friendly face available. Whatever gets her through this.* After a few minutes her breathing settled into a sleeping rhythm, and I let out a breath of relief. I began to realize I was also tired, but my mind was still preoccupied with the matter at hand.

*I have to do something to get her out of here. She probably doesn't realize it, but being used as leverage like this, she's in a lot more danger than just being bored and hungry. Hopefully they leave her be for the next day, at least. They probably want to make her sweat, get her all worked up...*I cut the train of thought early. *It won't come to that. I will NOT let it come to that. But for now...sleep. I'm not thinking at one hundred percent.* Slowly, I curled back up under the sheet and attempted to get comfortable. Sleep came quickly, but it was not the restful relief I had hoped for.

Rastor Ashedown slammed his fist down hard on the wooden dinner table. "You are NOT going to the castle, Elden! We talked about this yesterday, and my decision is still the same." *He grimaced at me, his huge bearded face a mask of anger and stubbornness.*

I paced back and forth across the stone floor, my fingernails digging into my palm as my fists continued to clench. We had been arguing on and off all day, and it had finally come to a head after an uncomfortably quiet dinner. "How can you say that, knowing she's in danger? You just let them walk in here and—"

"Don't you DARE put that on me! The only reason any of this is happening is because of you." Ashedown stood in a rage, his full six foot eight frame shadowing me. "You know as well as I do what would've happened if I had resisted those guards. Things would be a lot worse than they are now, for her and for us."

"Oh, don't give me that bullshit! We could've left town at any time and been out of their reach, but no, you couldn't leave your precious forge." I yelled up at him, unphased by his threatening presence. "It's good to know where your priorities lie. The family business before the family."

Ashedown poked a massive, callused finger into my chest. "You better watch your tongue, boy. I gave you everything you have, and I can damn well take it all away."

I slapped the hand away, surprised by how much force it took. Ashedown's arms were corded with muscle, gained through decades of swinging a blacksmith's hammer. "Don't you get it? They already took it away! I'm just trying to get it back!"

"You know why we can't do that!" His face contorted, the mask of anger showing just a flash of regret and sadness. "If you give them what they want now, what's stopping them from pulling this again down the line when they want something else? They'll run roughshod over this entire town if we let them win here."

"I don't CARE!" The anger finally boiled over, my words coming without second thought or restraint. "I don't care what happens to you, or anybody else in the damn town! I only care about her!" If looks could kill, I would've glared a hole straight through his face. "I thought you cared about her too."

I had crossed a line with that. Ashedown lumbered over me, clamping a huge hand down onto my shoulder and shoving me roughly back against the brick wall. "That's enough out of you!" I struggled to move away, but he was leaning his weight into it now, and I was well and truly stuck. He lowered his head down, our faces only inches apart. Veins were bulging in his neck and his face was beet red. "Don't you EVER question my loyalties again! I care about her more than a punk like you could ever imagine!" He was shouting now, his composure lost just like mine. "She's my DAUGHTER!"

"AND SHE'S MY WIFE!" I smashed my forehead into his nose, bringing stars to my eyes. He grunted in pain as he *recoiled, giving me enough space to slip out from beneath his hand. I spun quickly underneath the outstretched arm and kicked hard at the back of his knees, sending him toppling forward against the brick wall. With Ashedown momentarily disabled, I turned and ran to the rack next to the door, unsheathing my sword.*

Turning, I held up the blade just in time. Ashedown had recovered and was charging me with a bulging fist held high. He stopped as I raised my weapon, the point dangerously close to his trunk-like neck. Although my body was coursing with adrenaline, my face was completely calm. "I'm going to get Amaya back. No discussion. End of story. If you don't like that idea, you'll have to kill me." I turned the sword, pressing an edge to his cheek. We locked eyes for a long moment in silence. "While there's life in me, she will not sit imprisoned. Not another second longer."

All at once, Ashedown's strength left him. He staggered back a step, paused for a moment, and then collapsed into his chair. Covering his face with his hands, his shoulders bounced weakly as he began to sob. Blood and tears leaked through his fingers, dripping down to the stone floor to splash too loudly in the silence. Slowly, I turned and retrieved my cloak, sheathed my sword on my belt, and opened the door. Rain was pouring down in the darkness outside, but I didn't care. I had to go.

I stepped outside but stopped and turned to look back at Ashedown for a moment. "She's going to be okay, Rastor. You both will." With that, I pulled up my hood and walked out into the night. Wind was whipping the rain straight into the back of my head, instantly soaking through the thin woolen cloak and into my undergarments. With dark clouds covering the sky the night was an impenetrable black, but I still knew where I was going. Far in the distance, through the town past rolling hills, small orange lights flickered against the darkness atop what I knew were the stone walls of the keep.

As I trudged through the mud, I reflected on the events of the past few days. The guard had come alone at first, carrying a contract from Lord Eadric, the presiding lord protector of the surrounding townships. It implored Ashedown to forge twenty of the finest sets of plate armor, shields and longswords. More curiously, it specifically asked for me, by name, to come to the keep at once. The offered price on the contract was insultingly low, and Ashedown had refused out of hand.

The next day the guard returned with a new contract and five additional men. The new proposal stated that the work would be done for free as a favor to his Lordship, and that I would be escorted back to the keep upon acceptance. Ashedown refused again and told the guards that if he were to do any work at all for Lord Eadric, he would have to show up himself and offer a fair price. He also made it clear that I would not be accompanying the guards back to the keep, although I didn't understand what role I had in any of this.

When they returned the following day, they were led by a man in flashy crimson plate armor. He rode atop a powerful black destrier and had an impressively ornate lance on his back. Without a word the men had kicked down the door, grabbed Amaya from where she sat sewing by the fire, and carried her out in chains. Ashedown had raged at the men, although when I moved to stop them, he placed a hard hand on my shoulder to hold me in place. When Amaya was in irons, roughly set atop a horse, the commander called down to us in a dismissive, arrogant voice. "If you ever want to see her again, fulfill the contract, and send the boy to us."

I had fought with Ashedown for six days after that, each one escalating in intensity as I pleaded for him to at least send me to speak with Lord Eadric. He stubbornly refused but wouldn't elaborate as to why I couldn't leave other than repeating, "If we give them what they want now, they'll do this to everyone in town to get what they want." He had continued working on other smaller jobs, refusing to start a single blade for the contract.

I didn't know why the Lord wanted to see me, but I didn't care. Amaya was in trouble through no fault of her own, and I couldn't leave her scared and alone in some holding cell within the keep. Though I was soaked to the bone and freezing I continued to trudge up the last hill on my way to the keep. Ashedown must have had a reason to keep me away, though he wouldn't explain them, and I knew his points were valid about giving in to these types of threats, but I couldn't help myself.

When I finally reached the gate I was surprised to find that despite the terrible weather, two guards were still standing watch outside the heavy wooden doors. As I approached, one held out his hand to stop me. "Whoa there, stranger. What business do you have at the keep this late at night?"

Calmly, I rested my hand on the pommel of my sword as I turned to face the guard. "My name is Elden Graham. I'm here to get my wife back."

I awoke with a start, gasping sharply as I sat up. It took me a moment of panic to realize I was still in my stone cell, sitting on my cot. Closing my eyes again I inhaled and exhaled deeply a few times to settle my frazzled nerves. *I guess I shouldn't expect all of my dreams to be happy ones.*

Remembering the early morning's meeting I turned to find Lia still asleep across the hall from me, undisturbed by my rude awakening. I found it comforting to see her sleeping so peacefully despite her situation. *I promised I wouldn't let this happen again. Yet here I am, watching it happen to someone else, right in front of me.* I rubbed my eyes and sighed heavily. *I guess it's decided then. It's time to get out of here.*

***

7. UNITY

A loud yawn from across the hall pulled me from my meditation. I cracked one eye open to spot Lia sit up on her cot and stretch lazily. Closing my eye once again, I thought over the list of questions I had for her. A prison break was dangerous and difficult enough solo, but depending on how helpless or useful Lia could be, it might become even harder. *Oh, let her wake up before the questioning starts, at least.*

Lia cleared her throat, though whether it was an attempt to gain my attention or unblock some phlegm I couldn't tell. That is, I couldn't tell until she did it a second time, much louder and more obviously than before. Suppressing a grin, I stayed quiet with my eyes closed, curious to gain some insights into her personality. When I didn't react, she began to hum softly to herself and shuffle around her cell. After a while, she gave up on that tact as well.

"Good morning, Lux!" She called out cheerfully. I opened my eyes to her beaming at me happily between the bars of her cell.

"Good morning, Lia." I replied. "You seem to be in a particularly good mood for an innocent girl wrongly imprisoned in a dungeon. Did you sleep well?"

Lia's face reddened, and she became overly interested in straightening the sheet on her cot. "It's not like I'm happy to be here, it's just...I was just thinking, it could have been a lot worse if I were down here by myself." After very carefully adjusting the thin sheet, she turned back to me. "And yes, I did sleep well, actually."

"I'm glad to hear it." I gave her a small smile. *Alright, that's enough time.* "So, Lia. Tell me about yourself. Before you were so rudely removed from your life, what did you do day to day?"

She blushed an even deeper red. "About myself? I-I don't really know what to say..."

I looked at her in puzzlement. *I understand that a friendly face and kind words goes further than normal in a situation like this, but...what's this about?* Lia's gaze continued to fix on everything around her aside from myself. Scanning down over myself, I came to a sudden realization. *Right. No shirt.* My bare chest was exposed due to the lack of prison garments I had received, and my muscular physique was particularly accentuated due to both the lack of food and the abundance of exercise I had been doing. *Ah shit.*

"Yeah, just anything about yourself. Day to day life, the things you like, any special skills, that sort of thing." I tried to prompt her along, doing my best to move past the awkwardness I was beginning to feel. *I can be nice to her and not be leading her on. She needs somebody like that right now.* I did my best to rationalize the thoughts in my head. While it was true that she was an attractive young woman with wide hips, a full chest, big amber eyes, and a lovely disposition, it was also true that I had no interest in her in any sort of sexual or romantic manner. *I haven't felt that way about somebody in a long time.*

Lia finally regained some composure. "Right. Well...I'm 25, and I live with my parents outside of the city to help my father with his trading business. I can't really move the crates around, but I keep track of the figures and manifests. My parents were never taught to read and write when they were young; I helped my mother learn the basics, but Father got frustrated and gave up, saying that we could just do it for him." She paused for a moment, staring off into empty space with a smile. "When I'm not working with Father, I guess I just find ways to keep busy otherwise. Cleaning, knitting...oh, I love cooking! Once I get out of here, I'll make you a meal of—"

She stopped herself mid-sentence with a contrite look. "I'm sorry, Lux, I didn't mean to...What I meant was..."

"It's alright. Unfortunately for that meal, I don't think I'll be getting out of here when you do." I smiled reassuringly.

"If you don't mind me asking...why are you down here?" Her voice was softer now, as if the delicate subject would be overheard by the empty cells around us.

"Oh, just a misunderstanding, really. I was being robbed at knifepoint, after the girl was let into my room at the inn by the innkeeper, and to protect myself I ended up cutting her hand off." The statement felt outlandish hearing it out loud for the first time, but I just chuckled lightly and continued. "The guards didn't seem interested in my side of the story, though. I was never even questioned, come to think of it. They just dragged me down here, took all of my belongings, and left me. I've been down here for about a week." I stopped, thinking. "Well, I assume it's been about a week. It's hard to tell without any windows."

Lia's face had paled over the course of my explanation. "That's...that's terrible! Why didn't you try to tell them what really happened? I'm sure they—"

The sound of a heavy, creaking door interrupted her. Footsteps began to approach from down the hallway, a single person from the sound of it. I motioned for Lia to be silent. *Please, let this be breakfast, and not an unwanted visitor.* An agonizing ten seconds passed as the steps grew louder, coming closer to our cells. I had never felt more relieved to see such a miserable plate of food in any of my lives once the guard finally made it to us. "Mealtime, prisoners." The gruff voice called out as always while he shoved the trays in through the delivery slots.

Once the guard had made the trip back to the door and left us alone once more, I let out a heavy sigh of relief and retrieved the tray of food. "I'm sure this isn't anywhere near the quality of what you're used to eating, Lia, but I suggest you finish it regardless. It might be bland and stale, but it'll help you keep your strength up." I set the bread to soften in the soup for a moment, almost a necessity with how stale it was.

"Lux...I'm sorry that you're stuck down here. I'm sure you'll get out soon, too!" Lia tried to sound uplifting, but I could still see the worry on her face.

"Oh, you don't have to worry about me." I called out between mouthfuls of food. "I'm sure they'll want to give me some sort of punishment eventually, and at that point we'll get everything cleared up. Truth be told, I'm much more eager to see you out of here than myself; I'm sure you have lots of family and friends that are worried about you."

"Well, not really." Lia admitted as she began to pick over her tray with disinterest. "I'm sure Mother and Father are worried sick about me, but other than that, I don't have many friends that would even know I'm gone." She took a bite of bread and struggled a long while to get it down. "Most of my friends from childhood have gotten married and moved away. It's really just me and my parents now." This didn't seem to upset her based on the way she said it so matter-of-factly.

I finished the rest of my meal in silence, unsure of how to respond. After I had sponged up the last of the soup and pushed the tray back into the hallway, I finally had something to say. "If there's one person out there worried about you, it's one person too many." I clapped my hands together and hopped to my feet, starting in on my pre-workout calisthenics. "But that's enough talk about that for now. Why don't you join me in doing some post-meal workouts? It's a great way to pass the time, and it'll keep your strength up too!" She didn't stand to join me, but I proceeded with my stretches regardless.

Lia watched me for a long while in silence. "Hey, Lux. Why are you doing this?"

"Well, I've found that if you're going to be stuck somewhere for a long time, it's best to keep both your mind and your body engaged as much—"

"No, not the workout." Her tone was markedly more serious than normal. "Why are you being so nice to me?"

That caught me by surprise. *Well. She's much more perceptive than I gave her credit for. Though, I don't know if I should burden her with what I think is really going on...or am I just being too protective of her with that as well?* I slowly sat down cross-legged in the middle of my cell. "Do you really want to know what I think?"

"Yes." Lia's face was a mask of determination, and her eyes were locked on to mine as she stood opposite me.

"I believe that you were taken to be used as leverage over your father. If he's been resisting the usual shakedown that the corrupt guards have been giving him, they were most likely looking for a new way to control him." I swallowed hard. "If that is indeed the case, I'm worried for your safety down here. Those guards...if they were able to take you without repercussion and are allowed to put you down here in the lower dungeon without cause, I believe they'll be coming to pay you a visit within the day. And it won't be a pleasant one."

To her credit, Lia never broke eye contact with me as I spoke, although I could see the beginnings of tears welling in her eyes. Even so, I continued. "I wasn't lying when I said you would probably be let out soon. I'm sure your father has given them whatever they wanted, even if they raised the price. But if these guards are really the scumbags I think they are, they won't pass up the opportunity to hurt you, and use it to ensure your father never defies them again." *Can I really trust her with this?* I lingered on the thought for a moment as she took the words in.

"Lia." Finally decided, my words were resolute. "I promise that I am going to get you out of here. I promise that those guards aren't going to hurt you in any way. And I promise that they will leave you and your family in peace from now on."

Her face was a mixture of shock and happiness as she stared at me with tears on her cheeks. "Lux, I...I don't know what I did to earn this from you. I'll never be able to repay you."

"A long time ago, I made a vow. I vowed that I wouldn't let those in power take advantage of the people they were supposed to protect. Not while I could do something about it." I motioned to my surroundings. "Clearly, it's time for me to step up and fulfill that vow."

Lia slowly fell to her knees and began to weep. I could vaguely make out the words, "Thank you...th-thank you..." as she cried I moved to respond, but thought better of it. Clearly, she needed some time to process the information. I turned to face the back wall of my cell to give her the most privacy I could, given the circumstances, and resumed my calisthenics. After a few minutes, as I was finishing up my routine, I heard her attempt to clear her throat as she sniffled.

She was sitting on the edge of her cot now, looking down at the floor as she swung her feet back and forth lazily. "So...what are you going to do?" She was avoiding my eyes again, but it didn't seem to be out of awkwardness. "Do you know someone in the prison that can help you out?"

I laughed, surprised by the line of questioning. "Ha, no, I don't. To be honest with you Lia, I don't necessarily have a fully formed plan yet." Walking to the front of my cell, I examined the steel bars as I continued. "Before you were brought here, my initial plan was to continue experimenting for a while, until I figured out a way to break out of here without alerting any guards. With the advanced timetable, though, it might be a little more..." I knocked on the bars lightly. "...A little more hectic."

"Experimenting?" Lia cocked her head to the side, curious. "I'm not sure what you mean."

"Lia, do you know anything about magic?"

The question caught her off guard. "Magic? No, I don't really...well, I mean, I've heard about it, and I know what it is, but I've never met anybody who could do it before."

I suppose it was too much to hope that the prisoner I'm about to save would be able to teach me how to control this world's form of magic. "I'm pretty unclear on the specifics as well. But, over the past day or so, I've made some helpful discoveries that might aid me in getting out of here." Holding my palms out flat before me and calling on my mana, I wrapped my right fingers down until I felt the familiar grip of my sword and pulled the weapon from the ether.

Lia jumped to her feet, her eyes wide with shock and excitement. "You're...you're a wizard!"

I grinned and shook my head. "No, I'm not a wizard. Or at least, I don't think I am." I stopped, tilting my head and thinking for a moment. *I'm not a wizard, right?* "It's a bit of a long story to explain, so I'll just say, I am very slowly teaching myself how to use magic, and I'm most likely doing it all wrong." Moving to my cot I sat down to face Lia, setting the blade next to me. "My experimenting has mainly been trying to figure out how magic works in this world, and how I can use it to escape from here."

For the moment, it seemed as though Lia's mind was focused on thoughts other than the potential dangers coming tonight, and I was happy to keep it that way for as long as I could. "So, can you cast some sort of...unlocking spell, or something?"

"No. At least not yet." I tapped on the sword. "I use this sword as my casting implement. Unfortunately, I don't know how to use magic that affects other objects yet. I certainly have some ideas to test on that front, but I haven't gotten to them yet." Tracing my finger absentmindedly along some of the runes on the blade, I gave Lia a smile. "While I start working on that, can you try to think of anything you've heard about magic that might be able to help? Even the simplest things you've heard about it could end up being extremely helpful."

She nodded enthusiastically. "Of course! I'll do my best to make a list of everything I know!" Lia leaned back on her hands, staring through me off into space as she began to organize her thoughts. She seemed engaged in the task, at least for now, which was all I had hoped for.

I took a moment to join her in thought, organizing my list of ideas to test. *Now that I have someone else around, I should probably be a bit more careful with my testing.* Of all the ideas I had to test, more work with runes seemed to be the safest for now. I winced pre-emptively at the thought of cutting my hands to write again, but I couldn't think of a better option. *Finding ink should be higher on my list of priorities after this.*

Turning away from Lia, I pricked a finger on the tip of my sword. After my last experiments I had realized that the amount of blood needed to trace out a simple rune was relatively small, and the cut I had made on my thumb was much more excessive than was necessary. I took the small woolen pillow from the cot and walked to the back wall, settling down on the floor next to it. Welling the blood up to the tip of my finger, I carefully began to draw the rune for fire on the face of the pillow.

Once I was satisfied with the symbol, I held the wool in both hands and began to tap into the energy in my core. It felt sluggish at first, like trying to flex a muscle the day after a hard workout, but my years of practice won out in the end. With the mana now flowing, I channeled it up through my arms and down to the tips of my fingers. As I expected, it seemed to pool there, unwilling to move out of my body and into the cloth.

No giving up this time. Figure it out. I closed my eyes and calmed my breathing, slowing my thoughts to gain some clarity. *I can channel mana through my sword to activate magical effects. I can't channel mana through this pillow. What's different? What's causing the issue?* I ran a hand along the scratchy wool, taking in all the bumps and grooves.

The sword was forged from manasteel; Metal, folded and forged while constantly channeling energy through it. I had been wielding it for so long that it felt like a natural extension of my arm. *I know every crease of the leather grip, the position of every rune along the blade. When I'm moving mana through the metal, it's as though I sense through every inch of the weapon itself.* I paused for a moment. *If I could know the material I'm trying to channel into as well as I know my sword, I bet I could do it!*

I turned the material over a few times in my hands, observing it closely. *Wool. Animal hair, spun and woven into yarn. A microcosm of interlacing strands with air filling the gaps left in between.* Looking over at my sword, an idea struck me. *I can channel mana through my sword. At a molecular level, the metal is pretty densely packed, with no gaps in between. Maybe, instead of just trying to push the mana through like I'm used to, I could...feel the fibers, and only move the energy through those?*

I almost laughed at the thought. *Boy, I'm really stretching with this one. I doubt this world has much knowledge of molecular theories though, so I should leverage every advantage I have...right?* I settled back into a meditative stance and tried to clear my mind. With exaggerated care, I channeled my mana back down into my fingertips. *Just take your time. Visualize the path the mana will take...like a river, flowing through me and into the woolen fibers.*

Without any way to measure time, I couldn't say how long I sat meditating against the back wall of my cell. It was a comforting exercise, consciously circulating my energy reserves across my hands as I slowly attempted to probe out into the wool. There was a new sensation tickling the tips of my fingers, which grew more pronounced as time passed: It was as if my mana was sending out exploratory tendrils, which gradually dissipated the farther they traveled.

Just as I was about to take a break, energy shocked my arms unexpectedly. I could feel the mana between my left and right hands, buzzing frantically as it began to build connections between the wool fibers. The tendrils of energy whipped out with an increasing fervor and I supplied the increasing mana cost eagerly. *This is it! I'm doing it!* My eyes snapped open, and I focused on the fire rune stained into the fabric. All at once the mana between my fingers channeled across the surface of the pillow, and the rune burst into crimson flames.

"Yes!" I jumped to my feet, still holding the burning wool. Cutting off the flow of mana, I dropped it to the floor before I burned my hands a second time. The flames went out immediately, but the surface of the wool where the rune had been was still smoldering. Lia bolted upright across the hall, startled by my sudden exclamation.

"Did you figure something out?" she asked, hopping off the cot to try and get a better view of my cell.

"I have indeed!" I proclaimed proudly. "It's not much, and it certainly isn't practical in an emergency, but progress is progress." I picked up the pillow and tossed it over to my cot as I walked up to the bars of my cell. "Have you thought of anything you've heard about magic that might be helpful for me?"

She shrugged, frowning. "A couple things, I think, but most of it is just really common knowledge that everyone would know, or a couple of fairy tales." Lia kicked at the ground, uncertainly. "I don't think it'll be able to help you at all."

I smiled. "You'd be surprised at how much I don't know. Why don't you just tell me what you're thinking, and I'll stop you if anything sounds unfamiliar. Okay?"

Lia nodded. "Okay. So, I know that to use magic, people have to say some sort of spell, and then whichever Primeval Elemental they called on gives them the—"

"Woah woah woah, hold on," I chuckled, stopping her mid-sentence. "A what elemental?"

Lia had a funny look on her face, as though she were simultaneously concerned for my mental wellbeing and trying not to laugh at it. "A Primeval Elemental? You know, from the Unity Church? Those Elementals?"

Oh, shit. Magic is a religion here. "I'm not familiar with the Unity Church. I take it that's the main religion in Yoria?"

"You're not familiar with..." She trailed off, clearly confused. "The Unity Religion is followed throughout the entire country of Kaldan. And in most of the surrounding ones, too." We sat in silence for a while; I was waiting for her to ask the next logical question, and Lia was trying to find the words for it as she twiddled her thumbs anxiously.

"Where are you from, Lux?" The question finally came. "If you haven't heard of Unity, you must be from...really far away." Lia's face was turned down towards the floor, but she was peering up at me sheepishly.

"I know it's a dissatisfying answer, but could we keep it at 'really far away' for now?" I tried to give her a small, reassuring smile. "Once we get out of here, I'll give you all the details you care to hear. But for right now, I'm still very interested in this Unity Church. What does it have to do with magic?"

"Right, of course!" She nodded. "The Unity Church says that, a long time ago, the world was created by the Primeval Elementals, or big powerful beings made purely of the elements. The Primeval of Earth made the ground, the Primeval of Water made the oceans, the Primeval of Wind made the air, on and on until the whole world was made." Lia was telling the story with fervor complete with emphatic hand gestures and voice changes, seemingly repeating words she had heard all her life. The whole scene was pretty cute, our present situation forgotten.

"Finally, all the Primevals came together, and by combining all of the elements, they made the living creatures that live throughout our world. With their jobs completed, they all got together and went back to their home, far away from here." Satisfied with her storytelling, she smiled at me. "Does that help at all?"

"Well, it was a very good story!" I gave a small round of applause. "I don't really see how it relates to magic, though."

"Oh, I forgot the best part!" Lia said excitedly. "Even though the Primevals left, they still like to watch and listen to the things we do. Sometimes, if people practice and train hard enough, they can ask the Primevals to give them a part of their abilities, and then the magic happens!"

I cocked an eyebrow. "So, if you pray hard enough, these Primevals will give you the ability to do magic?"

"It's not like that!" She sounded slightly frustrated. "You work really hard, making sure your body is strong enough to handle their energy, and then you ask for their help. If you're good enough, they'll give you the energy to cast a spell! Sometimes, you can even cast two or three spells, if you use the right words."

There it is. I nodded. "I think I understand now. Do you happen to know what the words are?"

Lia shook her head. "I've never met anybody who could do magic before, so I've never heard the words." She reddened a bit. "Well, actually, I do know one thing, but it's probably not even real. It's the words from a story my father used to tell me when I was little."

I couldn't help but smile. "Anything is helpful at this point. You've already taught me a lot today!"

She looked up at me, and then away again. "Alright. I guess..." Lia cleared her throat and shifted around nervously. "The story says that a long time ago, the country of Kaldan was under attack by a giant dragon that nobody could defeat. The greatest wizard of the city of Yoria went on an adventure to try and get the help of some of the Primeval Elementals. When he returned to the city, the dragon was attacking, so he cast a giant spell..." She trailed off for a moment, then took a deep breath.

"PRIMEVAL OF ICE, I BESEECH THEE, CAST THROUGH ME THE MOST POWERFUL STORM TO FREEZE

AND BLAST AWAY THIS BEAST, SO I MAY SAVE MY BELOVED CITY!" Lia shouted with a theatrical, booming voice.

Laughter burst out of me, completely taken by surprise by Lia's commitment. She scowled at me. "Don't laugh! It's just a silly kid story, and that's always how Father did it!" Her face went beet red and she ran to her cot, hiding her face in her hands.

It took a while for my laughter to subside enough for me to talk clearly. "I'm sorry, that was just unexpected is all!" My words did little to assuage her embarrassment. "Really, Lia, it was good! It was good! And I definitely think it will help me learn about magic, too!" She was sitting on the edge of her cot now, knees drawn up in front of her with her arms crossed on top. Cautiously, she peered over her arms, brow furrowed.

"It better have!" Lia pouted at me. "And you better remember it, because I'm not gonna tell you the story again!"

"I promise, I will!" Chuckling, I paced over to my cot and flopped down onto my back. Despite everything, I was enjoying my time here with Lia. The looming dark clouds of what was to come later still lingered on the periphery of my thoughts, but for now I kept them at bay. *I've got to get her out of here. No matter the cost. I promised, didn't I?*

***

8. A PLAN IN MOTION

The rest of the day passed relatively uneventfully. I chatted with Lia on and off about various things: favorite foods, weather, fond memories, whatever came up. If she was feeling apprehensive of the future, she was doing well to hide it. Any time that wasn't spent on conversation was used to formulate a plan to escape my cell.

Not knowing when, or if, the guards that imprisoned Lia would come to see her, it was difficult to come up with an effective strategy. I had no doubt that given enough time and energy I could break through the bars in front of me, either through fire or force. But if the cell were broken when our usual guard came to deliver our next meal, I would no doubt be moved, questioned, and watched. On the other hand, using any sort of magic on the bars themselves would take far too long in the moment itself, and I couldn't be assured I would succeed at all.

My plan was to somehow manipulate the lock of my cell door before any danger were to happen, but in such a way that wasn't noticeable by our regular guard. Over the course of the afternoon, I had spent a long time meditating with my hands on the metal lock, trying to analyze it from the inside by channeling mana through it. I had originally expected it to be a somewhat easy task, having already succeeded in my tests on wool earlier, but it was giving me trouble.

I found that in comparison to my sword or the yarn, the lock was much more complex. Initially, imparting energy into it had gone faster than expected. As I was so familiar with channeling through metal, it only took a few small adjustments for the different elemental makeup. However, I found that as soon as my mana reached an unknown mechanism within the lock, I couldn't correctly visualize the structure and the energy immediately receded back into my fingers.

With a large amount of patience and at least an hour's worth of meditation, I had built a relatively accurate mental map of the internal mechanisms of the lock. Every time I reached a new twist or curvature I would have to start over again, but with a slightly clearer picture in mind. At the current moment, I was taking a quick break to wipe sweat from my brow. *I've never had to channel energy for this long before, and certainly not through a new material. I guess there's always new avenues to improve...I'll add "New Channeling Materials" and "Continuous Channeling" to my practice routines.*

With a heavy sigh, I placed my hands on the face of the lock and closed my eyes again. Reaching out once more the energy moved quickly through the surface, but I dialed it back as it pushed into the more complicated sections. *Alright, gently now. Keyway...tumbler, tumbler, little crack in the shaft, tumbler, bolt...*

My fingers abruptly warmed with a buzzing energy as the mana encompassed the entire structure of the lock. "Finally!" I threw my hands up over my head in triumph. I was sweating and out of breath, but it was the most satisfied I had felt in a long time. Lia turned around to face me from her position on the floor, having finally agreed that physical exercise would be of some benefit.

"What did you do?" she asked, smiling up at me. Her face was flushed from the exertion of her latest set of push-ups, a strand of hair stuck to her damp forehead.

"I mapped the internal structure of the mechanisms in my cell's lock!"

Lia tilted her head, staring for a moment, and then laughed. "I don't really know what that means, but...great job!" She laughed and clapped her hands.

I chuckled, rubbing my face. "I think I should be able to get my door open in an emergency, should the need arise." There were still things to test, but the groundwork was finally set. I took a moment to stretch my neck and arms, after being in the same meditation positions for so long. "How is your workout going? It's nice, right?"

She rolled her eyes. "Yes, Lux, it's actually pretty nice. And it's something to do, which is also nice."

"Well, I won't distract you from it any longer than I already have. I should probably finish up my testing before I forget everything I just learned." I knelt in front of the door and pressed my hands against the back of the lock again. Now that I had a decent mental map of the mechanisms, I attempted to channel a small amount of energy into the lock without using the added support of meditation.

Surprisingly, the process worked much more easily than I had expected. It took about thirty seconds, by my estimation, to fully surround the lock with mana. It certainly wasn't the almost instantaneous suffusion I could achieve with my sword, but it was minutes better than I had achieved earlier. *I need to get this down to single digits if it's to be of any real use.* With a clear goal in mind, I set to work on constantly suffusing the lock with energy as fast as possible, withdrawing the mana, and repeating the process.

Though the work was tedious, I found a certain joy in it. It had become my passion over my previous lives to work on discovering new ways to use mana and reveal new insights never before found in the field. Based on what Lia had said of the world, I found it hard to believe that anybody capable of using magic would be using a pillow or a jail cell lock as their catalyst, and that thought excited me. Plus, the idea that I had made dramatic progress on my magic research two days in a row continually reinvigorated me in my task.

By the end of my experimentation, I was able to completely suffuse the lock with magic in just under seven seconds. I could even carry a simple conversation with Lia while doing so, though it dramatically increased the amount of time the process took due to the distraction. Finally satisfied with my performance, I slumped down against the bars to take a rest. *Now, on to the next hurdle: actually doing something with the mana.* The thought created a small knot in my stomach; even though there was no definitive proof anybody would be coming down to harm Lia, the idea continued to drive me harder and harder as time went on.

I let out a hearty sigh, relieved to have even a small moment to rest. From behind me, I heard Lia call out to me. "Lux? What is it you're doing, exactly? I thought you already did the...internal...map thing."

Turning to face her, I tried to think of a simple explanation. *There is no concept of internal energy or mana here. And unless I want to try and disprove an entire religion, I don't think there's an easy way to explain it.* "Well, it's sort of hard to explain. Basically, I'm trying to cast magic through the lock, but I don't know what magic to do, so I'm just practicing. Does that make sense?"

Lia considered for a moment. "Yeah! Well, kind of!" she laughed. "I wouldn't mind learning more about it, though. I still don't really understand how you're doing magic without saying anything."

"Of course!" The idea of teaching somebody else about magic in the same way that I had learned it was exciting. "When we're out of here, I'll tell you anything you want to know." I stood and walked to my cot to retrieve my sword. *Now to pick a rune to get through this lock.*

"You'll have a lot of talking to do when we get out of here, if you keep promising me that," Lia teased. "Anything else you want to add to that list?"

Break? That seems sort of vague. Destroy? No, that's the same thing as Break. Unlock? I'd probably have to know all of the right positions for the tumblers for that to work. "Hey, I told you I'd tell you anything you wanted to know, right? That's already the biggest list I can think of. You should start making a list of things you want to ask me." *Shatter...yeah, that could work.*

Out of the corner of my eye, I noticed Lia blush and look away. Distracted by my train of thought I didn't follow up, but instead took the opportunity to cut my finger on my sword again while she wasn't looking. With my hand behind the locking mechanism of the door I sketched out the rune for shatter on the metal. *There. Done, finally.*

Sucking on my bleeding fingertip I returned my sword to its scabbard, wherever it was currently being kept. A gurgle from my stomach, clearly audible in the silence of the dungeon, alerted me that it was most likely time for dinner. "I suppose that means food should be on its way. Are you hungry, Lia?"

"Yeah, really hungry." She frowned. "I used to eat three times a day. You said they only give you two meals here?"

"That is sadly the case. Or at least my best guess." I chuckled. "It sort of felt like two meals until I got tired for the day." *Although, I usually don't feel this hungry by the time my next meal is arriving. Has it been longer than normal?* I didn't vocalize the thought.

Lia pouted again in a half-joking but still a bit upset sort of way. "Well, I hope he comes soon. I don't like going to bed hungry, but I'm feeling a bit worn out." She shot an accusatory glance my way. "Maybe it's from all the working out."

I put my hands up to accept the blame. "Maybe it is! But I think in the long run, you'll thank me for it." My gut had started to turn, but now from anxiety instead of hunger. I couldn't pin down exactly why the lingering dread was getting stronger, but it was reaching uncomfortable levels.

Unfortunately for Lia, dinner didn't arrive anytime soon. We both sat in an increasingly uneasy quiet, neither wanting to point out the fact that we might not be eating tonight. Finally, I broke the silence with a less-than-convincing yawn. "Well, I think I'll just go to sleep for now. Maybe I'll wake up to a lukewarm tray of food delivered straight to my cell!" I stretched for a moment and then laid down on my cot, resting back on my elbows. I didn't feel tired at all; in fact, I was as wired as I had been since being locked up. *Don't let her see you nervous. She doesn't need that.*

Lia eyed me for a moment, then shrugged in agreement. "I guess you're right. If the food comes and I'm still asleep, you'll wake me up right?"

"It's a promise." I gave her a thumbs up.

She smiled back at me. "Goodnight, Lux."

"Goodnight, Lia." I laid back onto the pillow, now slightly less comfortable than it had been the night before. Angrily, I flipped it over so the scorch marks faced downwards and gave it a few punches to try and fluff it up to no avail. My entire body was tense now, and I stared at the damp stone ceiling in silence. *Get it together, Elden. Just because you thought something could happen doesn't mean it will happen.*

My mental disciplining did little to calm my frayed nerves and I rolled from one side to the other restlessly for a long while. I took a small comfort in the fact that Lia was most likely sleeping now, her breathing slow and even, but it wasn't enough. *I promised.* My hands started to clench reflexively into fists at the thought. *I promised I wouldn't let it happen again, but here we are. I'm not going to make myself a liar.*

I could feel my heart pounding in my chest, beating in arrhythmic spasms. My breathing was ragged and strained, and sweat was beading up on my brow. *Is this a panic attack?* Swinging my legs out of bed, I stood shakily. Staring down at my hands I could see them clearly trembling. *No...this is something else. I wouldn't be thinking so clearly otherwise.* Every muscle in my body wanted to move, needing to relieve the extreme stress coursing through me. *This is pre-battle adrenaline.*

The state I was in suddenly made sense within the new context, although I couldn't figure out why it was happening to begin with. Nothing was immediately a threat, but I was reaching for the grip of my sword out of habit. *Danger.* The klaxons were ringing in my head, screaming a red alert to every inch of my form. *Danger!* I wanted to shout, "THERE IS NO DANGER!", but my body wouldn't allow it. *DANGER!*

A familiar squealing of metal from down the hall cleared my head. *The door. This is it.* It opened and shut, and footsteps echoed towards me. My blood turned electric as the adrenaline fully took hold of my panicked mind and body. *Two sets. Not the normal guard.* Quickly, I moved back to my cot as stealthily as possible, sitting down at the far end to face the hall. As the footsteps approached, I heard some murmured speech. "...our rewards for this...not going last..." They shared a laugh.

Two unfamiliar men entered my field of vision. They were both dressed in city guard attire complete with iron caps, shields on their backs, and weapons on their hips. One of them lazily spun a half-full keyring in his hand. Both men stopped when they reached our cells. The man with the keyring began sorting through the keys, while the other stood in the middle of the hall, apparently keeping guard. Casually, he turned his head towards me, and the look on his face told me he did not expect another prisoner.

"Oi!" He yelled, elbowing his buddy with the keys. "What's he doin' here?"

"Ah, fuck 'em. Dungeon trash." The man with the keys replied, laughing to himself.

The first man walked up to the bars of my cell. "You go on ahead and forget we were down here." He tapped his helmeted temple and gave me an insistent look. "Understand?"

"What do you want with that one?" I heard my voice reply cool and collected, as though someone else were speaking.

The guard looked taken aback. "Did you not hear what I just said? Turn your head the fuck around, and I won't bash your face in. You understand that?"

"Aye." Casually, I leaned up against my cell wall and stared off into space past the guard.

The conversation had woken Lia. "A-are you coming to take me home?"

With a snide laugh, the man with the keys responded. "No, sweet thing. The boys upstairs want to have a look at you." He settled on a key and moved to her cell door. "If your Daddy keeps doin' what he's told, and YOU do what YOU'RE told, maybe we'll take you home at weeks end. 'Spose that also depends on just how well you do." He put the key into the door and turned hard, shifting some well-aged tumblers. "Oi, shithead! Come over here and help me with the girl!"

The man watching me turned and stepped across the hall to assist with the door. In one swift motion I lunged from my cot, crossed the cell, and put my hands around my door's lock. Mana shot down my arms and suffused the lock in a second flat, and I activated the rune. It glowed with an angry orange light, and I could feel the energy draw from my reserves. The metal under my hands began to vibrate, and the internal mechanisms began to fracture. *No, NOW!* I flooded the metal with a tidal wave of mana far greater than I had before. The small cracks turned to fissures, and the metal splintered between my fingers with a loud *crack!*

Hearing the sound, the closer man turned and saw me standing over a small pile of metal fragments. "What the fuck are you doing?" He shouted at me, taking a step towards my cell while drawing his sword. I reared back and kicked my door at center mass, flinging it open to catch him in the chest. The sound of the wind leaving his lungs hissed as he toppled sideways. Drawing my sword from an unseen hip scabbard, I strode into the hall as the guard with the keys had successfully opened Lia's door. He had only just begun to react to the noises behind him when I held my blade up to his throat.

"Lia. Out here, behind me. Now." I pulled the guard out of the way, easily overpowering his weak attempts to break free. Lia complied, scurrying out of the cell to hide further down the hall behind me. "Good. Close your eyes." The look on her face was one of pure terror, but she obeyed. Satisfied, I moved my head to my current prisoner's ear. "Now, why don't you tell me exactly where you were planning on taking the girl."

To his credit, the man continued trying to fight. "Fuck you!" He aimed a headbutt back where my head was, but I was already moving, having anticipated that mode of attack. I pressed the sword harder into the flesh of his neck, now drawing tiny drops of blood. Every breath he took was painful, indicated by the terrible rasping sound he was making. "They're goin' to kill you for this, bastard!"

"No, they aren't." I replied calmly, drawing the blade hard across his throat. A dark red wave gushed from his neck as I let the man fall. He clutched in vain at the wound, trying to stop the giant spurts of blood from pulsing out. With a hard kick, I sent him toppling into Lia's now empty cell.

Turning to the man on the floor, I was surprised to see him propped up against the wall clutching his side. Clearly, the door had done more damage than I had initially thought. I crouched down to eye level and he recoiled pitifully. "Don't kill me!" he cried out, holding his other hand out in front of his face.

I cocked my head to one side. "Why would I kill you when you know so many things that I want to know? No, you're too useful to me at the present moment. If you'd like to stay that way, and not go the way of your friend there, you can start telling me what you want with the girl."

"W-We was just comin' down to get 'er, for the boys upstairs. It wasn't my idea, honest, they just said I had to come down and bring 'er up." He was trembling as he spoke, his earlier gruff tone long forgotten. His speech began to slur as he continued. "She's just down 'ere until 'er Pops falls in line. He wasn't payin' the tolls, a-an' we had to do somethin' to change his mind, elsewise other folks might stop payin' too."

Sighing, I nodded. "Yes, I know that. But what did they want with the girl *right now?*"

The man averted his eyes, talking now to the floor. "I-I don't know."

The tip of my sword whipped up to his chest, flicking droplets of the dead guard's blood onto the man's face. "You're shit at lying." He looked back up at me, eyes wide and face completely pale. "Try the truth this time."

He gulped hard, looking around in desperation to find anything that could save him. "T-they wanted to 'ave some fun w-with 'er is all. W-wanted to tell 'er dad some stories, keep 'im from doin' it again." Suddenly he looked up to me in a panic, eyes watering. "I wasn't goin' to touch 'er! Swear on the Primes I wasn't!" He sniveled, tears and snot beginning to run down his face. "J-just don't kill me!"

Greater Sharpening. I pressed the tip of my blade down into his boiled leather jerkin, instantly piercing the material and cutting into the man's chest. "Where are these men now?"

Crying out in pain he tried to wiggle away, but his broken ribs stopped him. "Just upstairs. Through, uhm, the door at the end of the hallway, up the stairs and, er, to the left. First door. They gave the normal guards a night off, so it's just, just them." Finally, he gave up squirming and slumped back against the wall, defeated. "That's everything I know, I swear! Just let me live, I'm b-begging you!"

I rolled my eyes. "Why do they always say that? If that's everything you know, you're not of use to me anymore." The man's face changed to one of pure horror. "I don't want anybody to know what happened down here." I tapped the side of my temple. "Understand?"

The man nodded vigorously. "Right! I w-won't tell a soul, I p-promise!"

"Good." With unnatural ease, I ran the sword through the man's chest, impacting the wall behind him. He spasmed once, then let out a long low sigh. I withdrew the blade and gave it a quick flourish to remove some of the blood dripping along its edge. With the threat currently dealt with I put away my sword and moved to search the bodies. The man in front of me held little on his person aside from a small coin purse in his vest pocket. I took it, not bothering to look inside, and moved to the other man behind me.

A large puddle of blood had pooled underneath him, coating the bottom of my feet in a warm, sticky residue. I pulled the keyring from his pocket, as well as another coin purse, but found nothing out of the ordinary otherwise. The roughspun pants I was wearing didn't have pockets, so I moved down the hallway towards Lia.

As she heard me approach Lia recoiled, eyes still closed. "Lia, it's okay. It's just me." I moved in close, blocking her view of the hallway. "You can open your eyes."

Slowly, her eyes flickered open. She was trembling, and her face was stained with tears. "L-Lux..." She managed to get the word out before choking on a sob. Lunging forward, she hugged me around the waist and cried into my bare chest. Her face was hot with tears, and her arms were locked tight around me.

    I put a hand on her head, stroking her hair. "It's alright. It's alright." I gave her a few seconds to cry before I continued. "We have to start moving now. Can you do that?" She nodded wordlessly into my chest. "Good, that's great. You can just close your eyes again, and I'll lead you out. Okay?"

    She nodded again, but didn't move to leave. *Give her a damn break. This isn't normal for most people.* I patted her head again. "You're going to be okay, Lia. I promise." Pulling away, I took her hand and began to walk towards the exit. Lia followed slowly, sniffling. I did my best to avoid the spreading pool of blood as we began our journey upwards. Lia gave a small gasp, confirming to me that she hadn't closed her eyes as I had asked. *Welcome to the real world, Lia. Sorry it had to happen like this.*

***

9. REUNIONS

After a moment of searching I found the key to open the heavy iron door sealing the dungeon closed. With a hard push it swung open, revealing a narrow set of dark stairs leading up to a hallway. I paused for a moment and turned to Lia. "Lia, I need you to do something for me. Can you carry these?" I offered her the two pouches of money and the ring of keys.

She nodded meekly and accepted the items. "Thank you, Lia. Now, just follow along close behind me, okay? It won't be long now, we're almost out of here." She nodded again in silence. *Poor girl. She didn't deserve this.* Recalling my sword, I turned and started up the stone staircase.

The air was heavy with the smell of damp stone as we ascended from the dungeon. A single torch burned dangerously low at the halfway point, obviously deemed unimportant in the normal prison upkeep. Reaching the top, a hallway ran both left and right, lined with various wooden doors labeled in an unfamiliar language. *First door on the left.* I took a calming breath, then turned and headed down the hallway. I stopped before reaching the first door.

"Lia." My voice was a low whisper. "Things might be dangerous in this next room. Do you want to stay outside in the hallway until—"

"No." Lia cut me off, her voice surprisingly strong. "I'm coming in with you. Those men are in there." She scowled, in amusing contrast to her red, puffy face. "I'm not closing my eyes any more."

She ran out of tears. All that's left is anger now. I nodded to her. "Stay behind me." Turning to the door, I knocked twice.

A familiar voice yelled back. "About time, you fucken' half-wits! Bring her in." There was a chorus of laughter from within, at least three other distinct voices. "How hard is it to grab a girl from a cell? If she gave you trouble, I swear I'll never let you hear the end of it."

I opened the door and entered the room, and the laughter stopped. Five men sat around a large table, playing cards and drinking from steins. A fireplace crackled to their left, filling the room with a pleasant aroma and dancing shadows. There were long tables with benches shoved up against the far wall in a disheveled pile, moved hastily out of the way for what looked like a new addition to the room: A single bed frame with a well-used mattress. Ropes were tied to each post, currently sitting piled in the center.

Initially, I had planned to enter with some quippy line about a lovely reunion, but my jaw was clenched so tightly shut with rage I could hardly breathe. *It was all true. I was right.* The thought echoed around my otherwise blank mind, stunned by the scene before me. My stomach turned in disgust at the idea of what they had planned to do.

"Who the fuck are you?" The tall man asked, standing. The rest of the men followed suit, reaching for various weapons on their belts or on side tables. I was about to take a step forward when I felt Lia brush up behind me, peeking out around my shoulder. The fat man, positioned beside his partner, raised his eyebrows in surprise. "He's got the girl, Jack."

The tall man, apparently named Jack, rolled his eyes. "Oh, does he, Porks? I appreciate the update; I wouldn't have known." His words dripped with venom, but Porks seemed oblivious, just nodding his head. Jack turned back to me. "I'm not sure who you're supposed to be, but if you hand us the girl, we'll let you go last." Two men at the front of the table laughed in unison. They looked like a mirror image of one another, aside from a large scar running across the right man's forehead.

I felt a small hand on my back as Lia's hair brushed over my shoulder. "That's them," She whispered in my ear. "That's all of them." My body was taut as a drawn bowstring, but I managed a nod. Every muscle burned with pent up energy, and my blood was boiling with fury. Lia retreated a step, and I heard the door creak closed behind me.

"Do you understand anything I'm saying?" Jack asked of me, waving a hand in front of him. He spoke slowly, with exaggerated emphasis. "You. Fuck. Off. Now." I stood statue still, my face a blank mask watching them. Jack laughed. "Looks like he forgot what he was doing. Alby, break his fucken' teeth, and then grab the bitch so we can get started."

I finally reached my breaking point. All at once, mana suffused my body and the runes on my sword dazzled brightly. There was no plan, no composed strategy; every enhancement I knew flicked on at once, something I usually found difficult to do. Tossing my sword up into the air, I caught it with a sideways grip and threw it like a javelin at the closest target, an unfamiliar man with dark hair and fox-like ears. It crushed through his chest, embedding itself up to the crossguard in his mangled flesh. He screamed for a moment, but blood erupted from his mouth and cut it short as he toppled backwards over his chair.

"BY THE PRIMES, KILL THIS FUCKER!" Jack screeched, jumping further back into the room to take cover behind the bed. The twins rushed forward, trying to take advantage of my weaponless state. Porks ran to a table by the fire and picked up a crossbow, fumbling with a pouch of bolts. "PORKS, SHOOT HIM!"

My vision was tinged with a pulsing red light, highlighting each man left standing in the room with a radiant crimson glow. It was an unfamiliar sensation, but I was long past the point of intellectual curiosity. Plus, it felt...good. Rocketing forward, I dodged an overhead blow from a mace. The man seemed to be moving at a snail's pace, at least to my accelerated viewpoint, and I let his momentum carry him past me as I spun around behind him. A flash of red energy shone brilliantly from his belt and I noticed a small dagger sticking out, previously hidden to me. I reached in, yanking it up and out, sending it directly into the bottom of his jaw.

With the first twin out of the way, I rounded on the second. His face was a mix of strong emotions: rage from seeing his brother fall to his knees in agony, confusion over how the plan had gone so wrong, and fear. The fear was...delicious. He held a longsword and a shield to bear against me, but his form was sloppy. The shield was too low, and his footing was terrible. Even though I was bare handed, he was hesitant to approach. *The fear of death is taking him.* A dark smirk spread across my face as I reached out an empty hand between us.

In a flash, my sword disappeared from the wrecked chest cavity of the first man and materialized before me. Somewhere behind the overturned chair, there was a sickening wet squelch as the gaping wound collapsed on itself. The blade was glowing a monstrous red, a combination of the blood from the dead guards and the combat enhancements I had used. It shone and dimmed menacingly in the flickering firelight.

With a quick cut, I lashed out at the twin's head. He barely caught it with the corner of his shield, just in time to save his face. The force of the blow sent him stumbling backwards, and he tripped and fell over one of the haphazardly pushed out chairs. I was about to follow up and confirm the kill when an all-to-familiar *click* of a loaded crossbow echoed in my ears. Turning, I saw Porks had finally loaded and readied a bolt, the deadly end of the weapon pointing directly at me.

Or, almost directly at me. His arms were shaking, and I could see that any shot taken from his current angle would fall far wide of me. Even so, when the bowstring snapped, I found myself moving unconsciously forward, directly into the line of fire. The bolt connected with my left shoulder with a hard thud, spinning me backwards and down to one knee. When I went to stand, I found myself face to face with a horrified Lia. *That bolt would have taken her between the eyes.* A new layer of fury took hold of me, and I let out a roar of pain and anger.

The second twin was scrambling to his feet on my right, and Porks was hastily reloading the crossbow behind the table on my left. Instinctually, I regained my footing and pointed the bastard sword at the twin. "FIRE!" The fierce bellow left my lips as I poured the full force of my mana through my right arm. The blade erupted with a swirling column of flame, jetting across the room to engulf the approaching foe. Shadows lengthened and danced frantically in the deadly crimson light.

A horrible scream came from the flaming figure as he flailed desperately against the licking fire. Without a second thought, I turned my sights to Porks, still fumbling with the crossbow. Behind him, Jack had paled to a ghostly white, and was kicking benches and chairs down to fill the space between us. He was shouting incoherently at Porks, which only seemed to confuse the fat little man even further.

I crossed the length of the room in three steps, a product of my Windstep and my driving anger. Porks looked up at me, his face contorted in frustration over the difficulty he was having with the crossbow. By the time he realized he was under attack, he was already dead; a deadly quick slash lopped his head from his neck without resistance. It bounced off the corner of the table next to his decapitated body and rolled up to Jack's feet. He looked down at it in horror.

"What the fuck ARE you?" he shouted, trying to retreat further into the room. His progress was quickly blocked by an overturned table, trapping him in a corner with the bed frame.

Silently, I stalked forward. Blood was running down my left arm, dripping onto the floor to mark my progress across the room, but I hardly felt the wound. The pain would come later, after the adrenaline and the bloodlust had subsided. Right now, my singular reason for being was to destroy the man named Jack standing before me.

He held out a dagger before him in one hand and wielded a longsword in the other. I observed from his stance that he had more combat training than the others, but I was unconcerned. "Just stop. STOP!" Jack was screaming now, any sort of confidence or composure he had moments before long lost to him.

For some reason beyond me, I stopped walking. I was only ten feet from him, easily within range of a deathblow, but some dark part of me needed to know more about him. Standing in silence, I slowly raised my blade to point at his face. "Why are you doing this, you maniac?" He shouted at me, clearly unnerved. Without a word, I pointed my sword to Lia, still standing by the door, and then to the bed.

"What, are you some kind of hero? Is that it?" Jack sneered at me. "If you're so heroic, you aren't going to kill me, right? I'll be taken in for justice?" Somehow, the man had convinced himself that even though there were four fresh corpses before him, he was somehow special. Unfortunately for him, he was right.

Through my clenched jaw, I managed to choke out a few words. "You...don't deserve...death."

Jack's face shifted, first to fear, but quickly to a false facade of confidence. "Oh, I see. She your little girlfriend or something? Trying to save her from the bad men so she'll love you better?" He pointed his longsword towards her. "I'm going to kill you, bastard, and then I'm going to tie her to this fucking bed, and I'm going—"

I couldn't understand why he said what he did, and I was long past the point of caring about conversation. A man like Jack probably lived his life getting under people's skin until they made a mistake he could exploit. In our situation, though, Jack failed to realize that I wasn't operating with any form of reason or planning that could be abandoned.

The blood along the face of my sword began to bubble and hiss violently as my vision narrowed with the pulsing red light from before. An ominous black energy swirled around the blade, shimmering like a nearly invisible flame. It came completely unbidden, drawing heavily on my energy reserves, but I could feel an overwhelming power in the unknown effect, and I allowed it to continue. With a cold, menacing look, I stared Jack down and hissed, "Suffer."

My blade snapped up quickly, an arcing upward slash sent towards his dagger side. A small grin curled Jack's lip, most likely believing he had goaded me into an unwise attack. He moved, so incredibly slowly, to flick away the attack with his dagger. At this point I was running on pure combat instinct, and his actions seemed so obvious. He would attempt to redirect my strike outwards, and then follow up with a slice to my unguarded side.

As soon as my sword connected with his parrying dagger, I gripped the pommel with my empty hand and wrenched the strike inward. The redirect caught him by surprise, catching his dagger at an awkward angle as he struggled to repel the blow. The attack had less power behind it due to the change in direction, but it was enough to draw the tip of my sword across his chest.

The instant the blade made contact, Jack shrieked with pain. He stumbled backwards, dropping his weapons as he scrabbled at his jerkin in panic. The creeping black energy from my sword was seeping from the cut in his armor now with a faint hissing sound, increasing in volume by the second. Jack collapsed to his knees and convulsed as thick, dark lines began to work their way up his neck. They curled and wound around the base of his jaw, sending black tendrils racing across his face. His screams of agony were blood curdling as he desperately tried to find relief.

After another second of torture I released the energy from my sword. His wound stopped smoking, and the corruption slowly began to recede down his neck back towards the source. It left dark tracks in its wake that spiderwebbed across the entirety of his face and neck, most likely a permanent disfigurement on his skin. Jack curled into a ball on the floor, still screaming in pain. My vision began to uncloud as my senses slowly returned to my control, and I found myself viewing the man with a surprising amount of pity.

"Lia." I turned, calling her over from the doorway. She had pressed herself up against the wall, but judging by her expression, she had watched the entire encounter unfold. "Come here, Lia." Cautiously, she picked her way around the carnage before her and came to my side. The entire time, her eyes were locked on Jack's sniveling form. "He's yours."

She looked up at me, confused. "M-mine?"

"Yours." I nodded. "Forgive him. Kill him. Condemn him." I pushed the tip of my sword into the floor and leaned the grip towards her. "Whatever closure you need from this, it's yours to take."

Setting the keyring and purses down on the floor, Lia placed her hand on the pommel of my sword, tilting the weapon towards her. As I stepped back to give her space, I noticed my hands had started to tremble again. It wasn't surprising; it was the most mana I had expended at once in years, and I had lost a fair amount of blood from the bolt currently sticking out of my shoulder. I did my best to calm them, hiding any signs of weakness from both Lia and Jack.

Lia took a cautious step forward, dragging the sword along the floor as she moved. After a pause, she took another, more confidently this time. Reaching the point where Jack was curled on the ground, she heaved the weight of the sword out in front of her, lifting it with both hands to point at Jack. "I will *never* forgive you for what you've done." The pathetic form before her whimpered, weakly attempting to scoot away.

"But I won't kill you, either." The words surprised me. If it had been me in that situation, I would have killed Jack without a second thought. I had imagined that Lia would leave him whining pathetically in the corner, preferring to get out of this wretched place as soon as possible. There was a harshness to her tone as she continued that I hadn't heard from her before. "You'll live with this for the rest of your miserable life. As a lesson to what happens to people who take advantage of others."

With that, Lia turned and walked back to me, handing the sword back. She looked up at me with tears in her eyes and nodded. I placed a comforting hand on her shoulder and nodded back. "Wait here."

I passed her and walked to Jack, crouching down to his level. "Where are my things?"

Jack recoiled, hiding his face. "Just...kill me...please."

"You heard her. You have to live with this now." I dragged the sword out in front of me and pressed the tip into the back of his hand. "Now, unless you'd like the pain to come back, you'll tell me where they've stashed my things, and how to get out of here."

When the point of the sword contacted his flesh he screamed, most likely imagining the pain to be returning. In truth, I had no idea what I had done to the man, and certainly had no way of recreating the effect now. But Jack didn't know that. He shook violently for a while, then calmed enough to speak. "Door marked 'lock-up'. That's where it should be." A brutal cough interrupted him, and I waited in silence until he could speak again. "Then, the 'West Tower' door, to the right." He looked up at me with empty eyes. *Those are the eyes of a broken man. He won't last a week.*

Without another word, I turned and left him there. "Let's go," I said softly to Lia. As we left, I noticed a small dish on the center table where the men had been playing cards before we arrived. It was filled with coins, mostly crowns, with some silver peeking out here and there. I put away my sword and grabbed it with my right hand, leaving my left arm dangling limply at my side. Blood continued to flow down my arm, leaving it more red than white at this point.

I cautiously opened the door to the hallway and took a careful peek around the corner. The hall was still empty in both directions. I let out a sigh of relief. *I don't think I'd be able to handle much more in this state.* Looking around at the doors nearby, I quickly remembered that the language here was not my own. "Lia, can you read these signs for me?"

Lia popped out into the hallway behind me, keeping close as we checked the doors. "Barracks...Files...Oh, Lux, here." She crossed in front of me to a door, pointing to the placard. "Lock-up." I nodded and moved to the entrance. Before opening the door, I took a deep breath and summoned what remained of my strength to put on an imposing look.

I swung the door open and was immensely relieved to find the room empty. It was dark aside from a single candle sputtering on a table against the far wall, so I pulled the torch from the wall sconce in the hallway. Bringing it into the room, the light revealed a row of chests against the side wall with a large symbol engraved into the top of each one. *Of course. I didn't check for symbols on our cells.*

"This one should have your things, Lux." Lia walked to the third chest in the line. She flipped the lid open, and I could see the supple black fabric with silver embroidery of my cloak folded inside.

"Thank you." I took a step forward, then paused. "How did you know this was mine?"

"It has the same number on it as your cell door did. I just sort of figured it would have your things."

"Right. I...don't remember what yours was." I felt a bit embarrassed by the admission. *A week in that cell and I didn't even notice writing on the door directly across from me? I thought I was more observant than that.* "Sorry."

Lia shrugged. "It's alright. I didn't have anything with me when they took me, aside from my clothes."

"In that case," I said, setting the torch into a nearby holder, "Why don't you start looking through the chests for your clothes while I take care of..." I pointed to my shoulder. "This situation."

Her eyebrows were drawn tight with concern, but she simply nodded and went to work looking through the few dozen chests against the wall. I half sat, half collapsed into a chair and gently poked at the wound. The pain was immediate with the numbing effects of adrenaline fully gone. *Okay, standard medieval style crossbow bolt. Puncture is through the lower shoulder muscle, luckily avoiding the major arteries. Most likely a plain metal tip, but in the case those fuckers were using barbs...*I grimaced at the thought of what was to come.

Scanning the desk I sat in front of, I replaced the bowl of coins I currently held with a small, leather bound ledger. The words on the front were, as usual, alien to me, but I wasn't interested in reading them anyways. I put the journal into my mouth and braced my feet solidly on the floor. My right hand slowly raised to my shoulder and I rested my fingers gingerly on the tail end of the bolt. I took in a deep breath and counted down in my head. *Three...two...*

I gripped the bolt and twisted hard, sending a shockwave of pain through my arm and chest. Involuntarily, I let out a loud moan, biting down hard into the leather. The taste was unpleasant, a mix of old dust and new blood. Lia spun to face me, worried, and our eyes met for a moment. I knew that she wasn't okay, with the trauma of the night obviously still filtering through her head, but neither of us had the energy or desire to talk about it. She turned back to the chests, continuing her search.

Although it had increased both the bleeding and the pain level significantly, I was pleased with the overall situation. The bolt had spun mostly unimpeded, signalling to me that it was neither barbed nor lodged directly in the bone of my shoulder. Without delay, I gripped the tail end hard and ripped it from my arm. I let the bolt clatter to the floor, the pain too severe at the moment to do anything but bite into the book and try not to scream.

Blood was pouring from the now-open wound, and I was beginning to feel light-headed. As quickly as I could, I reached out and pulled for my sword, which drew a small clatter from the open chest in front of me as it flashed into existence. "Major Sustained Self-healing, Wounds," I muttered, spitting the leather notebook out into my lap. My sword and shoulder shimmered a bright green, overpowering the light from the single torch. There was a lurching feeling in my gut like I had missed the last step on a flight of stairs, and I almost lost control of the mana flow. *This spell pulls a lot of energy.*

I monitored the wound as the magic worked. Bit by bit, the gaping hole sewed itself shut, flesh mending back together as though it had never been split. My head was spinning, though if it was due to an overuse of energy or a loss of blood, I couldn't tell. As soon as the cut was closed, I dropped the evocation and began to pant heavily. *The wound is closed, but...*I rolled my shoulder gently, but stopped with a groan when it spasmed in pain. *That's going to require a lot more healing than I can give tonight.*

"Hey," I managed to rasp out through my labored breathing. "Did you find it?" She stood, holding up a blue dress with white lace cuffs and a pair of shoes. "Okay...good. We've got to...get changed and then...we can get out of here." I stood and stumbled my way over to the chest of my belongings. "We can't be...walking around the city...in prisoner's clothes...right?" I smiled weakly.

She blushed, and it took my dazed brain a few extra seconds to figure out why. "Lia...I just killed seven guards...and you're worried about me...seeing you naked?" I let out a wheezing laugh. "I think we have...bigger problems right now...don't we?" Lia reddened even more, either from continued sheepishness or embarrassment for it being pointed out. She nodded and set the dress down on the floor, beginning to disrobe.

I turned back to my crate of possessions, doing my best to give her some privacy. *I guess modesty about one's body is the same everywhere.* Using my sword as a support, I pulled the roughspun pants off and kicked them away. Luckily, the guards had allowed me to keep my underwear which, with their anti-fouling enchantments, were by far the cleanest part of me. *Oh, to be in a warm bath right now...*

As I bent down to pull the cloak from my chest, I felt a sudden rush of dizziness come on. My legs folded under me and I toppled forward, bouncing hard off of the wooden chest and onto the stone floor. My vision swam with stars as I rolled to my back, trying to take stock of myself. *What a pathetic showing. Only seven guards and I'm already as good as dead. I've fallen out of practice.*

Somewhere, I heard Lia calling out to me. I looked from side to side, unable to pinpoint her location with sound alone, until I realized she was standing directly in front of me, leaning down in worry. "Lux! Lux, what's wrong?" She reached down and tried to tug me up, but she grabbed my left arm. I hissed in pain and rolled away, groaning.

"Not...that arm...please." After taking a moment to regain my bearings, I managed to roll up to my knees. "I'm...fine, really...just a bit...tired."

"No, you're not fine!" Her voice broke as she shouted at me. I squinted up at her face and realized she was crying. "You're hurt, and it's my fault. It's all my fault..."

"Lia, no, no..." I fought awkwardly to gain my footing for some time as the room spun around me, finally standing up enough and put a hand on her head. "I'm here because...I wanted to be...not because you made me. It's my fault...they hit me at all." Lia impacted my chest hard, almost sending me toppling over again as she hugged me. She cried into my chest, shaking her head. *This is happening too often. She shouldn't have to do this.* I leaned my head forward, resting my forehead on the top of her head as I returned her embrace with my good arm.

She was muttering something into my chest, but I couldn't make out the words. "We're going to be fine...I just have to...get dressed, and we'll be out of here." I gave her a light squeeze. The bare skin of her back was hot against my arm, comforting in the cold air of the stone room. My brain, struggling to keep up with even basic input and thought, was slow to connect the dots.

This time, it was my modesty that brought on embarrassment. I broke off the hug and looked away awkwardly. "You can go...get dressed. I'll be fine...on my own." Shifting over to my box I tried to fish out the cloak with my sword to no great success.

Lia followed up behind me, grabbed the cloak and pushed it into my arms. "I think we have bigger problems right now, don't we?" She echoed my words back at me. I coughed out a laugh and nodded. I piled my cloak and sword on the nearby table as she fetched the rest of my clothes for me. Although I tried to avert my eyes, it was hard not to see her standing right in front of me. Her skin, slightly paler where her dress would usually sit, looked smooth and firm, the muscles underneath toned but not defined. Her chest was well endowed, giving her a very classic hourglass figure combined with her wide hips. Aside from a small pair of underwear, she was completely naked.

In another situation, at another time, things might have been different, but in the moment I felt...nothing. Just pained, dizzy, and tired. After the initial awkwardness had passed it was easy to forget that anything was out of the ordinary.

Once she had stacked all of my belongings beside me, she paused. "Do you need any help getting dressed?"

I shook my head. "No, I'm fine. If I can't...get myself dressed, we're probably...in a lot more trouble than I thought." I flashed a small smile. "You go get dressed, and I'll...do the same." Having sat down for a while, I was feeling a bit more confident in my balance than I was before. Pulling my pants from the pile I stood and put them on, using the table for extra support. By the time I had them fastened with my belt, Lia was already back, clothed in her blue dress.

I pointed to my coin purse on the table. "You can transfer all the coins...from your bags, and that dish on the desk...into that purse." I slipped into my undershirt, wincing over my left arm and skipping most of the buttons.

Lia looked doubtful. "I don't think they'll all fit."

"They will. Just put them in one at a time." As she did so, I shrugged into my leather chestpiece and strung the bandolier over my shoulder. By the time she had finished, I was lacing up my boots.

"How did everything fit in here?" Lia shook the coin purse, listening to the contents jingle inside.

"Magic." I picked up my scabbard and secured it to my hip. "I know that sounds sarcastic, but it actually is magic. I can...explain later, if you'd like. Add it to the list." Finally reunited with my full kit I sheathed my sword, sending it away. After finessing my way into my cloak one-handed, I moved toward the door. "Now, I think...we should get out of here."

She nodded in agreement and handed me the purse. Together we re-emerged into the hallway and continued to the right as Jack had instructed. Lia stopped me at the second to last door. "West Tower," she said, pointing to the placard. I nodded and pulled the door open. A tight stone staircase spiraled up into near darkness with only the vaguest hint of light flickering somewhere above us.

Stepping through the door, I turned to Lia and offered a hand. "Let's get you home."

***

10. THE LONG ROAD HOME

It felt as though we had been climbing for ages. As we ascended through the near darkness of the turning staircase, the only indication I had that we were making progress was a new scent in the air. After being under so many layers of stone for a week, it was like smelling the most beautiful perfume in the world: fresh air. The stale, dusty air was mixing with the smell of rainfall, and I could feel the humidity increasing with every step. *Petrichor,* I thought with a wistful smile.

Finally, at one of the rare torches, we found a doorway. I pressed my ear to the heavy wood and listened for a long time in silence. The only sound I could hear from the other side was the constant pattering of rain on stone. When I was finally convinced the door was clear, I lifted the handle and slowly led Lia outside.

We stepped out onto a small stone porch overlooking a lake. Rain was pouring down around us, draining off the sides of the roof hard enough to splash up onto my boots. After having climbed for what seemed like forever, I was surprised to see we were at ground level. The easily recognizable city wall of Yoria stretched off in both directions, connected to the guard tower behind us. With the storm clouds covering the night sky I could barely see twenty feet down the wall before it faded into hazy darkness.

"I know that lake!" Lia said excitedly. "If we're at Alott Lake, we're still two or three hours from home, but I know how to get there!" She moved to take off down the stairs to the well rutted dirt road below, pulling me by the hand.

I resisted, albeit weakly. "Is there any way we can get there without using the main road?" I pointed backwards over my shoulder. "Those men might have cleared the floor for a while, but someone will inevitably go down and find them dead, and us missing."

She stopped for a moment. "Well, we could work our way through the trees for a while." Lia pointed off into the black night, at some unseen thicket. "The forest thins out before we get to my house, so at that point, I'm not sure what we'll do." Her eyes flashed with concern. "Do you think we can make it back?"

Smiling, I nodded. "Of course. I wouldn't get us this far just to fail now." I hoped that my bravado seemed genuine to her because in truth I felt as though I could pass out at any minute. The combination of the blood loss, physical overexertion due to adrenaline, and extreme mana usage had sapped me beyond my normal limits. I carefully took a step down to her level and nodded towards the darkness. "Lead the way."

Lia nodded and pulled me out into the rain. My cloak provided some respite, keeping me mostly dry and comfortably warm, but the wind was whipping the water angrily into our faces, quickly numbing my nose and cheeks. We trudged through thick, sinking mud for a while as we followed a dirt offshoot towards the forest. The effort required was quite taxing on me, and by the time we finally broke the treeline I was panting again.

We continued deeper into the trees for a while, enjoying the light cover from wind and rain the leaves above us provided. I was impressed at Lia bravely leading me forward into the total darkness of night without any hesitation. Having finally escaped the hell that was the dungeon and its occupants she had perked up a bit, perhaps finally seeing some light at the end of the tunnel. *I'm leaving the rest in your hands, Lia. I've got nothing left to give you tonight. Or for a while after this, I imagine.*

Eventually, at some unseen junction, Lia turned and led me off the worn path into the brush. Our pace slowed considerably now having to carefully step over roots and through the undergrowth. She never seemed to trip or lose her footing as we traveled, and on multiple occasions warned me, "Watch out for this root," or "Big rock coming up." *I've really underestimated her at every turn. Just because she's a pretty girl I've been assuming she's needed my help the entire time I've known her.*

As I followed behind her, stumbling clumsily through the trees, the thought lingered in my mind. *The entire time I've known her...For as well as I feel like I know her, I only just met her a day ago. Is that right?* I reviewed my memories since she was first brought down to the cells. So much had happened in such a short period of time that I felt like our time together had been weeks, not hours. *Time has a funny habit of never working the way it's supposed to.*

From somewhere through the trees a distant bell began to ring. It chimed quickly and without rhythm, clearly too fast to be marking the hour. *I guess I'm a fugitive now.* Lia didn't outwardly react to the sound, but I felt her hand grip mine a little harder, and her pace quickened. I had trouble keeping up with the new speed, but I didn't complain as I continued to stumble on through the darkness in pained silence.

The hand Lia was leading me with began to tremble as we walked on through the forest. Garbed in a simple wool dress, she had quickly become soaked when we first stepped out into the rain, and although we had some cover from the downpour now, the wind was still blowing aggressively. "Lia," I croaked out hoarsely, throat raw from my raspy panting. Over the wind and rain, she didn't seem to hear me. I tugged softly on her hand. "Lia."

She stopped and turned to me, her face set with determination. As soon as she saw me, though, worry washed over it. "Oh, Lux, you look so pale. Are you okay? Do you need to stop?"

The question unsettled me. "Do I look...that bad? I'm feeling...better than ever." The grin I forced felt unconvincing, even to me. "You should...take my cloak. It'll warm you up."

Lia shook her head. "I can't do that. You need it more than I do."

"I think the rain...will do me some good. Besides...I'm relying on you...to get me out of here. I need you at...one hundred percent." Without waiting for her to accept, I slipped my scabbard from my back and shrugged the cloak off. I draped the hood over her head, and she begrudgingly put it on. The cloak ended near my calves when I wore it, but on Lia it was long enough to brush the ground behind her.

A few moments after putting on the cloak, Lia's face changed to one of wonder mixed with a small bit of confusion. "It's so warm!" She tugged on the wet fabric, admiring the stitching and make. "How is it so warm?"

"It's a very...nice cloak. And...some magic." I smiled, taking her hand again. She eyed me a raised eyebrow for a moment, but turned around and resumed our trek through the trees. The dripping rain and biting winds felt so much colder now, but I welcomed it gladly. My eyelids were growing heavier by the minute, and the freezing weather certainly woke me up.

At least, it did for a while. Time was hard to track in the darkness, but it wasn't long until my head began to droop again, even through the elements. I was stumbling harder and more often, causing Lia to look back in worry. I would smile and nod, doing my best to continue walking until I stumbled again. *We must be nearly there by now...I'm sure it's just...another few...*

I woke up to a shooting pain in my shoulder. I cried out in agony, but immediately clamped my jaw shut and put my hand over my mouth. Apparently, I had fallen asleep while walking and woken up when I landed hard against a protruding root. Lia was crouched over me, trying to help me up. "Lux, oh...Lux, I-I don't know...I don't know what to do." It looked as though she was about to cry.

"It's...fine." I rolled over onto my back. "You should...keep going. I'll...stay here...get some sleep." Although the situation was serious, I couldn't help but laugh. *What a pitiful display.* "They won't...find me out here. And they won't...be looking for you..." Having correctly guessed her captor's plans so far, I felt confident that there was no record of Lia being kept down in the dungeon. *They won't be looking for her. Just me.*

"You know I'm not going to leave you out here." She knelt down next to me, taking my hand in hers. "You know that, right?"

I closed my eyes for a long moment, but miraculously opened them again without falling unconscious. "Yeah...I know. Even though...you should." I smiled. "You really should."

Lia smiled back at me. "I still have a list of questions for you. You don't get to avoid it that easily." She sprang to her feet and looked around, searching for something I couldn't see. Whatever it was she seemed to find it, running off into the darkness for a moment before returning with an excited look on her face. "If you can go just a little farther, I've found somewhere you can sleep."

Grunting, I took a few tries to roll onto one knee, and with Lia's help, I regained my footing. "This better be...worth it. That root...was really...comfortable." In all my lives, I had never felt as drained as I did in this moment. It took every ounce of willpower, plus a heavy dash of support from Lia's shoulder, to walk me the short distance to the spot she had found.

A large, gnarled tree stood before us, some sort of strange amalgam of branches and trunks from multiple plants wound into a single structure. Lia led me towards the base, shrugging out from under my arm as I gripped onto one of the branches for support. "Look in here!" She pointed to the base of the tree in front of her. From my angle, it just looked like any other strange tree, and I failed to find any significance in her discovery. As I pulled my way along the branch, I came to see that near the base of the tree where two of the trunks wound together there was a small gap where a person just might be able to squeeze through.

"What am I...looking at here, Lia?" I let go of the branch and plopped to the ground roughly, my head swimming. My eyes were staying closed longer and longer every time I blinked, and I knew that it wouldn't be long until I fell unconscious.

"It's a hiding place! I think it should be big enough for us to fit inside." Lia pointed in between the two tree trunks. "The wood twists around enough to make a little hollow area inside. Nobody will see us in there!"

"So, it's...still us, then?" I coughed hard, bringing stars back to swim before my eyes. "I can...slip right in there...and you can go home." I was doing my best to hide just how bad of a state I was in, but I knew she could see right through me. "We must be...close by now."

She walked up to me with an irritated expression. "Get in the tree, Lux."

I sat in stunned silence for a moment, then chuckled. "Yes, ma'am." Crawling my way to the hole, I slowly removed my effects and passed them through, then followed suit myself feet first. It was a tight squeeze around my waist, but I was able to wiggle my way through into the interior of the tree. From inside, I could see that the whole structure was composed of three different trees, all having grown from nearly the same spot in the ground.

The chamber was composed in such a way that I could half lie, half lean onto the wood behind me, creating a recliner-like bed. It wasn't comfortable by any means, but it wasn't painful either. I had just enough room to lay out straight, only having to slightly curl my legs. Once I stopped fidgeting, Lia came to the entrance. "I'm coming in now." Where I had taken around half a minute to awkwardly shimmy my way into the hollow, Lia gracefully slid through in mere moments. With me already inside, there wasn't enough room for her to easily adjust her position, so she gently leaned back against me, curling up into my chest.

I let out a long sigh, finally able to relax my aching body. Although we weren't in the most comfortable of circumstances, I found Lia's slight frame curled up against me soothing. My hazy mind began to wander, and I found myself forgetting where I was and who I was with, living multiple lives at once. I was daydreaming, sleeping lazily under a tree with Amaya. I was curled up by the fire with Alda, hiding from the bitter cold outside.

Lia's voice caught me a moment before I was gone. "Lux?" I couldn't see her face, but her voice cracked as she continued, and I realized she was crying. "Lux, I'm so sorry...you wouldn't be hurt if it weren't for me. You don't even know me, but you risked your life to help, and I...I can't ever repay that debt to you." She squeezed me tightly, her head nestling up under my chin. "Are you going to be okay?"

Softly, I wrapped my arms around her and returned the hug. "You don't owe me anything." The words were almost a whisper. "You're a...good person, Lia. I couldn't have lived with myself...if I didn't help you." My eyes closed, and I knew they wouldn't open again for a long time. "I'm going to be...fine. I just need...some sleep."

She let out a stifled sob and nodded into my chest. "Okay. I'll take care of you...I promise."

I smiled. "Thanks, Lia." My energy left me all at once, and I fell into a deep sleep.

Pain and darkness. Those two things were the entirety of my world. How long had it been? Time was meaningless in darkness, and pain could warp time any way it chose. It felt as though every molecule of my body was splitting apart, filling every inch of me with a torment I had never even imagined could exist.

How did I get here? What even was...here? Had there been anything before this? It was difficult to think. After an unknowably long time, my brain began to cope with the pain. It wasn't diminished in any way, but I found some small corner of my mind to hide in, somehow thinking in tandem with it.

There was a before. I had been sitting at my desk, working on my computer. I was alone, as usual, listening to music in the dark as I stayed up far too late for my own good. No, that couldn't be right. If that was right, how did I get here?

To this world of pain and darkness? Had there been a flash of light, or a burst of noise? I couldn't remember; it had found me again, and it punished me for thinking. It didn't like when I existed and sought to remedy that immediately.

More time passed. It felt as though my body were dissolving away into the darkness, and the pain surpassed my physical form. I could feel it everywhere now, not just in my body. I was just void and agony, nothing more. The idea of escaping from this place was useless now; I hadn't had control of my body when it had first started, and now, I wasn't sure I even had one.

My mind tried to convince me that it didn't hurt anymore, that this is what existence felt like, and that it wasn't truly pain any longer. That's when the darkness morphed into a new beast. It was similar to the heat of a fire, except I could feel it everywhere, and it was blazing so hot that I should have burned away to dust. Except I was darkness, and darkness can't burn.

The cycle continued, my world changing every time my mind tried to adapt. Eventually, I gave up and accepted life for what it was: Pain and darkness. It suffused my essence, and, in a way, it gave me peace. That's when the world changed again.

The darkness was gone, replaced with abstract morphing colors and shapes. The pain was gone, and I could feel my body again, every piece back where it should have been, seemingly unharmed. I felt like I was falling, tumbling end over end through this new reality. My stomach was lurching as my brain tried to reconcile some sort of horizon, but the light was too bright, and nothing stayed in place for long enough. Wind was raging at my ears, screaming louder than anything I had ever experienced.

I closed my eyes and clamped my hands over my ears, trying to block out all sensation. Spinning blindly, my disorientation amplified and I wretched, spitting up bile and stomach acid. Perhaps this was just another trick, and the pain and darkness would return to catch me off guard. In a way, I longed for the known evil over the unknown terror.

In a flash so bright it blinded me through my closed eyelids, everything changed again. The world wasn't spinning anymore, and I felt a hard impact along the front of my body. It was comfortably warm now, and I could smell grass and dirt around me. Somewhere nearby, I heard a man screaming.

Perhaps, I wasn't alone in this experience after all. As my senses slowly returned to me, I realized that the screaming was close by, and the voice was somehow familiar. It was my voice, and I was screaming so loud I tasted blood.

My eyes opened, revealing a shockingly normal scene before me. I was lying in a field of grass. The sky was bright blue with a few puffy white clouds and a shining sun. Somewhere ahead I could see trees swaying in a gentle breeze, multi-colored flowers ringing their trunks. In the distance, metal struck metal in a rhythmic cadence.

I tried to sit up, but my body was shaking violently. Although the pain was gone, my mind could still remember it, and it paralyzed me with fear that this pleasant reality could be ripped away again in an instant. "HELP!" I screamed out in vain, hoping that somebody would find me. My voice carried out over the field, fading into nothing in the wind.

After a time, my trembling lessened, and I was able to clamber to my feet. Not too far behind where I stood, I saw a wooden palisade with a large gate, currently open. Faint sounds of a crowd floated towards me, along with the continued ring of metal. Staggering at first, I made my way towards the signs of civilization, following a dirt road to my right.

When I approached the gate, I saw that there was a crowd of people just inside, looking out down the road. They fell silent as I entered, all of them staring at me with hard looks. I stared back in stunned silence. Many of the people in the group looked...strange. Some had tails and ears, like those of a dog or cat. One man had a small set of wings protruding from his back. "You...you aren't real."

It was the only thing I could think to say. Obviously, what I was seeing was wrong, somehow. Everything about this was wrong: the pain, the blackness, the flashing lights, and now, this crowd of impossible looking people. "Am I...dead?"

"Dead people aren't as loud as you!" A woman shouted from the back of the crowd, drawing a laugh from those around her.

"Alright everyone, show's over. Just another vagrant passing through." Another voice from the crowd. The people began to disperse, giving me one last glare as they went on their way. Now that I had passed through the palisade, I saw that I was in a small village. Houses lined the main street,

mostly made of wooden planks and logs. Ahead the road encircled a large well, where another group was gathered, carrying buckets or walking with baskets.

"No, wait..." I reached out weakly in front of me. "I need help, I need...something..." Shuffling forward, I watched as the remaining few people scurried away, sending worried glances back over their shoulders at me. In the distance I could see people pointing at me from the well, and before I knew it, the main street was completely empty. "No, please, I'm not...I just need some help!" I called out to the empty street.

My body began to tremble again, and I leaned up against the corner of a nearby house for support. I slid down into the dirt holding my head in my hands. "No, no, no...this isn't real...it was all just a dream." I didn't believe what I was saying, but I was trying my best, and failing, not to fall into a complete panic. "No, no, no, no..."

"Are you alright?" a soft voice spoke out to me. Startled, I skittered backwards, bouncing my shoulder hard off the corner post behind me as I moved. Looking up I saw the voice had come from a young woman standing in the middle of the road. She had long, golden hair and wide purple eyes. Two rabbit ears protruded from the top of her head, folded slightly under their own weight at the top.

"I...I'm not...I don't..." I trailed off, certain that I was not alright in any sense. Looking at her helplessly, my vision blurred as I began to cry. I shook my head meekly. "No." A single, choked sob escaped my lips. "No, I'm not."

She approached slowly, bending down to put a hand lightly on my shoulder. "Come with me. We can help you, I'm sure of it."

"How?" I didn't believe that she was real. She must have been a hallucination, a true indicator that I had snapped. "Where?"

The woman tilted her head to the side and smiled. "Home."

I felt as though I was floating in darkness. I had fragments of at least fifty different memories, all half formed and out of order in my head. My body ached from head to toe, and for a moment I was unsure as to whether the whole thing was still together or not. Somehow, I felt as though I *could* move my arms and legs if I wanted to, but there was just no need. It was at that moment that I realized I wasn't lying in the dark, but instead lying on the ground with my eyes closed. I was in a loose-fitting pair of pants and a thin shirt, neither my own.

It took a significant amount of effort to open my eyes, which I found disconcerting. Directly above me was a ceiling of wooden boards filtering down a hazy light. The walls and floor were cobbled grey stone, unadorned and ill-kept. All around me, the ground was stacked with crates and barrels all marked with a similar sticker labeled in an unfamiliar language. I could feel cracks over my lips, and my mouth was extremely dry. With a mighty grunt, I slowly stretched my arms and legs, drawing a dull ache from my left shoulder. My hand grazed something as it moved, and I heard the clatter of wood on stone.

Rolling to my side, I saw that I had knocked over a pitcher of water which now spilled out over the stone floor. It slowly seeped towards me, soaking into the thin bedroll I was laying on. *Where...am I?* A small gasp caught my attention, and I looked up to the entrance of the room to find a woman standing in shock. In her hands she held a tray of food and a similar pitcher to the one I had knocked over. Her hair was straight and black, with small grey rounded ears protruding from the top of her head and a puffy dark tail curling around behind her. I couldn't place why, but her features looked...familiar somehow.

Without a word, she turned and quickly ascended a flight of wooden stairs in the next room. I heard her footsteps pass over the wood above me, stopping somewhere close by. A second set of footsteps joined her hurriedly, moving back to the staircase. She reappeared, and Lia followed close behind her. When she saw me sitting up staring vacantly at them, a huge smile spread across her face.

"Lux!" Lia ran into the room, sliding down onto the floor beside me to dive into a headfirst embrace. The force knocked me back to the floor, winding me, but I was happy to see her. She pulled back a second later having realized that the hug had become more of a tackle. "Sorry, I just...I thought you weren't going to wake up, and I got carried away." She was still smiling, running her hand down the side of my face.

"Lia, how did I get here?" I looked around the unfamiliar room. "More importantly, where is here?"

Lia tilted her head to the side, tears running down her face even as she smiled. "Home."

***

11. HOME

"Just start from the beginning. At the tree, after I fell asleep." I sat up against one of the wooden crates, holding a cup of water and a slice of bread with jam. I had only taken a couple bites of the food, but I already felt stuffed, so I sipped slowly on the water instead. The cool liquid felt amazing on my dehydrated palate. Lia sat on the floor across from me and the woman, who I had correctly guessed to be Lia's mother, stood in the doorway.

Lia nodded. "Well, after you fell asleep, the bell in town kept ringing for a long time. I thought I might have heard people in the forest, so I pulled up your cloak and tried to be as quiet as possible. Nobody ever came near the tree, though." She paused for a moment to think, then continued. "I guess I fell asleep, because when I woke up, the rain had stopped, and the sun was up. You were still sleeping, so I decided to just stay inside and wait a while." She frowned. "Eventually, I thought I should get you up so we could leave, but...I couldn't get you to wake up. I tried really hard, but nothing worked."

I scratched the back of my head and looked away. "Yeah, sorry about that."

Lia shook her head. "No! It's just that...well, I was worried. If you didn't wake up, I knew I would have to try and feed you and get you water, and the tree was so small, so..." She looked down at the floor, wringing her hands. "I left." After the admission, she looked back up to me quickly, clearly flustered. "It wasn't for very long! I promise! I just knew I needed to do something, so I started walking."

I couldn't help but laugh, which drew a glare from Lia. "It's not funny!" she pouted, turning red in the face. "We weren't too far from the edge of the forest anyway, so I ran home." Lia looked to her mother who thus far had stood watching us in silence. The woman smiled, and the resemblance between the two became uncanny; aside from the small ears poking out from her hair and the puffy tail behind her, the two could have been mistaken for twins at a quick glance.

"We were amazed when Lia came home. We tried to get her to tell us what happened, but she just kept insisting we had to go somewhere immediately and wouldn't say anything else." She laughed softly. "We had no choice but to just indulge her and hope she would explain later."

Lia was glaring at her mother now. "You don't have to say it like that!" That drew a laugh from me as well, much to Lia's chagrin. "I made Father follow with his wagon, because I knew we wouldn't be able to carry you ourselves. Especially if the guards were looking for you." Her expression changed to one of suppressed amusement. "You were still sleeping, and I didn't want to risk anybody finding you, so...well, we..."

Her mother finished the thought for her. "We packed you into a produce crate and shipped you back here." she laughed. I had to admit, picturing the two of them pulling me out of a tree and stuffing me into a wooden box was certainly amusing.

"And I've been down here ever since?" I asked, curious. "How long has it been?"

Lia responded first. "It's been almost three days since we brought you here. I was worried that you weren't waking up, but Mother said if we kept you in a safe place to rest, you'd come to eventually." She smiled proudly, puffing out her chest a bit. "I helped her get you cleaned up, and I even wrapped up your shoulder myself!"

I put a hand to my injured shoulder and noticed for the first time it was wound in tight strips of cloth. "Thank you for that, Lia. It's feeling much better than before." I turned to her mother. "I'm extremely grateful to you as well. You risked your safety to look after a complete stranger. I hope I can pay you back somehow."

Her mother shook her head. "We didn't have much of a choice, really. Little Marlia was so distraught over you that we knew you must be someone very important to her." Lia's face turned fuchsia, and she let out an exasperated, wordless yell as she stomped out of the room. I laughed heartily at her reaction which only sped her retreat up to the top of the stairs where she slammed the door shut behind her.

Lia's mother chuckled as she walked over to where I was sitting on the floor. She knelt down and took my hand in hers, and I saw her face was now completely serious, all levity from moments before gone. "Lux. You brought my daughter home to us. I don't want to hear you speak of repaying us for kindness again; We will be indebted to you for the rest of our lives." A stream of tears cascaded down her face. "We were so scared after those men took her. We knew the kind of men they were, and what they might do to her..."

She trailed off, staring straight through me at some terror far away in her mind. I stayed quiet, and after a moment she snapped back to reality. "Please, tell me. Did they...did they hurt her?" I took a long, hard look at her, trying to get a good measure of what type of person she was. *There's no need to hold back the truth.*

"No." I met her gaze as I spoke. "They didn't. They had plans for her...awful, unspeakable things. They tried to..." I hesitated a moment, but continued on. "They tried to hurt her, and I killed them for it. I killed all of them." The memory played back in my mind in fuzzy fragments. Everything was blurred with a red haze as I watched them die again. *What...what did I do to them? That tunnel vision, that spell...what was that?* It made me shudder. Without the adrenaline pumping through me, remembering that night made me feel unclean.

"Good. They were evil men, and the world is much better off without them in it." She stood, wiping away the tears that had welled up in her eyes. "Now, I should go calm down Lia. She's just so easy to tease that sometimes I get a bit carried away." Giving me a small smile, she turned to leave, but stopped at the door. "All of your things are in the crate against the back wall. If you're feeling up to it, dinner is almost ready upstairs. You're welcome to join us."

"Thank you...oh. I'm sorry, but I never asked for your name," I realized mid-sentence, feeling slightly rude.

"No need to apologize, you've only been awake for a few minutes. My name is Hana Corell, and my husband's name is Marten Corell." Hana gave a small, respectful nod. "Thank you for saving Marlia, Lux." She turned to leave, but I called out to stop her.

"Hana. Have any guards come by while I've been asleep?" It was an awkward question to ask out of nowhere, but I needed to be sure my theory was correct.

Hana put a hand to her cheek, thinking for a moment. "No, not as far as I know." Her eyebrows raised in worry. "Should we be expecting them?"

I shook my head. "No, they shouldn't have any idea where I went." Giving her a pleasant smile, I bowed my head. "Sorry to bother you." With that, Hana turned and went upstairs, leaving me alone in the basement. I breathed a sigh of relief. *I guess that confirms it. Lia was never a real prisoner. They just locked her up down there where nobody would think to look for her.*

I stood and moved to the crate Hana had indicated, taking a quick inventory of my things as I started to dress myself in my own attire. My clothes, armor, and personal effects seemed to be all accounted for. As I got dressed, I found my left shoulder to be sore, but not unusable anymore, for which I was extremely thankful. Apart from the aches and pains of malnutrition, I felt surprisingly good. *Once I get some real food down and drink more water, my head should finally clear up.*

After I had dressed in my normal clothes, leaving my armor and effects in the crate, I made my way to the wooden stairway in the next room. It was clear to me that the basement was only used to store materials for Lia's father's trading business, and a rough path to my resting area had been shoved aside in a hurry. *Had the guards come looking for me, it would have been easy to hide me among the dozens of boxes down here. Well played.*

I climbed the stairs and pushed open the wooden door at the top, wincing as the full light of day shone down on me from an opposing window. I was in a small den with a few cloth chairs around a table and a large animal pelt rug splayed out on the floor. The walls looked to be composed of a plaster-like substance coated with a bright yellow paint. Here and there along its expanse hung decorative wooden carvings and woven wreaths, giving the room a very homey feeling.

To my left, I could hear voices floating out from around a corner, so I set off in that direction. Walking through an unfamiliar house by myself made me feel as though I were a home intruder, sneaking around to steal valuables while the family ate in the other room. I did my best to shake off the feeling as I rounded the corner, entering what was apparently the dining room.

The first thing I noticed was the heavenly aromas wafting from the open kitchen directly past the dining table. The smell of roasted fowl, fresh baked bread, and boiled greens made my mouth water, and I had to stop and take a prolonged inhale to satisfy the initial cravings. Lia and her mother were working together on something I couldn't see, though I could hear the tapping of knives against a cutting board. Directly in front of me, a stout, hairy man sat at the round dining room table watching them work.

I immediately felt uncomfortable again, standing unnoticed in the corner of the room. *Should I...leave? Wait around the corner for them to start eating, and then come in again? I don't want to startle them, maybe—*

My thought was cut off abruptly by my stomach gurgling loudly, apparently convinced by the lovely smell of food to be hungry again. The man in front of me spun around in his chair and let out a small shout of surprise when he saw me standing behind him.

"By the Primes, you scared me!" He let out a hearty laugh. "My heart nearly jumped from my chest!" Lia and Hana were also laughing, most likely startled by the yell.

"Lux, you're up!" Lia shouted happily. Instantly, she put a hand to her mouth, looking stunned by her own exclamation. She shot a sideways glare at her mother, then quickly turned back to whatever she had been working on. Hana covered a laugh and turned back with Lia, leaning over to whisper something in her ear. Although I couldn't see her face, I could tell Lia was feeling sheepish.

"You know, I didn't think you'd ever wake up. When they dragged you out of that forest, you looked pretty rough." The man stood from the table and approached, stopping to give me a hard look up and down. I met his gaze and stood silently, unsure as to whether he expected me to respond. After a long moment, he grinned and extended his hand. "Glad to see I was wrong."

I took his hand and laughed. "You and me both." He squeezed my hand hard and shook it up and down vigorously. His arms and legs were close to twice the thickness of mine, though he stood shorter than both his wife and daughter. He had a large bald spot on the top of his head but was otherwise covered in coarse brown hair, from his bushy beard and mustache to his impressively hairy arms. "Marten, I presume?"

"Indeed I am. You must be the famous Lux." His face broke into a wide grin, and he turned so he could see Lia. "We've heard so much about you." In the kitchen, I saw Lia's shoulders tense, and the force of her chopping audibly increased. Hana laughed, shooting Marten an amused look as she shook her head. He chuckled and turned back to me. "You must be starving. Come and sit down, dinner is just about ready."

"I'd love to, sir. It's been a while since I had a proper meal." I moved to the table and took the chair beside Marten's. Four places had been set out around the edge, each with an unadorned ceramic plate, a knife and fork, and a small cup of water. As if on cue, Lia and her mother carried over platters from the kitchen and set them at the center of the table. My stomach growled loudly again as I took in the sight, drawing a laugh from Lia's parents.

My eyes first fell upon a whole roasted bird about the size of a small chicken, glistening with fresh juices in the late afternoon sun. Next to it was a platter of fresh bread, sliced and arranged around a dish of brown gravy. A large pile of skewers caught my attention next; bright red and purple orbs about the size of ping pong balls, skin broken and charred, were packed tightly onto wooden sticks. They were piled on a bed of some sort of thick leafy plants, which were a pale orange and yellow in color and sliced into thin strips. A pitcher with the faint aroma of alcohol rounded out the offering, with a small stack of mugs next to it.

I eyed the meal hungrily, feeling like a king at a feast in comparison to the meals of prison gruel I had endured over the past week. Lia took the seat next to mine, and Hana sat down opposite me. I realized my face must have let on how much I was anticipating the meal when Marten laughed and clapped me on the shoulder. "Help yourself, lad!" Everybody began to load their plates with food, and I eagerly joined in.

Whatever had been suppressing my appetite before was gone now, and I ate voraciously. The meal was delicious; I quickly gave up any pretense of being civilized and stuffed myself with food, grease running down my chin unchecked. The strange skewers were a standout among the spread, and unlike anything I had ever eaten. Initially they seemed to be like a pepper with a thin skin and crunchy flesh underneath, but after biting into one I found they were filled with a thick jelly. It had a rich savory flavor reminiscent of a spiced brown butter, which I hadn't expected from something I assumed was a vegetable.

Over the course of the meal I hardly said a word. When it became clear that I was completely focused on the food, Lia and her parents talked amongst themselves, discussing various aspects of the trade business or some gossip about the neighbors. Every now and then one of them would glance at me out of the corner of their eye with an amused smile on their face, but nobody seemed eager to interrupt my feasting.

Finally, after ingesting far more food than I thought possible, I sat back in the chair with a deep, satisfied sigh. I wiped my chin with the back of my hand, embarrassed by my previous display, and began to nurse my cup of warm ale. It was thin and weak, most likely watered down, but I didn't mind. The conversation at the table had hit a natural lull, so I took the opportunity to speak. "Thank you for the meal, everyone. It may have been the most delicious thing I've eaten in my life." *This life, for certain.*

"Oh, go on. It's nothing special really, but I am glad you enjoyed it." Hana nodded in thanks.

"Having not eaten for a few days, this could be a royal banquet as far as I'm concerned." I laughed, patting my stomach gently. "I suppose hunger does that to you."

"So, Lux," Marten addressed me in between bites as he picked a bone clean of its meat. "Where are you from? Forgive me for saying so, but you don't look like someone from around these parts."

I was hoping to avoid this question. "You certainly caught me. I must stick out like a sore thumb." I laughed a bit nervously, trying to buy myself a few moments to think of a satisfactory lie. Lia chimed in, saving me the trouble.

"He's from somewhere in Doram," she said casually, chewing on a slice of bread. I did my best not to react but made a mental note to thank her later.

Marten's eyebrows raised slightly. "It's not often we get Northerners in these parts. What brings you down from the mountains?"

I shrugged. "Sometimes you just need a change of scenery, you know?"

"And you're traveling by yourself?"

Nodding, I took a sip of my ale. "That's right. I've got no family or attachments to speak of, so I figured it was the perfect time to see the world. I didn't intend on staying in Yoria for long, I just happened to get…" I waved my hand, trying to think of a fitting word. "…Side tracked."

Marten shook his head, a grim look on his face. "Aye, terrible thing, what happened to you. Lia told us the general story. I've always said there's a real problem with the guards in Yoria, haven't I, Hana?"

"Yes, you certainly have, dear," she responded, with a look that gave me the impression it was a well-worn line of conversation. Marten grumbled a bit in response, seeming to suppress the urge to continue on about it.

"Well, regardless, I'm glad to see you out of there. We were so worried when our Marlia was taken, and to get her back so soon after...it's truly a blessing." He weighed his words carefully. It was clear to me that Marten was not a man to often wear his emotions on his sleeve.

"Don't talk about me like I'm not around!" Lia complained at him, squirming with awkwardness. "I'm right here!"

"That you are. Because of him." Marten met her gaze, pointing his thumb in my direction.

She scrunched up her face and stood abruptly, gathering her plate and silverware. "Mother, could you help me take care of the dishes, please?" Lia grabbed my empty plate from in front of me and retreated with haste to the shelter of the kitchen. Hana smiled as she stood to help her daughter, taking the platter of food away.

"Thank you for the meal, darlings." Marten got up from the table as well. "Lux, why don't you come with me? I'll show you around." Without waiting for a response, he turned and walked out of the dining room.

"Thank you again for dinner," I called back to the kitchen as I followed him out. He led me out the front door of the house into the fading light of the evening. I took a moment to look back at the house, admiring the quaint facade. A small garden was tucked up against the wall next to the door, though it was currently empty of all but a few small flowers, no doubt due to Jack and his men. It was quite a small structure, standing only one story high with a gently slanted roof. I got the impression that there could only be one or two more rooms inside I hadn't seen already.

Beside the house in the direction Marten was headed was a small barn. As we approached, I spotted a horse stabled inside next to a wagon. The space was barely large enough for both of them, and I found myself wondering how the logistics of getting both the wagon and horse in at once actually worked. Marten gave the room a once over, patted the horse on the side of the head, and closed one of the large barn doors. I pulled the other closed as well, allowing him to loop a chain through the door handles and secure it with a heavy padlock.

With the barn secured, Marten leaned up against the door, staring off into the sky in silence. I joined him, closing my eyes for a while and taking a deep breath of the fresh evening air. Eventually, Marten broke the silence. "Hana tells me that Jack won't be bothering us anymore. Your doing."

"Yes sir." The sky was a brilliant patchwork of pinks and purples as the sun set somewhere behind the Corells' house.

He was quiet for a while. "I wanted nothing more than to bash that man's face in with a hammer, but I knew it would do more harm to my family than to him. Besides, I'd heard the stories about him, about how fast he could move those swords of his. I'd never have gotten close." Marten paused. "But you killed him."

"Yes sir." Jack's face twisted in my mind, black lines running up his neck as he screamed in pain.

Marten nodded thoughtfully. "What will you do now?"

"I haven't had the time to think about that yet." I took a moment to consider. "If you'll have me, I'd like to rest for a few more days to get my strength back. After that, I suppose I'll be on my way. I don't feel like Yoria is finished with me, but I'm finished with it."

Silence, again. "And Lia?"

"Lia, sir?" I looked down on him, eyebrow cocked in confusion. "I'm not sure I follow."

He sighed. "You know she loves you, don't you?"

I was taken off guard by the question. "She doesn't even know me. She met me four days ago, and I've been asleep for three of them."

"And yet, here we are." He let the statement sit in the cool night air. "I know you've just met her Lux, but I've been watching over her since the day she was born, and she has never looked at someone the way she looks at you. We've tried to set her up with a good man in the past, Primes know we have. A girl her age shouldn't be stuck at home taking care of her parents. But she's refused every single one out of hand, always finding a flaw here, or a reason there."

Marten laughed. "And then she drags you out of a hole in a tree, crying and insisting we bring you back to our house. Sitting with you every day while you slept." He shook his head. "I've never seen her with so much drive...so much passion. As her father, it wouldn't be right if I let the source of that passion leave her behind."

His honesty stunned me. "But, *you* hardly know me. And you'd trust me with your only daughter?"

"Let me tell you what I do know, Lux." He finally turned to address me directly. "You helped an innocent girl out of a situation that didn't involve you in the least, knowing full well how much more trouble it would put you through. You killed the men that have tormented my family, and other families, for years. You walked with her into the darkness until it nearly killed you. You woke up in our house, and the first thing you could think to do was thank us for our hospitality. You didn't ask for repayment, or reward." Marten turned away to stare into the darkness again. "That's the sort of man I want Marlia to be with. That's the sort of man you are."

"I...I can't marry your daughter, sir. I've only just met her. I have no prospects and nothing to give her."

Marten let out a small laugh. "Who said anything about marrying her?" He laughed again, harder this time. "When you leave, take Lia with you. If you killed Jack and his men single handedly, there's not a safer place in the world for her than by your side. Just let her be happy with you. And if, once you get to know her, marriage is on the table..." He trailed off, tilting his head side to side. "...There will be a dowry waiting for you back here."

We stood in silence for a long time as I thought through everything he had told me. *Could I really do that? Take her with me, away from her family, and certainly into an even greater danger than before? Would she even want that?* The sun had completely set revealing a large swath of stars above us before I spoke again. "I'll...think about what you've said."

He clapped me on the shoulder and pushed off from the barn door. "Good lad." Marten started to make his way back to the house. "Now, let's get inside before our ladies begin to worry about us." Chuckling at himself he turned the corner to the front of the house, leaving me standing alone by the barn.

Is that really...what's best for her? Would she want to be with me, even if I can't reciprocate those feelings? It wasn't a question I could answer by myself. With that future conversation now looming before me, I jogged into the darkness to catch up with Marten. *I told Lia she could ask me anything she wanted to know. I guess a dose of honesty will do us both some good.*

***

12. HONESTY

Lia called to us from the living room as we entered the house. "Where have you two been? I was starting to worry something might have happened out there." She was sitting with her mother, a deck of playing cards spread out on the table before them. The room was lit by a few small candles on the table, and a larger lantern hung on the wall behind them. It gave the space a very intimate glow, making me feel once again like a stranger in their home.

Marten laughed as he walked over to them, placing his hands on Lia's shoulders and giving her a quick kiss on the top of the head. "Oh, I was just showing Lux around outside. He helped me put away the wagon and lock up the barn." He turned to me with an eyebrow raised in amusement. "Isn't that right?"

"I was interested in your father's trading business, so we got to talking and before I knew it, the sun had gone down." The lie came naturally to me, which made me feel a bit guilty. "Sorry if we worried you." I stood awkwardly in the entryway, not sure where I belonged.

The look on Lia's face gave me the impression that she didn't believe me, but she shrugged it off as unimportant. "I was just finishing my game of cards with Mother." She turned back to the table and shuffled a few cards around. "I was just *winning* my game of cards, that is."

Hana smiled sweetly and laughed. "It looks like you've bested me again, Marlia." She scooped up the cards in front of her, stacking them into a neat pile. "Shall we play again?"

Her husband cut in before Lia could respond. "I think we should be getting to sleep, darling. We have an early morning tomorrow, after all." From across the room, I caught a quick exchange of facial expressions between the couple, although the impetus and meaning were far beyond me. Hana stood, nodding.

"Of course. We're meeting with Tomas tomorrow just after dawn." She placed a similar kiss on the top of Lia's head, then moved with her husband to one of the two doors I had yet to explore. Hana gave me a small nod. "Goodnight, Lux."

"Goodnight, Hana. Thank you again for the meal." I nodded back to her. She entered the room, and Marten followed in behind her. He paused a moment in the doorway, turning back to look at me.

"Lux, you can stay with Lia tonight. I'm sure it will be much more comfortable than the basement floor." A wry grin curled its way across his face. Out of the corner of my eye I saw Lia stand, clearly flustered, but I just smiled and nodded to him.

"Thank you, sir." Clearly satisfied with himself Marten closed the door behind him, leaving me alone with Lia. I crossed the living room and sat down in one of the chairs opposite the table from her. "So, which room is yours?"

She busied herself with the task of cleaning up the remaining cards from the table, avoiding my eyes. Hastily gathering up the pile she moved to the far wall and set it in a small box on a hanging shelf. Lia stood facing the wall for a while, arranging and rearranging the same few knick knacks as she bobbed in place. Without warning, she turned and walked past me, tapping me lightly on the shoulder as she went by. "This way."

I followed her around the corner, back into the dining room. Directly behind the chair I sat in during our meal was another door, which I had somehow missed on my first sweep of the room. Lia pushed the door open, revealing a simply furnished bedroom. The door opened along the left wall of the room, leaving just enough space beyond it for a bureau with a mirror on top. A small but comfortable looking bed was set in the back-right corner, flanked by a nightstand with a single candle burning on top. There was a simple wooden chair at the foot of the bed, next to a footlocker. Small wooden shelves adorned the walls of the room, all decorated with tiny clay figurines. In contrast with the rest of the house, the walls in this room were painted a dark green, amplifying the shadows cast by the lone candle.

As we entered the room, a single thought was buzzing through my head. *That bed is not big enough to accommodate the two of us comfortably.* Based on her reaction to Marten's suggestion, Lia had been thinking the same thing. I moved to the foot of the bed, pulling the chair into the corner of the room to sit down. Lia fiddled with the contents of a small wooden box on her dresser for a while but eventually sat down on the bed, pulling her legs up in front of her to rest her chin on top of her knees. We sat quietly for a bit, mostly avoiding eye contact with one another.

"So..." I trailed off, speaking to the center of the room. "I suppose you have some questions for me now, right?"

"Questions?" Lia tilted her head, puzzled. It was clear to me that she had been worrying more about our immediate predicament.

"Yeah, questions. I told you that once we were out of the prison, and you were home safe, you could ask me anything you could think of." I motioned around the room. "We're both here, I'm finally awake, and we're alone. I figured now might be a good time to get some of that out of the way."

Her face brightened. "Right! I almost forgot about that with everything that happened. I've been making a list so I can—" I held up a finger to cut her train of thought short.

"I've got to ask you something before we go any further." Ever since I had made the promise to her I had been thinking about how to approach the situation. "Do you want to know the whole truth? Everything, with nothing left out or censored? Even if it might be uncomfortable, confusing, shocking or hurtful?"

It looked like Lia moved to respond, but she caught herself. Her eyebrows furrowed as she pondered for a while, suddenly unsure after the unexpectedly serious question. Once she looked to have settled on an answer, she gave a small nod to the affirmative, her face set with determination. "Yes. No matter what."

I took a deep breath and nodded back. *Honesty it is, then.* Turning the chair slightly, I kicked my feet up onto the edge of the bed and leaned back into a comfortable position. "Alright then. Ask away."

Now it was Lia's turn to take a deep breath, taking a moment to think about her first question. It seemed as though she might be re-evaluating what she wanted to know after my ominous prerequisite question. She shifted as she settled on one, locking eyes with me. "Where are you really from?"

"Right. I wanted to thank you, by the way, for covering for me with your father. I should probably learn the surrounding geography if I'm going to be lying about it." I couldn't help but laugh at the idea. "Now, for where I'm from..." I paused for a moment, trying to think of the best way to explain the situation. "I'm not actually from anywhere in this world. About ten days ago, I just dropped into existence right outside the city walls of Yoria."

Lia regarded me carefully, processing what I had said but not responding. "Before that, I lived in a place called Hedaat for a long time. It was cold, lonely, and dark for most of the day. Not a very pleasant place."

"So, this Hedaat place...that's where you're really from?" I was surprised that Lia seemed to be accepting something so fantastical.

"No. This world we're in now, it's actually my...fourth." It felt strange to talk so frankly about my past. It had been a long time since I trusted anybody enough to even bring it up. "I'm originally from a place called America. That's where I was born, and where I grew up. To be honest with you, I don't remember much about it anymore. I've done so many things and met so many people since then, whoever I was back then feels like a stranger to who I am now."

Lia was sitting cross legged now, leaning her elbows into her knees and resting her head on her hands. Whether she believed what I was telling her, or she was just humoring me with her questions now, I couldn't tell. I hoped it was the former. "How did you...change worlds? Did you use magic?"

I shook my head. "No, nothing like that. In my original world, magic only existed in stories. I wish I had a more satisfying answer for you, but I really don't know how it happens. I just...wake up in the dark, in a lot of pain. I don't know how it is I get there, or why, but I'm stuck there for a while. In the end, everything randomly turns to flashing lights, and I get dumped into a new world."

She watched me in silence for a while, barely blinking as she stared at me in deep thought. "I'm sorry you had to go through that. It sounds terrible." The statement cut straight through me down to my core; it was a feeling I had been suppressing, burying deep down inside me, and she had found it and brought it out. I felt a rush of emotions and my vision blurred slightly as small tears formed in my eyes.

Turning away, I coughed loudly to try and disguise a sniffle as I wiped my eyes. "Yeah...yeah, it really is." The lump forming in my throat strained my speech so I coughed to try and clear it, to no avail. "I've left a lot of people behind. People that I cared about." I felt the tears run down my nose and looked down at the floor as I pawed at them, annoyed at my lack of composure.

Before I could even react, Lia rose from the bed and crossed the room to where I was sitting. Standing over me, she embraced me tightly, her long black hair spilling over my face to block my vision. I didn't react at first, caught off guard by the gesture, but I slowly raised my arms and returned the hug. Burrowing my face into her shoulder I allowed my tears to fall freely as my thoughts ran unbidden to the memories of all the people I had loved who I would never see again.

We remained there a while, locked together in each other's arms. Lia didn't speak, but she ran her hand through the hair on the back of my head in slow, calming scratches. The feeling was so soothing I thought I might fall asleep right there in her arms. I took a few deep breaths to center myself, noting a faint, pleasant aroma of mint mingled together with the natural scent of her hair and skin. Giving her a slight squeeze, I pulled away and wiped my leaking nose and eyes. She smiled softly and returned to the bed, sitting at the bottom this time, only a few feet from my chair.

"Sorry about that." I gave a few harrumphing coughs to clear my throat and clapped my cheeks lightly. "I'm sure you have more questions for me, so please, ask away." Even though I still felt embarrassed about the outburst, I felt a lightness in my shoulders and chest that I hadn't experienced for a long time. *Maybe stuffing unresolved emotions down inside to hide from them isn't the healthiest way to live after all.*

"Lux, it's okay, really. I'm just glad I could be here for you." Lia scooted forward to the edge of the bed, dangling her legs over the edge. "I really appreciate that you're being so open with me."

I felt a small pang of guilt. "About that. There is one thing I haven't been honest with you about."

She tipped her head to the side, curious. "What's that?"

"My name isn't really Lux. That's just a nickname I got a long time ago in Alderea, the first world I was sent to." Although there was clearly a story to be told on the subject, I moved on with the current line of thought. "Ever since I...left that world, using my real name just didn't feel right. My name is Elden Graham. I would prefer if you kept calling me Lux, but...I just wanted you to know."

"Elden..." She tested the name out with a whisper. Just hearing it spoken aloud made the hair stand up on the back of my neck. Lia gave a curt nod. "I promise I won't tell anyone."

"I appreciate it." I gave her a small smile. "Now, with that out of the way, what's your next question?"

Lia considered for a moment, and then her face lit up with excitement. "You told me that you would help me learn magic!"

"I did say that, didn't I?" I laughed a bit, feeling relieved to be done with heavy conversation, at least for the moment. "What would you like to know?"

The question stumped her. "Well, everything, I guess! The magic that you do seems a lot different from the magic I've heard about in the Unity Church."

"I'm not sure we have time tonight to go over everything, but...let's see." I pondered the topic of magic, trying to find a good entry point. "The way that I cast magic might be different, but I think the end result is the same. In my experience, everybody has the ability to use magic, but you need to be taught how to access it."

"Even me?!" Lia leaned forward, buzzing with excitement.

"Even you, Lia." I couldn't help but smile. Her enthusiasm and passion were infectious, and I seemed to be developing a weakness for it. "If you practiced for long enough, I'm sure you could be just as good as I am."

She let out a small squeal, throwing herself back into the center of the bed. Wiggling around for a moment, she took a deep meditative pose, most likely imitating how I had been sitting in my cell. "Okay, I'm ready. How do I do it?"

Raising an eyebrow, I shook my head. "It's probably not something you'll be able to pick up immediately, Lia. It took me four days of hard practice to use my first spell, and I had an experienced teacher. I can't say I've ever had to instruct somebody before."

"You'll do fine! Just tell me." She bounced up and down as she clapped her hands at me in anticipation.

"Okay, okay!" I laughed, putting my hands up to calm her down. "Here are the basics. You either want to be standing with your feet planted firmly about shoulder width apart or sitting up straight like you are now. The most important place to start is your breathing." I sat up straight to mirror her, placing one hand on my chest and the other on my stomach. Quickly, she copied my position.

"Close your eyes and take a few deep breaths in through your nose and out through your mouth." I took a few of my own, over-emphasizing the noise as an example. "As you breath, direct the air down to your core, pushing out your bottom hand with your gut. Do your best to not move the hand against your chest. All of your power comes from your core."

I watched her quietly as she adjusted to the new breathing pattern. "That's good, Lia. Focus on the air moving in and out of your body and clear your mind of everything else." Standing, I circled to the side of the bed as I continued. "Now, everybody has the energy inside them they need to use magic; I call it mana. When it isn't being used, it sits like a small pool of still water, deep down in your core.

"This mana behaves partly like a muscle does; it gets stronger the more you work it. Most people don't even know it's there and it sits dormant, never moving or growing. What we want to do is break down the barriers our body subconsciously makes around it and let that energy flow." I thought back to the lessons Brusch had given me. "Once you've been able to clear your mind and focus on your breath, try to picture a river flowing through you. It starts in your core, where the mana lives, and flows up your spine, through your arms and down to your fingertips."

Sitting down gently beside her, I traced a line with my finger from the small of her back up to her shoulder in the same way Brusch had shown me, years ago. Lia squeaked quietly and blushed, taken off guard by the physical contact, but to her credit she quickly resumed the breathing exercise. Continuing the line, I drew my finger down the outside of her arm to the hand in her lap. It lingered there a moment before I withdrew my hand and stood up.

"This is what you want to practice. Get better at clearing your mind and focusing on your breath, and picture that river flowing through you. Once you feel comfortable with it, the last step would be to let that energy out through your fingers into an object used channel the mana and say the name of the magic you want to invoke. I use my sword because that's how I was trained. I'm guessing they use wands or staves here? Something to shoot the magic out of?"

"In my storybook, the wizard was holding a big glass ball. I think that people use gemstones too, if they can find them." Lia was still facing forward, eyes closed.

I nodded. *Something uniform and easy to map. Makes sense.* "That's really all there is to the basics. If you practice that, I'm sure you'll pick it up in no time."

Her eyes flicked open. "And after I figure it out, I'll have you here to teach me all the words!" The statement fell heavy on the room, creating an awkward silence as we both knew where the conversation would go next. I broke eye contact with Lia, looking down to the floor. "Lux? I have another question."

"Sure," I responded, particularly focused on an interesting knot in the wooden plank below my feet.

"What are you going to do now that you're free?" Lia's voice was somber now, any traces of the jovialness from before gone.

"I haven't really thought about it," I lied. "I think I should probably get away from Yoria. After what I did to get out, I don't think the guards will stop looking for me. Plus, wherever I show up in a new world, people always...know, somehow. They find me, and then they want to use me for something." My hands balled into fists at the thought. "It never works out well for me in the end."

"Oh." Lia sounded defeated. "When will you leave?"

"Probably in a few days, after I've had time to rest and regain my strength." *I can't just avoid this topic. Now's the time.* I looked up from the floor to find her eyes downcast as she absentmindedly twirled the ends of her hair. "Lia." Her eyes shot up to meet mine in surprise. I could see a wide range of emotions clearly across her face: sadness, fear, even longing. "Your father mentioned something to me while we were outside."

She rolled her eyes, her expression changing to somewhere between embarrassment and annoyance. "Don't let anything he says bother you too much. He likes to get under people's skin."

"He said that if I left, I should take you along with me. That you wouldn't be happy here after I was gone." I watched her face as I spoke, curious as to how she would react. Her eyebrows raised in shock and she sheepishly turned her face away as it burned red.

"O-oh," Lia managed to stammer out. She tapped her fingers together nervously. "What did you say?"

"Lia..." I trailed off, uncertain of how to respond. I saw teardrops fall down to the bed from her downturned face. "Oh, Lia, please don't cry." I stood to put a hand on her shoulder, but she turned and put up a hand.

"I'm fine, really." She flashed a false smile, diverting the rivulets of water running down her face. "Please, just answer."

"Listen, Lia. You're a fantastic girl. You're quick witted and charming, with an infectious smile I can't resist. You're caring and sweet, and you look so cute when you're getting teased." I chuckled. "On top of that, you're absolutely beautiful. Truly, anybody would be lucky to know you. I'm certainly glad that we met, even with the terrible circumstances of how it happened."

"Lux, please..." Lia sniffled, moving to the edge of the bed.

"I don't know where I'm going to go, but I know that it's going to be dangerous. There's no guarantee that I could keep you safe, or that we would always have a place to sleep and food to eat." *You can't keep protecting her feelings, tell her how you feel.* I took a deep breath. "I would be happy to have your company on the road, so you can obviously come along, but I—"

I was cut off when Lia dove from the bed in a tackling embrace, tipping my chair dangerously far backwards before I could catch my balance. Puzzled, I patted her on the back. *This didn't go exactly as planned.* "What, did you think I wouldn't let you come with me? It's not like I could have stopped you from following me regardless of what I said, right?"

Now sitting squarely in my lap after her leap from the bed, Lia leaned back to look at me, hands on my chest. "You were being so nice, it just felt like you were going to say that I couldn't come. It was like you were leading up to bad news."

"Well, I thought I was, sort of." I felt awkward, having her face so close to mine. "It's just, I've really only known you for a couple days now, so I didn't want to make you any promises I can't keep. I don't know if I can...return your feelings in a way that would make you happy, is all."

Now it was Lia who was puzzled. "My...feelings?"

"Yeah, you know...your father brought up a dowry, and I said I'd have to think—"

Her face quickly melted into disbelief and anger. "He said WHAT?!" Up to this point, we had kept our voices down as to not disturb her parents, but she shouted at full volume now as she sprang up to her feet. "He said WHAT?!"

My mind felt split down the middle: Half of me wanted to burst out into laughter at the misunderstanding, and the other half wanted to shrivel up with awkwardness. I split the difference and managed to choke out a meek half whisper. "A dowry? He said you...loved me, and that—"

Without hearing another word Lia stormed out of the room, stomping loudly through the house. I heard a door swing open and slam shut, and some very muffled yelling. I couldn't quite hear the responses, but after a few more rounds of shouting from Lia the door opened and shut again, and her footsteps thundered back to her room. During the entire ordeal, I only managed one thought: *Did this go better or worse than I expected?*

She re-entered the room in a huff, closing the door loudly behind her. Lia stood in place for a moment, then let out one last exasperated, wordless yell. After giving herself a shake to let the rest of the anger out she walked to the bureau and produced a thin, lilac nightgown from the top drawer. Without hesitation, she pulled her blue and white dress up over her head and tossed it to hang over the back of the mirror. I was surprised by the action, but by the time I was able to look away, she had already slipped into the nightgown. It was a formless thing, hanging by two thin straps over her shoulders down to about mid-thigh, but it looked well-worn and comfortable.

Lia moved to the side of the bed and pointed to the mattress. "It's time for bed."

I nodded. "I'll grab the sheets from the basement and—"

"No, you won't. You'll get into bed." Her tone was oddly serious for the topic.

"I will?" I raised an eyebrow in amusement.

"You will." Judging by her expression, Lia wasn't looking for a discussion.

I shrugged. "Alright then." Standing from the chair, I went through the process of disrobing, stacking each item neatly on the wooden seat. In the end, I was left in only my underwear, a

plain pair of boxer briefs. Looking to Lia, she pointed down to the bed again. I moved to the side of the bed and sat down, giving a small chuckle. "What's gotten into you all of a sudden?"

She stared daggers down at me. "Nothing's gotten into me! Now scoot in, I sleep on the outside." I followed her orders, sliding to the far side of the mattress. I happily noted that this bed was long enough to allow me to stretch out fully without hanging off the ends. On the other hand, I also noticed it wasn't quite wide enough for two people to lay comfortably without touching. As soon as I was on my side and out of the way, Lia snuffed out the candle on the nightstand and climbed into bed after me, pressing her back firmly up against my chest. Before I could react, she reached back and grabbed my wrist, hauling it over her waist and snuggling back into my forced embrace.

"Now, go to sleep. No complaining." My arm was draped over her waist, resting just above her belly button, and she held my hand in both of hers. "You have more questions to answer tomorrow." I went to make a witty remark but came up empty. Instead, I made the best of the situation and nestled deeper into the blankets and pillows, a welcome comfort compared to the floor, tree and prison cot I had been sleeping on prior. Lia's hair almost completely covered my face, but it didn't bother me; in fact, I found the light scent of mint calming.

This is...fine, right? We didn't have a specific conversation about her feelings for me, but I think I got the idea across enough for now. I'm not leading her on, and she's just pissed off at her father and is trying to take control of her life. I tried to convince myself that everything was alright, but I still had the lingering feelings of regret and guilt in my gut. *Everything is fine. We're just sleeping in the same bed, it's not a proposal. Get it together.*

A yawn caught me off guard, making me realize how tired I was. Having woken up only a few hours prior I hadn't expected to be able to get to sleep, but I found myself dozing already against Lia's warm figure curled up next to me. I was nearly asleep when she spoke into the darkness.

"Lux? I have one more question." Her voice was quiet and calm, lacking whatever fit of energy had possessed her before.

Suddenly too tired to move, I spoke into the back of her head. "Sure, Lia. What is it?"

There was a long pause. "Have you ever been in love?"

"Yes." With my eyes closed, I could see a perfect picture of Amaya before me, standing by the tree in the backyard of Ashedown's forge on a bright summer day. "It was a long time ago, in the first world I was sent to. Alderea." I sat for a long time in the darkness, thinking of her. "Her name was Amaya."

"What happened?" Lia's voice was practically a whisper.

"I got taken away again." The sadness and bitterness deep down started to rise up, as it always did when I thought about it. "I left her behind...I lost her."

Lia squeezed my hand lightly. "I'm sorry."

"It's okay." I squeezed her hands back. "I think that losing someone like that, though...it changes you. I can't be who I was back then anymore. I gave away that piece of who I was, and I never got it back. I hope...I hope that Amaya still has it."

I felt Lia nod. "She does. She would never let that go."

There was a hard lump forming in my throat. I nodded silently, unable to speak without losing the internal fight with my emotions. Eventually, I felt in control enough to whisper, "Thanks, Lia." I pulled her back against me tightly, steadying myself with the close embrace. It had been a long time since I had been in such close physical contact with another person, and as much as I had convinced myself I didn't need it, I knew now that I had been missing it dearly.

As I laid in the darkness with Lia wrapped up in my arms, I felt a small wave of relief in the back of my mind, like I had finally removed a particularly annoying splinter and stopped the incessant itch. I nuzzled my face through her hair, resting my forehead against the back of her neck, and let out a satisfied sigh. After years of loneliness and anger, I finally felt connected to something again. I fell asleep in mere moments to the rhythmic rise and fall of Lia's chest, a soothing metronome I hadn't heard for a lifetime.

***

13. PREPARATION

The pain was everywhere. I screamed, but no sound escaped my lips. The blackness rushed down my throat, filling my lungs with the choking embrace of more torment. The sensation robbed me of all conscious thought, but even still, a small idea played at the edges of my mind, unbidden. This was familiar. The pain, the darkness, the empty void of nothing. Had I been here before? As my body seemed to burn away into black smoke, completing my transformation into formless agony, the memory rushed back to me all at once.

This was the second time I had entered the void. It was a defence mechanism of my brain, maybe, that had locked away the memory of the pain before. Perhaps it chose to forget, cutting out any thoughts of it root and stem, to protect me from living in constant fear of whatever this place was. Whatever had happened, the memories had come back, and somehow, it made the experience more bearable.

Though the torture was still an all-encompassing field around me, it had less of a hold over my mind this time. I could think, and one singular thought anchored me to sanity: There is relief, somewhere on the other side of the void. Whether it would last for ten seconds or ten thousand years I couldn't say, but I had done it once before. I could do it again.

Another memory bombarded me, taking complete hold of my mental bastion. Amaya. Alderea. All of the things that had happened to me since my first trip through the blackness played out in front of me as I burned. I didn't have the capacity to feel anything about the memories; that part of my brain was well occupied with screaming in utter agony. But the memories were coming back, and I knew that it was important. When the world changed to howling winds and flashing lights, I knew the transition was almost complete.

All of my physical senses came back to me at once, and I collapsed down to my knees immediately. Touching a hand to my chest I felt that the cool, sticky blood was still there, splashed across my leather chestpiece and arms. My gloves were torn, and a stinging in my left eye told me my forehead was still sliced open. None of it seemed to matter as my mind raced through the last memories of Alderea.

"Amaya!" I screamed out into the dark winterscape around me. The night sky was covered in clouds, leaving little *illumination to aid in identifying landmarks around me. "Amaya! Jarut! Kel!" Even though I knew they weren't here, I wasn't ready to admit it to myself. "AMAYA!"*

I crumpled forward into the snow, blood and tears streaming down my face. I couldn't reconcile my memories of where I had just been with where I was now, which left my mind in a useless state of shock. My body was shaking, not equipped in the slightest for cold temperatures, and my fingers had already started to go numb. I just shook my head into the snow, wailing down at the ground. "I'm not leaving you, Amaya...You're going to be okay...I promise..."

The wind was blowing steadily across the snowy plains, mounding up fresh precipitation on top of me as I laid motionless. All at once my body gave up and I gave a sigh of relief as I sank further into the snow. "Amaya...I'll be right there...You're going to be okay..." My vision began to narrow, but I wasn't concerned; sleep seemed welcome to my weary mind. "I'm not...leaving you..." The last thought I had before I fell unconscious in the snow was Amaya's face, smiling back at me.

I awoke to the sound of footsteps creaking on the wooden floor outside. Sleepily, I raised my head to check out the noise, doing my best to shake Lia's long black hair out of my face. The door handle was slowly unlatching, and as it pushed open, I saw Marten and Hana's faces peering into the room through the small crack. They must have seen me staring at them, because they quickly withdrew, closing the door and shuffling away from the bedroom.

Still groggy, I lay back down into the bed, quickly forgetting why I had even woken up. I gave Lia's hand a small squeeze as I pulled her in close, readjusting to find the perfect position to fall back asleep. *Need more sleep...just a few more minutes.* Some combination of the noise and movement roused Lia, and she let out a short, high-pitched groan as she wiggled and stretched. Although my eyes were closed, I could tell she had rolled over to face me.

"G'morning," Lia yawned. The noise alone was enough to make me yawn reflexively back at her. "How'd you sleep?"

"Honestly, that was by far the best night of sleep I've had in my life." I cracked one eye open and found her staring at me lazily, still halfway in the clutches of sleep. "Well, this life, for sure." A small grin curled my lips as I closed my eye again, wrestling a pillow down into a more comfortable position. It felt good to be able to talk openly about having past lives, something I hadn't discussed with anybody in a long time.

My arm was still around her, so I abandoned the smushed pillow and pulled her close, opting instead for her shoulder. Her skin was soft and hot against my cheek, a much more comfortable resting surface than the old down pillow. I felt Lia's breath quicken in her chest, and she patted my head quickly before withdrawing from the bed to stand up. "W-we should probably get up soon, it must be morning by now." Her speech was awkward and her voice high-pitched, clearly flustered.

"Lia, wait." I put a hand on her shoulder and sat upright. Slowly, she turned to me, her face bright red. Arching an eyebrow, I gave her a quizzical look. "If I'm remembering things correctly, you specifically put my arm around you last night."

Her eyebrows shot up as she let out a small, shy squeak. "Y-yes, I did."

She's obviously new to this sort of thing. "But now, you're feeling embarrassed about it." She didn't say anything, choosing to instead look away and fiddle with the bedsheets. I chuckled and shook my head. "Listen, Lia. There's nothing to feel awkward about. Sleeping next to someone doesn't need to mean anything."

Throwing the blanket back, I scooted to sit next to her on the edge of the bed. "I apologize if I made you feel uncomfortable. I guess I didn't realize how long it's been since I had any sort of...real human contact, and obviously I got carried away with it." I patted her on the shoulder. "I don't want things to be weird between us, you know?"

Lia looked to me, wide eyed and shaking her head. "No! It's not your fault! It's my fault, really! Things aren't weird!" She wrung her hands in her lap. "It's just, I've never really slept in a bed with someone else, so when I woke up, it was just...startling?"

I laughed. "Yeah, I can imagine that might be startling." I stood and moved to the chair at the end of the bed and began to sort through my clothes. "I just wanted to make sure we're on the same page. I obviously wouldn't want to do anything to make you feel uncomfortable in any way."

She jumped up from the bed, her face bashful. "No, really, I'm fine! It was...nice." Lia looked away, but I caught a small smile on her face through the embarrassment.

"I'm happy to hear it." I shrugged on my plain white undershirt, working my way up the buttons. "I have to warn you, though. Judging by how things went yesterday, I think your parents are going to give you a hard time about it." Lia froze, her face becoming deathly serious. "They popped their heads in this morning before you woke up."

An angry pout spread across her face as she stomped over to her dresser. She changed from her nightgown into a comfortable looking white sundress, patterned with small red flowers. "You stay in here. I'll be right back." Lia went to the door, quickly slipping through before closing it behind her. As I continued to dress myself, I heard laughter from Marten and Hana, followed by angry, furtive whispers from Lia. About the time I had belted on my pants and slipped into my boots, Lia was back in the doorway. "You can come out now, Lux."

Chuckling, I exited the room with her into the bright morning sunlight of the house. Rounding the corner, I saw Marten and Hana sitting in the living room, both anxiously awaiting our appearance. Marten was grinning ear to ear. "Lux! How did you sleep last night?"

Lia stomped her foot and glared at her father. "I slept like a log. It's the first proper bed I've slept in in weeks!" Now that I knew Marten's personality better, it was easy to avoid his attempts to fluster me. "I have to thank you both again for letting me stay here, and for watching over me while I was injured. I'll certainly do whatever I can to repay you."

Marten waved a hand at me. "Oh, enough of that, Lux. You'll always have a place under our roof and at our table."

"Speaking of which, I was just about to make us some breakfast. Would you like some, Lux?" Hana chimed in.

"Oh, no thank you. I've never been much of a breakfast person." I smiled graciously. "I was actually hoping to take a walk around outside to help myself wake up."

"I'll go with you!" Lia bounced out in front of me, excited. "I can show you around the town!"

"Excellent." I turned to Marten. "Do you have a cloak I could borrow? Preferably one with a hood?"

"By the door." He motioned vaguely with his hand. "Be careful out there, you two."

"Of course." I moved to the basement door. "Lia, I need to grab a few of my things. You should have some time for breakfast before we leave, if you're hungry."

"Okay!" Lia dashed off around the corner to the kitchen. I shook my head and laughed, marveling at her energy. *Compared to her, I might as well be an old man again.* My belongings were still tucked away in the crate at the back wall of the basement, covered with a thin bed sheet. Searching through the box, I withdrew and pocketed my coin purse. I took a moment to stare at the rest of my gear. *If anybody is looking for me, I'll be most likely described wearing this gear.* With a touch of disappointment, I replaced the sheet and headed back up the stairs.

Lia was already waiting by the front door when I arrived, a large canvas bag slung over one shoulder. She was holding two pieces of bread with a pale orange paste smeared on top, one in each hand. She held one out to me when I approached. "I know you said you don't like breakfast, but you really seemed to like the asperfruits at dinner last night, so I made you some toast with asperfruit jam!" She seemed very proud of herself, a wide smile on her face.

"That sounds delicious!" I had made a mental note to find out what had been roasted on the skewers, so I was pleasantly surprised with the offering. I found Marten's cloak hung by the door, a thick, faded green wool with a deep hood. It was much shorter and scratchier than my own cloak, but I wasn't wearing it for fashion or luxury. I slid it on and took the bread from Lia, taking a quick bite. The savory, buttery flavor I remembered filled my mouth, but this time it was laced with hits of nutmeg and clove, adding a delicious layer of spice. "It's so good!" I said excitedly between bites, sending a few crumbs flying.

Lia giggled. "I'm glad you like it!" She opened the front door, revealing a beautiful blue sky outside. Hopping outside, she turned and smiled at me. "Let's go, Lux!"

I followed her out into the cool morning air, finishing the last bite of my toast. Turning left around the corner of the house revealed a rough dirt road, just wide enough for two wagons to pass by one another. The surrounding land was flat, with few trees or ground cover to get in the way, so I was able to see quite a long way in any direction. I could see a concentrated group of houses in the distance, which I assumed was our destination.

"So, this is the town of Tolamar," Lia began as we walked down the road. "Lots of little towns like this have popped up around Yoria. It's really expensive to live in the city, so most people like us live just outside, wherever there's room." I nodded, enjoying the sun and fresh air as we walked. We seemed to be a good five or ten minutes away from the town center, so I figured it was the perfect time to learn more about the new world I was in.

"I actually had a couple questions for you, if you don't mind. Being in a new world and all, I figured this would be a good time to clear some things up before I do or say anything too stupid." I laughed. "I know you're supposed to be the one asking all the questions, but maybe we could switch it up for the morning."

"Of course!" Lia was eager, as always. "What do you want to know?"

Let's get the potentially awkward stuff out of the way first. "Your mother. She's a demihuman, right? Is that the right word?"

She nodded. "Yeah, that's right. Why do you ask?"

I let out a sigh of relief at not having accidentally used some sort of racial slur. "Two reasons. Firstly, you don't really look demihuman. How does that sort of thing get passed on?"

Lia shrugged. "It's random, mostly. Sometimes when a demihuman and a human have a baby, it has the same features as the demihuman. Sometimes, they only get some of the traits, like me. I can see really well in the dark, but that's basically it." She looked up at me, curious. "Is that different from the other worlds?"

"A bit. In Alderea, if a demihuman has a child with a human, they always inherit the demihuman traits." I shrugged, logging the information away as a curiosity. "The other reason I ask is...well, are people nice to demihumans in this world?"

She looked confused. "I'm not sure what you mean. I don't think people are nicer to demihumans than anybody else."

"That's not exactly what I meant." Racism wasn't a topic I was particularly comfortable talking about. "Other races aren't hateful towards demihumans just because of the way they're born, right?"

"I've never met anybody like that before." Her voice sounded sad as she continued. "Did people hate demihumans in your world?"

"In the world I'm from originally, there were no demihumans. Alderea was like it is here, but Hedaat..." I trailed off, considering how much to say. "Humans and demihumans didn't get along there." We walked in silence for a while. *Hedaat was a shithole,* I thought to myself bitterly. "I'm glad things aren't like that here."

"Me too!" Lia laughed. "Was there anything else you wanted to know?"

We were approaching the town proper now, and I spotted a small signpost at the side of the road before the houses started. "I can't read the language here." I pointed to the sign. "What does that say?"

"It just says 'Tolamar'." She perked up. "I can teach you how to read, if you want! We have lots of books at home, I'm sure you can figure it out in no time!"

"That would be great. It's always tough to go back to square one in that regard." I thought back to all of the written languages I had learned over the years, all useless now.

"I just thought of something. If you can't read Kaldanic, how can you speak it? You don't have a weird accent or anything."

"That's a great question. Unfortunately, I have no idea." The language issue had been something I thought about a lot in Alderea, but with no way to really test it I had just accepted it as a fact of life. "I've never met anybody I couldn't understand, and they've always been able to understand me. I took it as a blessing and tried not to think about it."

Lia gave me a strange look. "You never tried to figure out how it worked?"

"Well, of course I did. But how would you go about testing something like that?"

"You could..." She trailed off, tapping her finger on her lips in thought. Eventually, she laughed. "I guess that's more complicated than I thought!" I nodded. We had finally entered the heart of the town, with the small wooden houses much more closely packed together along the road. Lia ran ahead, stopping at a side street. "This way!"

As we turned the corner, I found half a dozen wooden stalls lining the road on either side, all displaying various goods for sale. I was confused by the sight. "Lia, why are people selling things here? Wouldn't they get better business selling things in Yoria? I saw a huge market square when I was there that was packed with people."

"They definitely would, but it can be hard to get a trader's permit allowing you to sell goods in the city. It costs a lot of money and the guards hassle you all the time when you bring things in and out." Lia motioned to the street before us. It wasn't large, but it had a sizable number of people for the limited shops. "That's why these people set up here. Sometimes people who live in the city proper come out to shop, but usually it's just the people who live nearby."

We were nearly to the first stand now, and I could see it was loaded with what looked like fresh produce. "I see. Your father has one of these trader's passes, right?"

"He does! His business doesn't actually make any goods to sell, we just make contracts with local craftsman to sell their goods in the city and take a commission for transporting and selling." Lia spotted the produce stand and ran over excitedly. "Lux, come look at this!"

The table before us was covered in a wide array of food, some familiar to me and others completely foreign. I saw carrots, apples, radishes, and the round things I had now come to know as asperfruits in piles along the front. There were also large bundles of yellow and orange leaves that I remembered seeing at dinner, and some knobby blue tuber-like plants the size of softballs. I marveled at the vibrant colors of the offerings, and I felt a longing pang in my stomach at the thought of eating more asperfruits.

Lia scooped some of the blue tubers and a bundle of leafy plants into her bag and paid the woman behind the table with a few coppers she had produced from a small pocket in her dress. She looked back at me, a self-satisfied smile on her face. "Mother is going to cook this up for dinner tonight. I bet you'll love it!"

"I'm sure you're right!" I scanned over the other nearby tables. "Lia, is there anybody here that sells forged items? Stuff like weapons, armor, horseshoes, that sort of thing."

"Yeah, there's usually a man down near the end who does metal work. He doesn't sell a lot of weapons or armor though, and I don't think it would be anywhere near as good as the things you already have." Her brow furrowed. "I don't really like him. Father is the one who gets him his supply of metal to work with, and whenever I see him, he always looks...mean."

I chuckled. "Don't worry. I'll do all the talking." We headed down the increasingly busy street, now having to actively work to avoid bumping into people. As I scanned ahead for the blacksmith's table, my stomach dropped as I saw two city guards walking in our direction. They both seemed relaxed, casually chatting with each other as they walked, but I pulled Lia by the hand to the closest market stall to take cover.

Doing my best to look casual, I leaned over and whispered, "Everything is fine, but there are two city guards heading our way. I'm sure they aren't looking for me, but let's stay out of the way until they go by." I began to pick through the contents of the table in front of me, which was piled high with various bits of cloth and textiles. Lia followed suit, making benign comments about the color or softness of certain materials.

Out of the corner of my eye, I watched the two guards pass uneventfully from beneath my cloak's hood. After they were well past, I let out a deep sigh as we headed back into the street. "Sorry about that. I'd rather not take any chances, especially when you're with me. I wouldn't want you or your parents to get in trouble for harboring a fugitive." I scoffed grimly. *When is the last time I WASN'T a fugitive?*

After some meandering to check out interesting looking offerings, we found our way to the blacksmith's stall. The man behind the large counter had a tall, wiry frame, topped with greasy black hair and a large, crooked nose. He had dark sunken eyes and pale skin that looked like it barely stretched to fit over his bony form. *I can see why Lia doesn't like him.* As we approached he paid us no mind, casually sharpening a small knife against a whetstone as he stared off into space.

In terms of weapons, the offering was sparse as Lia had predicted. The main showing was two shortswords, each halfway inserted into leather scabbards, sitting front and center on the table. Beside them were a few simple daggers and hatchets, piled with much less care. A wooden buckler with a metal frame and rivets rounded out the weapons and armor display. Overall, I was unimpressed by the quality of the metalwork, but each piece would serve its purpose well enough. *Ashedown would have kicked me out on the spot if I had tried to pass off work like this for one of his orders.*

The rest of the table was covered in various implements and accessories which made up the bulk of the offered products. Building materials like hinges, nails and brackets, basic tools like hammers and tongs, and sharpened scissors and knives were all scattered haphazardly across the stall. I was annoyed at the lack of organization and was tempted to leave without inspecting the items further, but I had a feeling that this would be the only accessible smith I would meet for a while.

"Excuse me, sir. How much are you asking for the shortswords?" I reached down to the table and picked up one of the weapons, pulling it from the scabbard to inspect the full length of the blade. The man looked down his nose at me with a sneer.

He spoke with a slow, lisping voice that agitated me severely. "That would be ten steins, paid in full." Although I had little experience with Yorian currency, it seemed a steep price to me. *Sherman said one gold would pay for a season's worth of lodging and food at his in. One shortsword is worth the same as months of room and board?* I did my best to hide my distaste. *Not for this quality.*

I tried to pick the most diplomatic words for my thoughts. "That seems awfully high. I'm sure I could find a blade for less than that price at the pavilion in Yoria."

"Well, you aren't in Yoria now, are you?" For someone who was supposedly trying to make a sale, the man seemed determined to infuriate me.

"True, true." I looked over the stock on the table between us. "Suppose I was to buy both the shortswords, and one of these daggers too. Perhaps you could lower the collective price a bit?"

He stared me down with his cold, lifeless eyes for a while. "An imperium for the lot of it. I'll even throw in a sheath for the dagger, as a sign of my...generosity." The man grinned a sarcastic smile, revealing multiple gaps where his teeth had fallen out. Those that remained seemed ready to abandon ship at any moment, all of them yellow and cracked.

I pulled out my coin purse and fished around inside, feeling for the distinctive hole in the small gold coin signifying an imperium. I pulled it out and placed it on the table in front of him with a small grin. *Thanks, Sherman.* The man looked stunned, perhaps believing I didn't have the funds for such an offer. He quickly snatched up the coin and held it up to the light, inspecting its features carefully.

After a lengthy inspection he seemed satisfied enough to stash the coin in a strongbox behind him. Opening a crate nearby, he fished out a simple leather sheath and tossed it down on the table. I picked through the pile of daggers for a moment, finding one with the least number of nicks to the cutting edge, and slid it into the sheath. "What are you planning to do with all those?" He watched me through narrowed eyes, clearly suspicious.

"Oh, just practicing swordplay is all, really." I gave him an innocent smile. "One can never be too prepared, right?" Turning to Lia, who had been doing her best to hide behind me throughout the exchange, I handed her the dagger. "Put this in your bag for me, will you?" With my hands emptied, I took up both of the shortswords in my arms. "Pleasure doing business with you." He glared silently as we left the stall, walking back the way we had come.

Once we were out of earshot of the smith, Lia gave an exasperated groan. "I told you he was mean." She turned to look at me as we walked, a scowl on her face. "And what were you doing, paying him a whole imperium for that stuff? What do you even need it all for? Where did you even get that much money in the first place?"

I laughed at her. "Trust me Lia, I know they're not great. When I was a smith, I could forge better steel than this in my sleep. The money came from the innkeeper I met in Yoria, who tried to steal my things with that thief girl. He was kind enough to teach me the value of your coins here, so I figured taking that imperium was fair repayment for the inconvenience they caused me."

She thought on the information for a while. We had successfully made it off of the market street, and the crowd was thin enough now that we didn't have to worry about any guards sneaking up on us. "That still doesn't explain why you bought them in the first place."

"You didn't hear me back there? I wasn't lying to him." I took one of the shortswords I was carrying and carefully handed it to Lia. "They're for practice."

***

14. PRACTICE

"Hold out your hand. Palm flat, facing the sky, like this." I held out an upturned hand in demonstration. Lia was across from me sitting on a large barrel with her feet swinging just above the ground. She mirrored my hand movement, putting her small palm out next to mine. Nodding, I reached down the crate behind me and grabbed one of the two newly acquired shortswords. Holding the sheathed weapon by the blade I gently placed the grip into her hand.

"Alright. To hold a sword this size properly, you'll want to position your hand like this." Rotating it slightly in her hand I carefully wrapped each of her fingers around the leather grip to the correct positions. "The power of your grip will come from these first two fingers against the meat of your thumb, and the last two fingers will be loose to guide the blade and give you a bit of extra reach and dexterity." I tapped and squeezed each part of her hand as I spoke to emphasize.

Lia nodded, her brow furrowed in concentration as she observed her own hand. She had been bouncing with excitement the entire walk home after I had told her my plan to teach her sword fighting. While she saw it as a fun new adventure, I saw it as a necessity; my mind would be much more at ease while traveling if I knew Lia could defend herself in a dire situation. As I had no idea how the culture of this world viewed women learning to fight, I hadn't yet informed her parents of my plans. We were currently behind Marten's barn where he stored most of his empty crates and barrels, far out of view of the main house.

With Lia's hand firmly gripped on the handle I removed my hand from the opposite end of the blade. The full weight of the weapon made her arm drop, but she recovered quickly. I nodded to her. "Okay, time for your footwork. Hop up and show me your best battle stance." She slid off the barrel and stretched for a moment before settling into a rigid stance, pointing the tip of the sword out at me at a full arm's length.

Hiding my amusement, I walked around her to observe. "Not bad for a guess, really. Let's start from the ground up." With the tip of my boot I tapped the inside of her heels. "You should spread your feet out more, about shoulder width apart. Seeing as you use your sword in your right hand, you should keep your right foot forward, towards whoever you would be fighting. It's easier for you to move out with power that way."

I circled around to her side and pushed gently on her shoulders, causing her to rock forward before she could catch her balance. "Your legs are so stiff, it wouldn't take more than a light breeze to knock you over!" Lia put on a pitiful pout as she readjusted her footing. "You should have a slight bend to your knees and keep your weight more towards the balls of your feet. It lets you react faster to movement and helps keep you steady."

I moved to her front, lowering her sword arm substantially. "You'll want to keep your weapon a bit closer. If it's too far out, you won't be able to block an incoming attack as easily. Plus, your power comes from your core muscles as much as your sword arm, so you want to use that leverage as efficiently as possible." Placing my hands on her shoulders, I rotated her counterclockwise. "You don't want to face your opponent head on. That gives them the biggest possible target."

Lia cocked her head. "Where did you learn all of this? I had no idea there was so much that went into just...standing, in a fight."

"Well, I sort of learned from everything, I guess." I scratched the back of my head, thinking back to my first few encounters with a sword. "I started out on my own, just doing whatever felt right. Whenever somebody would come through town with a weapon, I'd ask them to practice with me." The memories gave me a good laugh. "After you get thrown in the dirt enough times, you start to learn a few things about what you're doing wrong."

She let out a small giggle. "Does that mean you're going to throw me into the dirt, too?"

"I guess that depends on how good you are!" In one swift motion I crouched and connected my shin with the back of Lia's knees, using my own momentum to spin and take a knee to catch her in my arms as she toppled backwards with a sudden yelp. The sword, still in its leather sheath, spun to the ground and landed with a dull thud. "Hmmm. Might happen a few times."

Lia shoved my chest playfully. "That wasn't fair! I didn't even know we were starting!" She stood up and retrieved her weapon, dusting off the leather.

"I'm sorry Lia, I couldn't help myself." I chuckled as I got up and patted her on the shoulder. "We won't be doing any real combat training for a while. You have to learn the basics before we get to fighting, or you'll make some bad habits that will be hard to break." Taking a few steps back, I sat down on a crate and watched her. "Do you think you can take that combat stance again?"

She nodded, taking a moment to reposition herself to face me. Initially she fell into a stance much like her original one, but she seemed to go through a mental checklist and one by one corrected the issues I had pointed out to her. "That's great, Lia! Soon enough, that will feel so natural that you won't even have to think about it. Now, let's move on to some simple strikes."

I ran her through a few cuts and slashes, trying to pick moves that were easy but worked different muscle groups to perform. Once I was satisfied with her demonstration of the cuts, I nodded. "Okay. The rest of your practice for today is to repeat those attacks as many times as you can. Just pick one of them, take your stance, do the full motion like we practiced, retake your stance, and repeat." I looked off into the distance thoughtfully. "Maybe...fifty of each one?"

Lia's eyebrows shot up, but she caught herself before she said anything, choosing instead to nod silently. *She probably thinks I'm less likely to leave her behind if she does what she's asked and learns quickly.* The thought made me uncomfortable, so I logged it away to bring up later. "Let me know if you have any questions. I've got a project to work on in the meantime."

Leaving Lia to her practice, I scouted the area for a set of like-sized crates. Stacking them two by two, I created a decently sized workbench for my next task. Reaching out, I pulled my sword from its resting place in the basement and set it down on the surface in front of me. Turning it in place I let it rest with the engraved runes facing up at me, the only marks on an otherwise unblemished surface. I ran my thumb across them, admiring my own craftsmanship. *Agility. Thought Acceleration. Sharpening. Heighten Senses. Windstep.*

Two smaller runes sat adjacent to the main column, reading *Greater* and *Lesser*. The idea of adding modifiers to my combat runes had come later, after engraving the main abilities themselves. It had taken some practice to perfect using enhancements with the modifying runes, as they weren't written directly next to each other, but now it felt like second nature. I moved to Lia's bag and dug the newly acquired dagger out, then tossed the leather sheath onto the work surface. *Time to expand my horizons.*

    I spent a moment examining the new weapon in my hand, taking note of the imperfections in the blade and the leather wrapped grip. Probing out with my mana, it was a simple task to suffuse the dagger with energy. Having used weapons as my sole implement for casting combat enhancements for all my lives, even a foreign blade felt familiar in my hand. "Greater Sharpening, Lesser Fire Blade," I intoned aloud. The blade flashed a dull red for a moment, then rippled with tiny crimson flames.

    Although I had already created fire multiple times through various means, I was still surprised when the invocation worked. I thought back to the fire I had created in my fight with the dungeon guards. The flames had shot out in a controlled pillar perfectly in the direction I had wanted them to go, completely scorching the man in front of me but leaving my sword hand unharmed. The memory puzzled me for a moment, but I shook my head and returned to the task at hand. *One thing at a time. Unravel the mysteries of the universe later, engrave the runes now.*

    The dagger's blade began to glow a dull red as it was heated by the dancing mana-fueled flames. Carefully guiding the pointed tip down to my bastard sword with both hands, I drew out a small curve of my first planned rune as a test. Between the heated metal and the spell-sharpened point, carving a shallow cut into the manasteel was easier than I had anticipated. *Well, it's not as clean as the engraver in Ashedown's shop, but I can make do.* With a slow practiced hand, I began to inscribe the new runes along the face of the blade.

    As I worked, I could hear Lia panting from exertion behind me. The sound from her routine fell into a simple rhythm that I unconsciously followed in my head. *Swish. Exhale. Reposition. Inhale. Swish. Exhale. Reposition. Inhale.* Time passed quickly as I worked, and soon enough I found myself finished with the first set of runes. Fire and Healing had been added to the main column, while Sustained, Self, and Blade were engraved in the smaller column. I cut the mana supply to the dagger and let out a satisfied sigh of relief from the constant concentration.

Tossing the dagger down to the crates I turned to observe Lia's practicing. She was facing away from me, currently engaged in a series of methodical overhead slices. After a few swings she stopped, bending over with her hands on her knees as she breathed heavily. Turning to look back in my direction with her face red and drenched in sweat, her eyes widened when she realized I was watching her casually from my spot back on the crate workbench. "Gah! How long have you been watching me?"

I grinned. "Not long, really. Just a few swings. Your form still looks good! How are you feeling?"

Lia fell back to land in the grass with a soft thud. "Exhausted! The sword isn't that heavy...but swinging it over and over again...it's hard work!" She set the blade down beside her and flopped back into the grass, letting out a long, low grunt. "I'm only halfway done!"

"Oh, you've done more than enough already. Fifty was way too high of a goal, to be honest." Her head popped up from the ground to glare at me, but I just laughed. "Now that you're done, why don't we try meditating for a bit? I find the best time to meditate is right after a hard workout." I moved over to the grassy area and sat down next to Lia, crossing my legs into a comfortable position.

She sighed as she pushed herself up and rolled her eyes. "But you didn't get a hard workout. I did." Begrudgingly, Lia moved to imitate my pose. Her eyes narrowed as she looked over at me. "I think you might be enjoying this a little too much."

"Maybe!" I closed my eyes and settled my breathing. "Alright, deep breaths now. Close your eyes. Breathing through your nose, down into your core, and out through your mouth. If your muscles are aching, focus on that feeling and the rhythm of your breath, clearing everything else out of your mind." As I spoke, I channeled mana around my body, extending it down to the tips of my fingers and toes, then back to pool in my core. It was an exercise I had found helpful back in Alderea both for increasing my control over the energy and for expanding the total pool of mana I had access to.

"Once you've cleared your mind, try looking inward to see your own energy. Picture a river, flowing out from your core in all directions, slowly trickling down to your fingers before it loops back in again." I cracked one eye open to peek over at Lia. She was still red faced from her workout with strands of dark hair stuck to her forehead. The rest spilled down behind her in a loose braid, almost reaching the ground. She was still dressed in her white sundress which, although fashionable and flattering, was not particularly well suited to combat and meditation. *I'll have to find her some proper combat attire.*

Closing my eye again, I continued with my guided meditation. "Now, don't expect any sort of fireworks or major breakthroughs. We're just practicing our breathing and relaxation techniques, which can help you in all aspects of your life. Keeping a blank mind can be difficult, so make a goal for yourself to stay focused for as long as possible. Every time we practice, it'll be a little easier."

I sat in the grass with her for quite a while in silence, enjoying the warm weather and gentle breeze until a distant voice roused us. "Marlia! Lux! Lunch is ready!" Hana called out from somewhere in front of the house. Yawning I stood and stretched my arms above my head, popping my shoulders. I helped Lia up from the ground, and together we made our way around the barn and into the house.

Lunch was a refreshing salad of unfamiliar greens topped with sliced apples, along with toasted bread and asperfruit jam. We sat in the living room and made pleasant conversation until late into the afternoon when Marten returned from the day's business. Lia took an inventory and marked down some numbers in a ledger while Marten and I unloaded crates and sorted the goods into their proper places. The rest of the day passed in a blur with work leading to dinner, which transitioned into playing cards around the table until the room was lit entirely by lamps and candles. Before I knew it, I was saying goodnight to Lia's parents.

"Thanks for your help today, Lux," Marten said as he stood from his seat at the table. "It certainly makes work faster with a second pair of strong hands around." He kissed Lia on the top of the head and clapped me on the shoulder as he passed us by on his way to the bedroom. "Now, you kids behave yourselves tonight, you hear me?" Before Hana could push him through the doorway and close the door, he shot me a wink.

"Of course, sir," I laughed, looking to find Lia red and pouting as I expected. Once her parents were closed away in the other room, I stood and looked down at her with my eyebrows raised. "You know, you warned me that he likes to get under people's skin, but he seems to be best at teasing you."

She hopped up, rolling her eyes. "Well, he's my father. Of course he gets on my nerves." Lia headed out of the living room around the corner, and I followed suit. "He thinks he's so funny, but it's just embarrassing." She suddenly stopped and turned back to look at me with concern on her face. "He didn't say anything weird while you were loading the crates, did he?"

"No, nothing like yesterday," I lied casually. In truth, Marten had brought up the topic of Lia and me again at the first possible chance: While we were alone moving cargo. He asked if I had made any decisions, and I told him that Lia wanted to come with me when I left as he had rightly guessed. Although he seemed to expect the answer, he was pensive for a while, but eventually laughed and said it was time she left home with a man. I reminded him that I had made no commitments, to which he just smiled and nodded in response. "We didn't talk much."

Looking somewhat relieved, Lia led me to her room and closed the door behind us. I took a seat on the wooden chair to pull off my boots while Lia changed into her nightgown. As she went to pull her dress over her head she stopped and recoiled in pain, letting out a weak moan; her arms had barely raised above shoulder level before the workout from earlier in the day took its revenge. Pitifully she turned and looked to me, giving her arms a gentle flop at her side. "Help," she half laughed, half whimpered.

I didn't laugh, but I couldn't stop a small grin from spreading across my face. "I suppose it is my fault, isn't it?" I hesitated once I crossed the room to where she stood. "What exactly would you like me to do?"

"I think I can get my arms up straight, so just...pull the dress up over my head. Please." Lia blushed, staring directly into my chest, well away from any eye contact.

Don't be weird. Just do it. "Right. Sure." Lia slowly raised her arms, laughing at her infirmity. Once she had both arms high enough with her forearms resting against the front of my shoulders for support, I gently hooked my fingers under the shoulder straps of the dress and pulled them up. I carefully bunched up the fabric and did my best to get her arms out without jostling her too much. Once she finally slid out of it I took a few steps back and handed her the balled up dress, making direct eye contact to avoid ogling her in her underwear. "I trust you can get into your clothes by yourself?"

She nodded quickly, turning away to hide her face. I chuckled, trying my best to relieve the intense awkwardness, and returned to my seat at the base of the bed. Lia wormed her way into her sleeping clothes, albeit in a much more involved manner than usual, and half lay, half fell onto her mattress. Crawling to the edge she propped herself up on her elbows and stared at me. I waited for a while in expectant silence, but she continued to quietly look me up and down. "Can I...help you with something?"

"I'm just thinking of what to ask you," She said casually, absentmindedly kicking her feet back and forth as a devious smirk came to her face. "Don't think you've gotten out of that after one night. I have a lot more things I want to know."

"Like I said, I'm an open book." I leaned back in the chair and kicked my feet up on the bed frame next to her. "Though I have to say, if you're going to be traveling with me, I should probably know more about you as well. Can't have a stranger watching my back, now can I?"

"That wasn't part of the original deal, you know." She rolled her eyes in an over exaggerated gesture. "But I guess that's okay."

Lia tapped her chin a few times, then perked up as she thought of a question. "When we were down in the dungeon, you said you made a promise to someone a long time ago. Something about keeping people safe. Is there a story behind that?"

I was surprised that she remembered the remark given the emotionally charged situation we had been in at the time. "Yeah, there is. It's probably good for this to come up now, actually, because it will most likely influence our traveling plans." The statement brought a confused look to Lia's face, but she waited patiently for me to explain. "It was a promise I made to Amaya. She was wrongfully taken prisoner to use as leverage, just like you were."

It felt strange to finally put into words a theory I had been thinking of for so long. "I don't know why I keep getting sent to other worlds, but there seem to be some rules associated with it. The first and most important is that no matter where I go, the ruling party of that country wants to use me to solve all of their problems. I don't know how, but they always seem to find me." Bitter thoughts from my life in Hedaat came unbidden to the forefront of my mind, bringing a scowl to my face. "And they seem to do whatever they please to coerce me into their plans."

Lia's face was painted in sadness as she continued to listen to the story. "The King of Alderea somehow heard about me, a nobody smith in a small town, and needed to meet with me immediately. He tasked the Lord of our township with arranging the meeting, and when I refused to go…" I trailed off, shrugging. "They didn't hurt her, at least. Lord Eadric was spineless, to be sure, but he wasn't cruel."

Seeing Lia's reaction made me feel a pang of regret. I did my best to perk up, moving on to more uplifting things. "I went to get her at the keep and made a deal with the Lord. Amaya got to go free, and after a month's time for preparation, I would head to the capitol and meet with the King. I made other demands, her safety chief among them, which were all accepted." I couldn't help but smile as I remembered the aggressively one-sided negotiation.

"I left with Amaya that night. I promised I would never let anything like that happen to her again, but she wasn't upset about the ordeal. Instead, she was worried that it would happen again, to someone else." Her passion still inspired me even when retelling the story so many years later. "So, I promised her that within my power, I would never let it happen to anybody again. And then, a couple lifetimes later…I ran into you." I gave Lia a quick smile. "Does that answer your question?"

She nodded. "Yeah, of course." Lia seemed to look off into the distance past my head. Her face still seemed to have traces of sadness, but she gave me a smile. "I guess I owe Amaya my thanks."

The comment caught me off guard. "I guess so." There was a long pause in the conversation as we both thought in silence. "I think she would've liked you," I said with a wistful smile. Lia looked embarrassed by the statement as she reddened and looked away. Clapping my hands, I sat up straight. "Okay. My turn to ask you a question." I narrowed my eyes and studied her face. She scrunched up her nose and stuck her tongue out, bringing an honest laugh out of me. "I've got one. Your father told me that even though he arranged a few suitors for you, you always turned them down right after you met them. Why is that?"

Lia stifled a gasp in shock. "Why would he tell you THAT?!" I raised my eyebrows and shrugged, chuckling. "T-that's not even important to anything! Why do you want to know that?"

"Oh, we can only ask the important questions now?" I asked mockingly, crossing my arms. "Maybe I'll learn something about your character from it. Now, let's hear it."

"Well, I just...I just didn't like them, okay? One of them seemed more interested in working with Father than getting to know me, and another one was so overly nice he wouldn't ever disagree with me about anything." She looked at me and let out an exasperated sigh. "I'm not just going to marry someone because my father told me to!"

"That's good! It's not something to be taken lightly, so you shouldn't compromise. You should be able to marry who you really want to, not someone who gets chosen for you that you've never met." My mind flew to a perfect memory of Amaya in a white dress, standing in front of the large oak tree behind Ashedown's forge. Lia stammered something incoherently, snapping me back to the present. She was bright red, looking at me with a nervous slant. "I'm sorry, I spaced out there for a moment. What did you say?"

Lia cleared her throat and seemed to settle down a bit. "I said, I answered your question, so now it's my turn." She pulled herself up and sat cross legged at the edge of the bed. "I want to know more about magic. I know I can't do it right now, but maybe if I learn more about it I'll figure it out faster."

I let out a low whistle. "That's a pretty big topic. Anything specific?"

She thought for a moment. "Maybe you could describe what it feels like when you do it. You said to picture a river running through me, but I don't really know what that means, and without having done it before I don't know what to expect." I stifled a laugh, which drew a scowl from Lia. "What's so funny about that?"

I shook my head. "Nothing! It's just...that's almost exactly what I said to the guy who trained me to use magic." Taking a moment to look inward, I drew on my mana reserves to reflect on what it felt like. "The first time you let your mana flow it's electric, like a new kind of energy you've never felt before is filling every inch of your body. You get this feeling that you could do anything." I closed my eyes and channeled the energy around my body, up and down my arms and legs.

"After you've done it a few times, moving the energy around feels like cool water rushing through you. You can open and close the gates that let it move, and it fills up the areas you tell it to go to." Letting the energy recede, I opened my eyes to find Lia staring at me in fascination. "I know it doesn't really make sense before you've felt it, but that's what I think."

She nodded. "I think that helps...I just wish there was a way to feel it before I figured it out. I'm sure I could control it if I knew what I was looking for." Lia laughed. "That sounds silly, doesn't it?"

Gears were turning rapidly in my head, caught by the sudden inspiration of Lia's thought. "No, that's not silly at all." *Try it. You know it will work.* "Lia, give me your hand." I sat on the edge of my seat and extended both my hands out in front of me.

"My hand?" She timidly extended her hand towards mine. I gently held it between both of my hands, focusing intently on the contact. Her skin was smooth and warm. The fingers of my right hand were resting on her wrist, and I could feel her pulse beating rapidly beneath them. Closing my eyes, I took a few deep breaths and called on my mana.

"Lia, try your best to clear your mind. Focus on your breathing, with the air going down to your core. I'm going to try to give you some of my mana, so you can identify what it feels like. If you notice any new sensations in your hand, try to find that same energy inside yourself, and just let it out." Moving the energy down to my fingertips, I gave her hand a small squeeze. "Alright, in three...two...one..." I pushed the mana downwards and was met with an entirely new and unique feeling.

As opposed to the steadfast resistance I felt when trying to suffuse mana into a foreign implement, the force I felt opposing me was...reactive. When I probed forward with my energy, the force would move out and intercept it, enveloping it with a rippling energy of its own. Whatever system of visualization I used in my own mind to help myself understand mana broke down at this alien presence.

I could feel Lia's hand trembling and her breath quickened as I increased the mana flow. "Tell me if you feel uncomfortable at all. I've never done this before, so I want to be careful." As I continued to test the opposing force, I could feel pockets where it was thinner, like it was spreading itself too wide to block me. Focusing my efforts on those spots, I gave a final push, and was rewarded with a small pop.

All at once, Lia's arm felt like an extension of my own. My mana surged like crackling lightning, racing up her arm to connect with her spine. I could feel the tingling sensation along every inch of her skin as it flew, crashing downwards towards her core where I could feel a small ball of tightly bound energy. When the energies collided, there was another small pop and her own supply of mana rushed out in all directions, suffusing her entire body with energy. As it commingled with my own mana, I could feel a similarity in the energy, but distinctly different elements I couldn't fully describe. For a brief instant my mind came dangerously close to being overwhelmed with sensory input, feeling both her sensations and my own simultaneously.

Lia let out a loud, wordless cry, startling me back to my senses. My eyes snapped open and I dropped her hand, severing the flow of energy to her body. When the contact broke, I had a moment of feeling hollow, like a part of my body had been abruptly lost. Shaking away the feeling, I knelt in front of her to make sure she was okay. Her breath was ragged and labored and sweat was beading along her flushed brow.

"Lia! Are you okay?" I put my hands on her shoulders, giving her a light shake. Her eyes fluttered open and she looked around confused as if she didn't know where she was. She smiled, and I let out a long sigh of relief.

"That...was incredible!" Lia jumped to her feet and held my head in her hands. "The electric feeling...I know what you meant now! You were just sitting there, and then all of a sudden, my whole body was just...full of energy! It was amazing!" She was laughing as she spoke, barely able to contain herself. "Was that what my mana feels like? Or was that yours? I don't really understand what you did, but it was amazing!"

Her enthusiasm was infectious, bringing a wide smile to my face. "That was your own energy. Everyone keeps their mana locked away inside before they use it for the first time. It might be a natural defense to put up the barriers so you don't accidentally expend all of your energy without knowing it. I think...I might have broken down those barriers for you." I stood up, still holding her shoulders. "How are you feeling?"

She took an uncertain step backwards. "Great! That was...woah." Lia's eyelids fluttered as she staggered back another step, bumping up against her bed. "I'm sort of...tired now..." Holding her tightly I guided her down onto the mattress just in time for her to fall backwards, unconscious. *That's about right.*

Laughing to myself I moved to the side of the bed and carefully shifted her up to the pillow, pulling the blanket up over her before lithely hopping to the adjacent open space beside her. Crawling under the covers myself, I marveled at all of the new avenues I had discovered. *That was...completely bizarre. Was I sharing her senses? Were those really her natural mana barriers? And her mana...it was different than mine. Does everybody have their own unique energy?*

I tried to put the thoughts aside for the moment, opting instead for sleep. I curled up next to Lia and wrapped an arm around her to pull her close. Although I had cleared my mind of the inquisitive thoughts, one thing remained as I drifted off to sleep: *I'm not alone anymore.*

***

15. WHAT THE FUTURE HOLDS

I lazily cracked an eye open to find the dim light of morning filtering in from beneath the door. Lia was still snoozing beside me, snuggled up warmly against my chest. Carefully pulling my arm back from around her waist, I rolled onto my back and stared up into the darkness. There was a feeling of disquiet that I couldn't quite identify as my brain slowly spun up to full speed, until finally the flash of inspiration hit me: *I didn't dream last night.*

The realization was deeply unsettling to me. Thinking back, I couldn't recall a night that I hadn't had vivid dreams of my past lives; even in my final years in Hedaat my dreams had been one of the few things I could count on. Whether or not they were pleasant dreams or nightmares was a coin flip, but they were always reliable. Regardless of the content it was the only steady link I had to my past lives, and now it seemed to be thrown into question.

So, I didn't dream for one night. Nobody dreams every night; it shouldn't be something to be worried about. The thoughts did little to dispel my discomfort. Even a tenuous threat to the brief time I could still spend with Amaya was enough to unsettle me. *There's nothing to be done about it. I'll go to sleep tonight, and everything will be back to normal.* I did my best to push the thoughts away, but they still nagged at the edge of my mind.

A small yawn from Lia snapped me out of my funk. She rolled over and, still asleep, threw an arm across my chest, resting her head against my shoulder. I rolled my head to the side to observe her through the near darkness, her face only inches from mine. She looked so peaceful sleeping with her eyes shut tight and the traces of a small smile on her face. For a moment I was able to completely forget my worries as I mirrored her smile. *Regardless of the terrible things that have happened to me so far in this world, this is one thing I did right.*

I fixed a small strand of hair that had fallen into Lia's face, tucking it gently behind her ear. My fingers brushed against the side of her face, causing her eyes to flick open. She blinked at me slowly trying to come to terms with having woken up. Eventually, she seemed to realize where she was and smiled. "G'morning, Lux. I...don't really remember falling asleep last night. We were talking about magic...and then..." She shot up abruptly, energized. "The magic! You gave me your mana, and I felt it just like you said, like a river, and then..."

"And then you passed out," I finished for her, chuckling. "I probably should have warned you about that. It seems to be pretty common thing for people accessing their mana for the first time."

Although it was dark, I could almost hear the pout Lia put on her face. "Yeah, you should've!" She twisted to punch me in the shoulder but stopped halfway through the motion, letting out a deep groan. "Oh Primes, my shoulders. Is this because of the mana, too?"

"No, that's from your sword practice." I sat up and slid behind her, putting a hand on each shoulder. Her skin was hot, and the muscles underneath were knotted tightly. "They probably hurt quite a bit now, but this should be the worst of it. We'll have to add a stretching regimen to the beginning of our practice sessions." I began to knead my thumbs into her tender shoulders, softly at first, which evoked a low hiss from Lia.

"Can't you just...I don't know, magic my arms back to normal?" She said, cautiously rolling her neck in a wide circle. "I'm not sure I'll be able to do any more practice like this."

I clicked my tongue at her in faux disappointment. "Nonsense. Now is the best time to keep working! It only hurts because you're working muscles you normally don't use. Every time you exert them, they come back stronger than before. Taking away the ache would make it a pretty hollow experience, don't you think?" Continuing to massage her shoulders I gradually moved down to her back and shoulder blades. "Plus, I don't know any magic that would help. I'm still new to it, you know."

Lia let out a small yelp as I pressed into a particularly hard knot in her back. "I didn't know it was going to be this hard."

"Rethinking your decision to come with me now?" I teased, already knowing the answer.

"Not a chance! You aren't getting rid of me that easily." She laughed and gave her shoulders a tentative roll. With her massage finished, Lia hopped up and crossed the room to her dresser, changing quickly from her nightgown to a long light yellow dress. I followed suit, moving to the wooden chair where I had piled my clothes.

"Make sure you drink plenty of water today. That will help reduce the pain faster, and help keep it at bay in the future." I slid quickly into my shirt and pants and followed Lia out of the bedroom into the full light of day. After taking a moment for my eyes to adjust, I found Marten sitting at the table eating a slice of toast.

"Mornin' you two. Sleep well?" He didn't turn to regard us, but he pushed out the chair next to him with his foot, which I took as an invitation to sit.

"As always," I grinned pleasantly to him. Lia rolled her eyes and moved to the kitchen to prepare something alongside her mother.

"I'm so sore this morning!" Lia whined, taking a moment to stretch again before she set to work slicing a small asperfruit.

"Oh? Long night?" Marten asked casually, staring straight ahead out the window on the opposite wall. His face was an inscrutable mask, but I could see a devious twinkle in his eyes. Lia whirled, sputtering and blushing a bright red.

"No! You know that's not what I meant! I-It's my arms, from yesterday! Lux is teaching me how to use a sword, a-and that's why...never mind!" She yelled at him, returning to her cutting board angrily. Hana laughed softly and leaned down to Lia's ear to say something I couldn't hear. They whispered back and forth as they worked, with Lia's side of the conversation seeming particularly more animated than Hana's.

"So," Marten spoke in a low voice, finally turning to address me, "when will you and Lia be leaving us?" The question sounded like a statement, as if he already knew the answer to follow.

"Three days from now, at my best guess. Regardless of where we're heading, I'd feel a lot better knowing Lia could handle herself in a dangerous situation." I realized my statement might seem disquieting to Lia's father, so I continued quickly. "Not that we're going out looking for dangerous situations, of course. Just trying to be prepared."

"Of course." He ran his hand through his beard thoughtfully. "Where is it you intend on going?"

"Any straight line leading away from Yoria, I think. To be honest, I didn't have any specific destination in mind." *Not that I know of any.*

"Anywhere but north, of course," Marten stated matter-of-factly.

"North?" The statement caught me off guard. "Why wouldn't I want to…" I realized too late that I had stumbled into a trap and recovered as best I could. "Oh, not to Doram of course, as I just came all this way from there." We shared an awkward silence staring into each other's eyes, refusing to be the first to look away. *I'm not sure you'd believe where I'm from if I told you, Marten.*

He raised his eyebrows and gave me a knowing look. "Right." Marten took another bite of his toast and looked off out the window again. "If I were you, I'd head west. Well maintained road, plenty of towns along the way to stop at, and the border is only a few weeks by foot that way. Lybesa is lovely this time of year, I'm told."

Finishing his breakfast, Marten stood and wiped his hands on his shirt. "I suppose I'll be leaving now. Lux, you'll be here to help me unload the cargo when I return?" He spoke much louder now, the conversation clearly intended to be heard by everyone in the house.

I nodded enthusiastically. "Of course, sir." Satisfied, Marten moved to the kitchen to give a quick kiss to Hana and Lia, then retrieved his hat from the rack by the door before exiting the house. Soon after he was gone Hana and Lia brought breakfast to the table, and we all enjoyed a pleasant meal together.

After we were finished, Hana excused herself to go work on restoring her garden, leaving Lia and myself alone at the table. "So," Lia chirped excitedly, "What are we going to do today?"

"The same thing we'll be doing every day for the foreseeable future," I replied, grinning. "Practice."

We quickly fell into a comfortable routine over the course of our last few days at the house. After breakfast was finished, I walked Lia through an extended stretching routine, followed by training with her shortsword. I showed her new forms and stances, explained which situations to use them in, and taught her new training drills to repeat. Once I finished instruction for the morning, she moved to practice the moves on her own while I followed suit with my own physical training next to her. If my injuries sustained in our escape from the dungeon had taught me anything, it was that I wasn't as sharp as I once was with a blade.

When the physical training was complete, we would retreat, tired and sore, into the house for rest and refreshment. Lunch usually consisted of small portions of some sort of game bird and assorted greens, which we ate voraciously to try and regain any bit of energy we could. After our meal we would return to our practice area behind the shed to meditate. With Lia's newfound knowledge of the sensation of mana, she made quick progress in the field. Though it was tiring for her to access the energy in a controlled way, she was able to practice channeling the mana to specific parts of her body in short bursts.

By the time meditation was finished, Marten was usually arriving back at the house with the day's cargo. I would set to work helping him move crates into the basement or repack an empty wagon, while Lia would take inventory and balance the numbers in her father's ledger. Hana always had dinner prepared for us by the time work was finished, and we eagerly ate anything she made. A game of cards would follow, the rules of which I had finally begun to grasp after multiple rounds of failing horribly, which would last until Marten and Hana turned in for the night.

Before sleeping, Lia and I continued our tradition of trading questions back and forth. The topics had become more mundane once we were comfortable with each other, and I learned a great deal about her hobbies, interests, and amusing stories from her past. In turn, I recounted stories of my time with Amaya, which Lia seemed particularly interested in. Thankfully, she seemed to avoid asking questions about my time in Hedaat, having picked up on my distaste for talking about the subject matter.

On the night before our departure, Lia was uncharacteristically reserved during dinner and our usual card game. I assumed she was nervous about leaving; traveling was a commonplace thing in my lives, whereas Lia had hardly ever left the town she was born and raised in. Adventuring with no particular destination in mind was no doubt an intimidating thought. When I asked her about it during our nightly exchange, I was surprised by her response.

"I've been wondering," Lia said uncertainly, pausing to search for the right words, "What is it you're looking for in this trip?"

"Nothing in particular, honestly. Now that I'm in a new world, I think I just want to see what it has to offer me." I was curious now. "Why do you ask?"

Lia looked away, clearly uncomfortable. "Well, it's just...With everything you've been through, I didn't know...I was wondering what you wanted to do. Not just right now, on this trip, but...after that." She reddened a bit, looking up at me with a worried expression. "I'm sorry, it's a stupid question."

"No, it's a great question." *What DO I want to do with my life?* It was a question I hadn't yet asked myself after arriving in Yoria. I had been living in the moment, not thinking more than a day ahead since my unfortunate run-in with Melrose. "I guess I should start thinking about the future, now that it's finally laid out in front of me to choose."

I kicked my feet up on the bed and thought for a while. "I think...I just want a normal, boring life for once." I smiled at the idea. "No grand adventures, nobody telling me what to do. Just all the time in the world to do what I want to." Waving my hand out in front of me, I pictured what it might look like. "I could build a farm, out in the middle of nowhere, and just...live." Somewhere in the back of my mind I knew it was an impossible dream, but I quelled the thoughts for the moment and basked in my thoughts of peace.

Lia's eyebrows shot up in disbelief. "A...farm?" She let out a small giggle. "I can't picture you as a farmer, Lux."

Giving an exaggerated huff, I spoke with indignation. "And why is that? I know a thing or two about raising plants and animals, thank you very much." We both laughed together, then fell into silence. "How about you? What's your big plan for life?"

"I-I guess I want what everybody else does," Lia said, stumbling over her words. "Find someone to start a family with and...do that." She tapped her fingers together, focusing intently on the task rather than looking at me. "But I don't want to do that here. I've been in Tolamar my whole life, and there's so much more out there that I want to see. I think...I should do that first."

"Well Lia, that's something that I can help you with." I smiled. "Starting tomorrow, I'll show you the world. Anywhere you want to go, I'll take you there. And after the adventures are done, we can live the rest of our lives however we want." Hopping to my feet, I held out my hand. "Deal?"

She stared up at me, her eyes filled with happiness. Nodding, Lia smiled and took my hand. "Deal!" She gave it a firm shake, then dropped my hand and lunged forward to hug me tightly. Although it was muffled, I could hear her talking into my chest. "Thank you, Lux. For everything."

I chuckled softly and patted her head. "Thank you, Lia." When she finally released the embrace, I rubbed my hands together eagerly. "Now, we should get some sleep. We've got quite the walk ahead of us, and don't think for a second that means you get out of sword practice!"

Lia looked at me with her face aghast. "No way!" She flung herself down onto the bed, rolling to face the ceiling. "Don't you think you're being a bit too hard on me?"

"Oh, stop whinging. You'll thank me for this someday, I guarantee it." I crawled up from the bottom of the bed to my spot beside her, laughing the whole way. We arranged ourselves into a comfortable sleeping position and drifted off for the night, our physical exertion of the past few days outweighing the excitement of the adventure to come in the morning.

Pain erupted across my chest; a sensation so extreme I could hardly recognize it. What had initially felt like a shallow cut was now throbbing in agony, sending ripples throughout my entire body. An unfamiliar foul stench filled my nostrils and my vision blurred and spotted. I could make out vague wisps of black smoke rising up before my eyes, obscuring the shadowy figure of a man before me.

He stood bare chested, covered in blood and pointing a black blade down at me. His face was hard, eyes blazing with anger under shaggy black hair. I tried to plead for help, but a scream erupted from my mouth instead as the pain increased. It was creeping up from my chest now, working its way atom by atom through my body towards my extremities. I clawed at the wound to no avail, trying to find some peace from the all-encompassing torture.

I collapsed to the ground, writhing as I screamed for the torment to stop. Somehow, I found enough control of my voice to whimper out to the man before me. "Please...kill me..." The figure turned, staring down with hate as he sneered at me.

"You...don't deserve...death." It spoke with hundreds of distinct voices, each echoing like thunder inside my mind. The smoking black pain had reached my eyes and my vision immediately darkened, leaving me in a perpetual void of agony. One by one, my senses receded, leaving me alone to scream in silence. In time, my thoughts faded away too, and whatever I was dissolved into black smoke, leaving nothing behind.

I awoke in a panic, bolting upright as I clutched my chest. My breath came in ragged gasps as I scanned the room, slowly taking in the information of my surroundings. *It was just a dream. I'm still here.* A small hand touched the back of my shoulder, soft and warm against my bare skin. "Lux? What's the matter? Are you okay?" Lia asked softly, her voice thick with concern.

"Yeah, I'm fine. I just had a nightmare. Sorry for waking you." I took a few deep breaths, trying to center myself. *What was that? It certainly wasn't a memory.* I slowly laid back down in bed, still absentmindedly rubbing my chest.

"It's okay, you didn't wake me. I haven't been able to get back to sleep for a while now." Lia rubbed my arm, rolling over to watch me closely. "What was the dream?"

"I...don't know. Usually, my dreams are memories from my past lives, but this was...different, somehow. It felt familiar, but it wasn't anything I can remember. Just the pain." I rolled to face her and let out a long sigh. She was barely visible in the darkness, only the faintest light sneaking through the crack of the door. "We've still got some time before the sun is up. Maybe we should get some more sleep."

"That's not gonna happen," Lia sighed, sounding resigned. "I'm too excited for today."

I smiled. "Well, if that's the case, I guess we can get a jump start on our preparations." Going through the list I had been making in my head I made a quick plan of action for the morning. "Put together a collection of anything you want to bring with you. Extra clothes, personal trinkets, whatever you want. Just remember: We have to carry it every day, everywhere we go."

"Aye aye!" Lia sprung out of bed excitedly and began searching through the drawers of her bureau. By the time I was up and dressed she had assembled a small pile of clothes on the bed and had changed into a dark belted tunic. Aside from a few extra dresses, the only other possession in the pile was a small, loosely bound leather book with a corked vial of black ink and a few writing quills.

I walked to the bedside and picked up the book. "Your journal?" I asked, turning it over in my hands. Lia turned from her place at the mirror and blushed upon seeing me holding it. She strode across the room and quickly took it from me before I had a chance to open it. "I'll take that as a yes," I chuckled, holding my hands up in defeat. She narrowed her eyes at me and stuck out her tongue.

"If you're all finished in here, we should try to find some traveling supplies around the house. A good length of rope, a lantern and tinderbox, a hatchet, and a bit of food would be a great start." I counted the items off on my hand as I spoke, making sure not to miss any of the things I considered essential adventuring gear. "Do you think we can find all of that?"

Lia nodded. "If we look through the basement, I'm sure we could find anything we need." We exited the bedroom into the dim pre-dawn light of the dining room. The house was suffused with a light purple glow as the sun considered breaking through the clouds on the horizon, setting a very mellow mood. Walking quietly over the wooden floorboards to avoid waking her parents, we made our way down to the basement.

It didn't take long for us to find the items we were looking for: Marten kept a small workshop in a room nestled under the staircase which held all the tools on my initial list. I made a mental note to repay him for the items, although I knew the response to the idea would be a derisive snort and a stark refusal. Lia took the items back upstairs to find a rucksack while I moved to the back room to retrieve my belongings.

I was still unsure of my decision to wear my full complement of gear on our travels. On one hand, I would certainly feel safer if I had my armor on in case of a confrontation. However, the distinctive patterns and superior craftsmanship would certainly stick out, making it more likely that a guard with my description would notice me. Safety had won out over discretion in the end, but it still worried me that I might be putting Lia in more danger by wearing it. *If I'm already wanted for murder, I suppose I shouldn't be worried about adding resisting arrest to my rap sheet.*

The thought of my crimes made me momentarily uncomfortable; I was doing my best to avoid the unpleasant memories from the night of our escape from the dungeon. Most of the events were obscured in my mind by a thick fog, most likely due to a combination of exhaustion, pain, and bloodlust. There wasn't a trace of regret within me for killing the men; the world was better off without them to be sure, and they weren't the first men I had killed by a long shot. It was the method of their execution that troubled me. *That bloodlust enhancement, and the black energy...I have no idea what that was, but it came so easily to me.* I shuddered and shook my head in an effort to get back to the task at hand.

Pulling the lid from the crate against the back wall of the basement, I let out a satisfied sigh at the sight of my possessions. Each piece evoked a powerful memory as I sorted through them which helped to comfort my uneasy mind. By the time I was fully equipped, everything troubling me seemed a little farther away and I was able to make my way back upstairs with confidence.

I found Lia in the kitchen, carefully packing some fresh fruits and hardtack into a canvas rucksack. She turned as she heard my approach, gave me a quick once over, and nodded. "Well, you certainly look the part of an adventurer now." Turning back to pack the last few bits of food, she giggled softly. "It suits you."

"Oh...thanks," I said with an awkward smile. "It does feel nice to be back in my gear."

Lia fastened the backpack closed and slung it over her shoulder. "Do we need to pack anything else?"

"If we end up sleeping on the road, you might want a blanket to bed down with, but that's up to you." I paused, remembering an important detail. "That reminds me, I wanted to ask your father if—"

"Wanted to ask her father what now?" Martens voice materialized from behind me, causing me to jump in alarm. I spun around to find his head poking out from around the corner grinning ear to ear.

"Were you just standing there listening to us?" Lia brushed past me to scold him.

"I didn't want to interrupt the moment" He laughed as he walked into the dining room and gave Lia a pat on the head, which she unsuccessfully tried to bat away. "What was it you wanted to ask me?"

"I was hoping you might have a map of the surrounding area, so I can get a better idea of where we're going."

"It just so happens that I have exactly what you're looking for. I wouldn't be a very good trader if I didn't know where I was going, now would I?" Marten motioned for me to follow him. "It's down in the basement, I'll show you." Turning to Lia, he gave her a small squeeze on the shoulder. "Marlia, dear, your mother wanted to speak with you in our bedroom."

Lia squinted, looking between the two of us a few times suspiciously. Eventually she sighed and nodded, and the three of us left the dining room. Lia closed the door to the bedroom behind her as I followed Marten back down to his workshop. He fished through the drawers underneath his workbench for a moment, producing a well-aged scroll of paper which he unfurled on the benchtop.

Looking over his shoulder I studied the unfamiliar world map. Although I couldn't read any of the labels written in the recognizable but unknown alphabet of the area, I was able to make a few assumptions with what little knowledge I had picked up. There was one large continent at the center of the map with a long chain of islands dotting a southern sea. The southern and western borders of the map were completely covered with ocean, but unlabeled land expanded past the north and east edges, either uncharted territory or unimportant lands for the purposes of this chart.

The main continent was divided into five distinct areas. An expansive mountainous region covered the northern portion of the map which I assumed was Doram, where I supposedly hailed from. A long spine of mountains ran south creating a natural border between the western coastal nation, most likely Lybesa, and the central country of Kaldan. A tiny country was

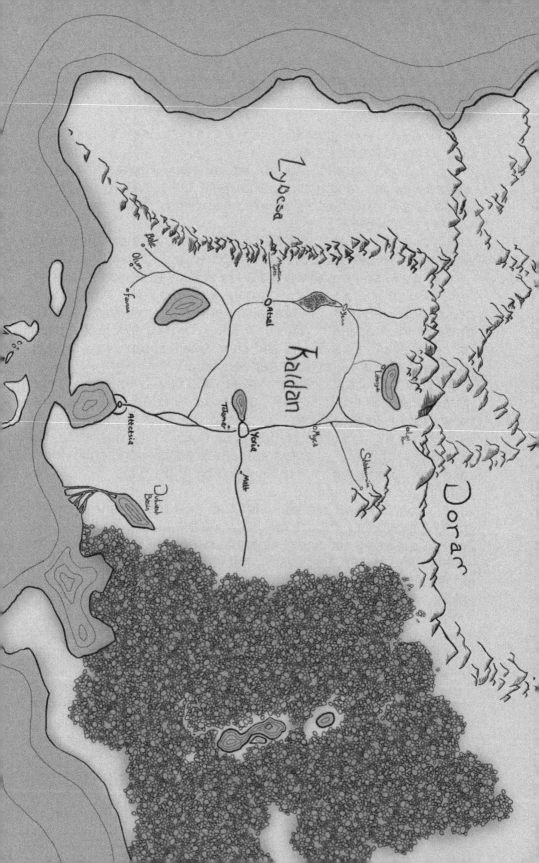

carved out along a bay on Kaldan's southern coast, its borders seemingly drawn along an encircling wall. To the east, a border line was drawn along the edge of a massive forest, which ran all the way to the edge of the map.

Marten pointed a stubby finger down onto the map, tracing a line along one of the marked roads in central Kaldan; it was clear to me that Yoria was a hugely important city to the country, if not its capital. "If you go west from here on foot, you should never have to travel more than a few days without making it to a village large enough to restock and rent a room. There's a large city...here, called Atsal, and then four days west from there is Lybesa's Mountain Gate. Depending on how fast you travel, you could make it there in just over two weeks."

I did my best to memorize all of the information in front of me. My lack of knowledge of the region's alphabet made this difficult, but just getting a rough idea of the geography we would be encountering was more than enough. Knowing how many days of travel we could expect between each settlement was extremely beneficial both in terms of physical pacing and for buying supplies.

"Now, I may not be the smartest man around, but I'd like to think I'm a good judge of character." Marten rolled the map back up and tossed it into the open drawer. "I know you aren't from Doram, Lux." Swallowing hard, I went to speak in my defense, but he held up a hand to stop me. "I'm sure you've got a good reason for lying, so I'm not asking for the truth. But I do need to know: Does Lia know the truth?"

I nodded to the affirmative, and Marten let out a relieved sigh. "That's good to hear." He drummed his fingers on the benchtop and stared off through the wall at nothing. "Marlia, she's the best parts of us. Me and Hana. In the end she's the only thing that matters to us. We've talked it over, and we think that leaving home with you is the best thing for her. It's certainly what she wants to do, so I don't think we could stop her, to be honest." He chuckled softly, then looked up to me. I was surprised to see he was misty-eyed, a far departure from his usual stone-faced look.

"I need you to promise me, Lux. Promise me that you'll keep her safe from harm. Promise that you think this is the right thing for her, and that you'll do what you can to keep her happy." He offered out his hand to shake but held up a finger before I could extend my own. "And promise that you'll never do anything to hurt her." I was taken aback by the request. It must have clearly shown through on my face, because Marten continued in clarification.

"You know what I told you is true; Marlia loves you. You must have seen it for yourself by now. Either that, or you're not as bright as I thought." He raised an eyebrow at me, and I gave him a small nod. "I need you to promise you won't take advantage of that fact. I'm not saying you have to love her back or pledge yourself to her forever, but don't hurt her. She deserves a lot better than that."

Can I make that promise? I've done my best to be clear about where we stand, but...is it enough? Is it fair for me to be so friendly and open with her, knowing how she feels about me? The familiar feeling of guilt was creeping back, twisting in my gut. I had been thinking on the topic on and off ever since I had woken up in her basement, but it was finally time to make good on my decisions. Grasping Marten's hand firmly in my own, I shook it. "Marten Corell, I promise no harm will come to Lia while she is with me. I promise I will do my best to make her happy, and I will never hurt her."

We shook hands in silence, regarding each other with serious expressions until Marten's mouth spread wide with a toothy grin. "You're a good man, Lux." He clapped my hand in his, then turned to leave. "With that business out of the way, we should head back upstairs. I'm sure the ladies are waiting on us."

Hana and Lia were waiting for us outside by the road. Lia was fully kitted for the trip, with the canvas rucksack on her back and her shortsword looped through her belt. The sun had just begun to peek out over the horizon, painting the two figures with a warm pink and orange glow. When we came into view, I caught a subtle nod between Marten and Hana. *I'm guessing Lia had a conversation similar to mine,* I thought to myself, smiling. *I should ask her about that, before she asks me.*

Lia huffed, tapping her foot with embellished impatience. "We've been waiting out here forreevverr!" She drew out the word, rolling her head around once for emphasis. "Did you get lost down there?"

I held my hands up in defence. "I was getting a good picture of where we're headed. You'll appreciate that once we get on our way, I think." Marten and I approached the pair, stopping next to them at the end of the dooryard. "Are you all ready to go, Lia?"

She nodded excitedly. "I've been ready for this for a long time!"

Marten stepped forward and planted a kiss on her forehead. "Take care, Marlia. Wherever you go and whatever you do, we'll always be here if you need us." He wrapped her in a tight embrace, squeezing her until she lifted off of the ground.

Hana stepped up behind Marten and tapped him on the shoulder lightly. "Alright, dear." He dropped Lia back down to the ground, clearing his throat as he stepped back. Hana took his place hugging their daughter, albeit in a much more gentle and delicate manner. She turned her head in close and whispered into Lia's ear. Whatever was said caused tears to well in her eyes, and she nodded hard into her mother's shoulder.

With the family goodbyes completed I took my place next to Lia. "Marten. Hana. Thank you again for everything you've done for me. Wherever we end up, I'll make sure Lia is well looked after."

"We'll hold you to that, lad," Marten said sternly. Hana said nothing, instead giving me a small nod and a smile as tears sparkled on her cheeks. The emotions were palpable between the family which made me feel both a bit out of place and choked up

Turning to Lia, I put a hand on her shoulder. "Well then. I think it's time to go." She looked up at me, face beaming with her infectious smile. Spinning in place quickly she ran off down the road, shouting over her shoulder.

"It's time to see the world!" I shook my head and laughed as I turned to chase after her, but I felt a hand catch my elbow. Marten was standing next to me holding out a small felt pouch. He tossed it to me, a soft jingle coming from the bag as it landed in my hand. It wasn't particularly heavy, but I knew the contents from the telling sound.

"An advance on that dowry." Marten's face curled with a wry smirk as Hana covered her mouth and giggled. "You'll get the rest whenever you bring her back safely." I was truly speechless, my head buzzing with a mix of embarrassment, appreciation, and annoyance. Instead of stammering an awkward reply, I simply nodded as my face burned red. "You better get going," He said, shooing me away with his hands. "I don't think she's going to wait for you to catch up."

Following his advice, I turned on my heels and jogged off after Lia. She had made it quite a way down the road, but finally stopped when she realized I wasn't close behind her. When I caught up, we matched our pace to a brisk but comfortable walk. We traveled in silence, appreciating each other's company as we were lost in our own thoughts of what adventures were to come.

Lia stopped as we reached a fork in the road. Turning back, we could see her parents still standing by the road off in the distance. She stretched up onto her toes and waved to them shouting, "Goodbye! I love you!" They waved back, but if they said anything in return it was lost to the morning breeze. Wiping her eyes, Lia righted herself and turned back to the split in the road. "We're really going, aren't we?"

I nodded. "We're really going."

She took a deep breath. "Okay. Let's go." With that, we turned left down the well traveled road into a thicket of trees, and home faded from view behind us.

***

16. ON COMBAT AND MAGIC

Our first day of traveling passed quickly. The road we would be following for most of our journey to Lybesa was wide and well maintained, for which I was extremely grateful. For the first few hours of our journey I felt on edge, constantly expecting a guard to pass us by and recognize me, but as we made it further and further from Yoria my nerves gradually began to relax. Traffic was heavy on the road but died down quickly as we left the comfortable traveling distance from the capitol. By the time the sun was low in the sky we had been walking alone for close to an hour.

Lia and I were casually chatting about the best way to prepare wildfowl when I spotted an enclosed clearing through the trees to our right. The surrounding countryside was covered in random patches of trees; no one grouping was thick enough to be truly considered a forest, but it was dense enough to block line of sight to any point from the road. Pushing aside some shrubs I led Lia off the main road and into the thicket. We only walked for half a minute, but once we reached the small clearing it was difficult to see back where we had come from.

"This spot should serve as a nice campsite for the night. I don't think we'll have anybody wandering through; I was pretty lucky to spot the clearing from the road." I sat down in the grass to give my feet a well-deserved rest after a long day of walking. Scanning the area, I estimated the glade to be about thirty feet across at its widest point, an ideal size to suit our needs. I unclasped my belt and carefully laid it out in front of me, sliding each item off in turn: our lantern, the spare shortsword I had purchased, and my own blade.

Lia flopped down beside me, spreading out with a high-pitched squeal. "I haven't walked that far in ages...maybe never!" Rolling over to the pack she had dropped on the ground, she fished through the main pouch and produced two apples. She tossed one to me before biting heartily into her own. "I'll sleep well tonight, I'm sure!" Lia said through a mouth full of apple, losing a few chunks in the process.

"I hope you weren't planning on going straight to bed, Lia. We've still got training to do." I bit into my own apple, watching for her reaction from the corner of my eye. She turned to me with a harsh glare, taking another large bite of the fruit and chewing in silence. I shrugged. "What? I warned you before, you're not off the hook just because we're walking all day. Just think of that as your warmup."

She let out a bitter laugh between bites. "It's going to take me forever to go through all my stances and practice swings. It'll be pitch black before I'm finished!"

Reaching out to pick up my shortsword, I stood and paced casually to the opposite side of the clearing. "Who said anything about practice swings?"

The expression on Lia's face changed instantly, the pouting replaced by excitement. "We're actually going to fight?" The core of her apple fell to the ground as she jumped to her feet, scrambling to where she had dropped her own sword. Pulling it from its sheath she held it in a ready position, but quickly dropped her arm with a confused look. "Won't we hurt each other?"

"Bruises, sure." I held the small sword out in front of me and pulled on my mana reserves. "Blunted blade," I incanted, sending a dull orange glow up along the sharp edges. I weighed the unfamiliar weapon in my hand with a few flourishes. *Center of balance is off. Shoddy work, indeed.* "I promise I won't injure you."

"Can you do that for mine as well? I don't know if I can use magic like that yet." Lia tilted her head to one side, still seeming a bit nervous.

I laughed. "If you can hit me hard enough to do real damage in our first practice, you've earned it." The look on her face told me she wasn't convinced. "Plus, if you do somehow manage to hurt me, it just gives me another chance to practice my healing magic. It's really a win-win situation."

She rolled her eyes. "Alright, alright." Raising her weapon again she tensed up awkwardly, clearly unsure of what to do next. "So, how do we start? Do we bow?" Lia gave a quick bow.

Covering my mouth, I tried my best to hide my amusement. "No, no bowing necessary. As long as I have this sword drawn and blunted, we're ready to go. We'll start by practicing your opening attack." I beckoned to her with my hand. "See if you can hit me. Anywhere on my body is a success."

Lia took a deep breath, using the moment to steady herself. After studying the situation she charged forward with her sword drawn back in both hands, shouting a wordless battlecry. It only took a few steps for her to close the distance between us, and she brought the weapon down in a crosswise cut aimed for my chest. Taking a small step to the side I knocked the slash aside with the flat of my blade, sending her stumbling past me.

"Not bad for your first go. Try to control your momentum and use it for extra power in your attack. If you're moving too quickly, any little adjustment could knock you off balance." We turned to face each other again. "Try a slower, more measured approach this time."

Lia nodded silently, taking a neutral stance as she approached, cautiously this time. Once she came within range she leaned forward with a quick stab pointed up towards my shoulder. I twisted quickly, allowing the blade to fly past me unimpeded to bring her into close quarters. With an open palm, I shoved her in the sternum, pushing us apart. She looked shocked by the counter, so I took the opportunity to bat her arm with my dulled sword. "Did you forget I have a second hand? Just because it's not holding a weapon doesn't mean it's not a threat."

To my surprise, Lia immediately launched into another attack, swinging her blade up in an arc at my hip. Her tenacity brought a smile to my face as I parried outwards. The impact of the two swords directly colliding sent a rough shockwave up her arm which seemed to stun her momentarily. My sword rose up quickly to rest in her armpit, stopping just short to avoid hurting her.

"That was a good one!" I jumped back a few steps. "You'll get used to the impact from clashing swords after a while, but it definitely takes a lot of energy out of you." Waving her back onto the attack, I smiled. "Let's try some of your low attacks."

The session continued on for a half hour following the same general flow: Lia would attempt some opening attacks which I would dodge or block, we would exchange some close combat blows, and then I would give her some critiques and suggestions. Lia performed valiantly, always accepting the pointers with a nod or a grunt and continuing on without a single complaint. By the end of the practice she was panting from exertion, shoulders rising and falling with every breath.

"Alright, let's call it quits for today." I tossed my sword to the ground beside me. Lia did the same before collapsing down into a heap, letting out a long moan. Chuckling under my breath, I sat down next to her. "You did a great job."

"I think my arm is going to fall off." She rubbed her right shoulder tenderly. "That didn't take nearly as long as my practice cuts, but it's so much harder!"

"That's true. It's easy to miss how much effort goes into a sword fight. Until you're the one doing the fighting of course." I stretched my arms out over my head, feeling the burn of lactic acid build-up. "I know a great cure for tired muscles, though."

Lia rolled to face me from her sprawling sideways position in the grass. "Really? Tell me!"

"Meditation!" I gave her a wide smile, then folded my legs into my usual stance and closed my eyes. Lia let out an irritated grunt, but after a moment I heard her shifting to an upright position. "Before you get settled, grab your sword and rest it across your lap, holding the grip in your dominant hand. We're going to start working on Combat Enhancements."

There was a small excited gasp as Lia rustled around to get into position. "Okay, I'm ready."

"We'll start with our usual routine. Clear your mind and take a deep breath down to your core, allowing the energy inside to start flowing. While it moves, try your best to direct it where you want it to go. Down your legs to your feet and back up again, all the way to your shoulders and down to your hands." I followed my own instructions as I spoke; manipulating my mana supply was a comforting relaxation exercise at this point and required little thought.

"After you're feeling comfortable, try to move the flow down your right arm and hold it in your hand." I opened my eyes and spun to face Lia beside me, observing her form. "When you're ready, try to hold an idea in your mind, letting everything else fall away. The sword in your hand is going to become dull, just like mine was before. Visualize what I did, keeping your intentions rock solid." Her brow furrowed and she readjusted her grip on the shortsword.

"Once you feel prepared, you just have to say the words. If your focus is right, the energy in your hand will know what to do." I extended my hand out slowly to hover over her sword and watched it anxiously. "Whenever you're ready." For a while, the clearing was silent aside from Lia's rhythmic breathing. I watched her eyes darting back and forth behind her closed eyelids in exertion as she struggled to find her focus.

"Blunted blade." The words were almost a whisper, passing from her lips in a tired sigh. A faint orange glow flickered to life along the edge of her sword, running from hilt to tip. Excitedly, I ran my thumb along the blade's edge and was relieved to find the skin unbroken. Lia's eyes fluttered open and she observed the fruits of her labor. The orange shimmer lasted only a few moments before fading away, gone as quickly as it had arrived.

"You did it, Lia!" I rocked forward onto my knees and embraced her tightly. "You really did it! You used magic!" She dropped the sword onto her lap and returned the hug, slumping forward.

"I...did it." Lia said lazily. She giggled as her head drooped forward momentarily. "I'm a...wizard now. A very...tired wizard." We both shared a laugh.

"Using magic for the first time takes a toll. I'm surprised you're still conscious, honestly." I leaned back carefully, lowering her to a resting position with her head in my lap. "After all your hard work tonight, you deserve a nice long rest." Gently, I ran my fingers through her silky black hair, lightly scratching the back of her head.

"Ooooh...That feels...nice." Lia rolled into a more comfortable position, looking up at me with drowsy eyes. "Thanks, Lux. For...everything." She smiled sleepily, then turned and pushed her head back against my hand, deepening the scalp massage. After muttering something too quiet for me to hear her breathing slowed to a steady rhythm as she fell asleep.

Scratching her head absentmindedly, I took stock of my surroundings. *Regardless of how well hidden this clearing is, I should keep watch for the night. Without knowing the immediate area, it would be careless to assume we're safe here. There could be unsavory characters traveling the road, not to mention the local wildlife...hmm. I should ask Lia about the types of wild animals they have in this world.* The idea that there could be monstrous beasts lurking in the darkness sharpened my focus and helped to keep me awake.

Although the sun had been fully set for nearly an hour, the grove was still well lit by the light of the moon and stars above us in a cloudless sky. A cool breeze blew across the meadow, causing the leaves on the thick trees around us to dance and shift in the shadows. I carefully pulled off my cloak and draped it over Lia. The cold evening air was a pleasant feeling across my uncovered head and back.

With a long night of keeping watch ahead I shifted as best I could under Lia's sleeping form to find a comfortable meditative stance. Staying alert for any signs of danger was drilled so far into my subconscious that I didn't have to actively patrol the campsite to feel secure, and I was confident I could move my focus to other topics without sacrificing our safety. I had been percolating some new ideas to test my magical abilities over the past few days, but until the present moment I had never found the time to explore them.

I took a deep breath and tapped into my mana supply. It was deeply satisfying to feel the energy back at full strength after my incident in the prison. After particularly strenuous use my mana reserves always rebounded back to more than they had been before, which over the decades had helped me to amass a massive, powerful pool to draw from. I let the energy flow where it wanted throughout my body as I thought about my plan of attack.

Of the two major ideas I wanted to pursue, one stood out as far more interesting. After I had helped to unlock Lia's mana, I had been constantly thinking about the sensation of feeling another person's latent energy. *If everybody has such a unique mana signature, it might be possible to detect it at range.* I felt the idea had merit, but it would require a different approach to mana manipulation than what I was used to.

I lowered a hand down to the ground, working my fingers through the soft grass and down to the topsoil. *In theory, it should be possible to channel mana across the surface of an object, instead of trying to completely suffuse it. If I keep the energy along the surface thin enough...*I closed my eyes and diverted my internal energy through my arm and down to the ground. The mana moved slowly, almost cautiously, spreading out in a circle from where my hand was planted firmly in the dirt.

A jolt of foreign energy up my arm caused me to jump, but I was able to maintain focus long enough to realize that my mana had encountered Lia's leg sprawled out in the grass next to me. The feeling of her energy was familiar; it was warm and soft, slowly churning just under the surface of her skin. As my own mana spread out further, it flowed up and around her sleeping form, tracing its way up her body until she was completely encompassed by it.

Even with my eyes closed, I felt as though I could still see Lia sleeping in my lap. Against the empty black backdrop of my mind, my probing energy field traced everything it touched with sharp white lines. They shifted and blurred together as the individual blades of grass bent in the breeze, filling my tiny world with a constant fluid movement. Lia's outline stood out in stark contrast to the phasing white grass as a consistent amber figure that glowed against the darkness. I could see the minute details of her clothing and gear displayed with perfect clarity before me, but there were also distinct traces underneath where I could clearly see the mana flowing inside her.

This is amazing! Is this what mana really looks like? Scanning down over my own body, the effect was entirely different than what I saw on Lia. A blinding electric blue light raced all along the surface of my skin, hard and distinct as opposed to Lia's soft yellow aura. *To think, I've been walking around all this time completely blind to an entire world of information. It's incredible.*

Excitedly I redoubled my efforts and continued to expand my mana along the ground, widening the area I could picture in my head at a rapid pace. My mind was racing as it tried to keep up with the new form of sensory input as best it could, but I was quickly overwhelmed by the raw data. The mana came rushing back all at once in a powerful surge, and I gasped audibly as my eyes snapped open and brought the world back to its usual focus. Although I hadn't actually expended any of the mana, I was still panting from the effort. *It seems as though I've found a new muscle to flex.*

A dumb grin spread across my face as I marveled at the new possibilities this ability could unlock. *Being able to see things in the dark, or outside of my line of sight...getting an estimate of a potential foe's magical ability...could this allow me to cast magic from distant locations?* The ideas continued to stack up faster than I could process them, and I had to take a conscious moment to breathe and take back control of my own thoughts. *One thing at a time. I should probably get some mastery over the ability before I try to base others on it.*

Extending my mana back out a short distance, I practiced various forms of control over the projection in my head. Concentrating the mana into a cone in front of me instead of a full circle made it much easier to project out to great distances. However, I found that the difficulty of maintaining the connection increased proportionally with the space traveled, regardless of how wide or narrow an area I was covering. The effect was always the same: White outlines of whatever the mana touched cutting a sharp contrast against the black slate of my meditative mind.

As I continued to play with the new ability, more interesting quirks revealed themselves to me. If I focused intently on a point revealed by my mana, I could observe it in my mind as though it were directly in front of me. Even though Lia was facing away from me, I could still see that her eyes were closed tightly when I pictured her in my mind. The intricate details of a flower halfway across the clearing were as clear as if I held it in my hands, given enough concentration.

A darting rustle through the tall grass behind me caught my attention. Reaching out towards the source, a small green outline appeared through the leaves of a small bush. A lizard about the size of a house cat licked its eyeball casually, head twitching to look in seemingly random directions. I was intrigued by the projection's coloration. *Does this mean...animals have mana too? Maybe it's an inherent characteristic of all living things, not just the "advanced" creatures like us.*

Curious, I tried to focus down on the dirt below the grass around my hand. As I looked closer, I noticed small lines of minuscule green lights bobbing along between the individual blades of grass. *They're ants.* With a shudder, I suddenly became overly aware of how outnumbered I was by the insects in the clearing. *I know that there's always bugs around, but to see thousands of them all at once...that's disconcerting.*

Completely lost in my mental world, I began to follow the actions of random insects. Ants carried small bits of food over mountainous pebbles and down into their nests. It was difficult to trace all the branching paths beneath an anthill with mana, but I relished the challenge, and eventually had an entire colony mapped before my eyes. A spider strolled by the entrance, and my focus shifted to follow it on a winding trek back to its web where dinner awaited. It bounded up a strand with ease and set to work munching on a struggling fly whose green light slowly faded away to a dull white outline.

A voice caught me off guard. "Mmmm...g'morning, Lux." Lia rolled over in my lap, looking up at me through one barely opened eye. She held up a hand in front of her face and laughed softly. "Why did you let me sleep so long? I thought we were going to leave before dawn."

I looked down at her, confused. "That's the plan."

She tapped me gently on the forehead. "I think you might have fallen asleep keeping watch last night." Sitting up beside me, Lia stretched her arms and rolled her head from side to side. Her movements looked odd to my eyes, as if she were somehow leaving a faint afterimage every time she shifted.

Oh. Much too late, I realized my eyes were still closed. Having been so enraptured in studying my new abilities I had momentarily forgotten that I was getting my "visual" feedback from mana. When I finally opened my eyes, Lia's statements made much more sense. The overcast sky above was lit a dull orange from the sun, which had clearly crested the horizon somewhere beyond the tree line. *Did I really meditate all night?*

"I guess I did fall asleep." I wasn't quite ready to explain my new discoveries to Lia; I still didn't understand everything about it myself. "Sorry about that. I promise it was only for a minute."

"You shouldn't be keeping watch all night in the first place. I can help, too." She tried to stand but winced halfway through the movement and fell back to the ground. I shook my head, chuckling.

"Trust me, you'll have plenty of time to keep watch. Once you get used to our new practice routine and have a bit more energy, we can start to split night watch duties." I hopped to my feet and offered a helping hand down to her. "As things stand now, I wouldn't feel right making you stay up given how worn down you are."

Lia playfully slapped away my hand and got up, barely concealing the grimace of a dozen sore muscles and joints. "I'm just fine, thank you very much!" She moved to start gathering her things, teetering dangerously for the first few steps, but managed to hold her footing.

I picked my cloak up from the ground and slung it over my shoulders. A wave of warmth rushed down the length of my body, a welcome relief from the long cool night. "Judging by the sunlight, it's still early. We should make it to the next town well before nightfall. That'll give us a chance to pick up some more trail rations and have a nice warm meal."

"A warm meal..." Lia murmured, rubbing her stomach forlornly. Reaching into her backpack, she pulled out a piece of hardtack and snapped it in half. She tossed a piece to me before nibbling on her own. After a few bites, she wrinkled up her nose and shook her head. "A warm meal sounds amazing right about now."

With our makeshift campsite packed up, we made our way back to the road through the trees and underbrush. As we broke the tree line, I could see that the sun was fully above the horizon, almost an hour past when I had intended on leaving. The road was still empty as far as we could see in both directions. I motioned down the road towards our destination with a small bow. "Shall we?"

***

17. WHO YOU REALLY ARE

Our day on the road was enjoyable, due in no small part to the wonderful weather and beautiful scenery. The sun was shining brightly, but just before it began to feel stifling a gentle breeze would sweep across the road to cool us down. The trees began to change around midday, shifting from mostly coniferous evergreens to a mix of brightly colored deciduous looking trees. Along the way we crossed paths with a few horse-drawn wagons, most likely trying to reach Yoria before nightfall.

I learned a lot about the surrounding area from my casual conversations with Lia. Remembering my thoughts from the night before, I had broached the topic of potentially dangerous wildlife and was met with a hearty laugh. According to her, the most problematic animal in Kaldan was the brown bear, which generally kept well away from human settlements. The stories of wildlife grew more fantastic as she described areas closer to the border mountains, reaching to the point of old wives tales about fantastic beasts like chimeras living in Doram or direwolves in Lybesa.

On the topic of weather, Lia taught me about the seasonal patterns of Kaldan. The country had a very temperate climate which had helped to establish it as an agrarian powerhouse compared to the neighboring nations. We were currently in the autumnal season with winter fast approaching. Snow wasn't uncommon near Yoria, but Lia said it never seemed to last very long.

Between the pleasant weather and interesting conversation, we made it to the outskirts of town in what seemed like no time at all. Passing by isolated homesteads at first, we had to continue for about an hour before we finally arrived in the town proper. It looked to be a small one-crossing town with a single populated drag of storefronts and stalls before the land quickly turned back to farmland and scattered houses.

Lia led me to a building which apparently was marked "Inn, Food and Drink" along the front in large, faded print. The wooden two-story building was obviously old with weathered planks and battered shutters clear across its face. Upon entering I was pleasantly surprised to find that the interior was well furnished, with plush rugs along the floor and comfortable looking chairs at the bar and tables in the common room. The large space was devoid of patrons, populated solely by a young woman sitting behind a counter directly ahead of us.

At the sound of the door the woman looked up from a book on the counter and eyed us through a thick pair of glasses. "Welcome to The Roadside, travellers. Are you looking for a place to rest for the night?"

"That, and a hot meal if you can manage it," I replied as we approached the counter. "One room, just for tonight."

She looked back and forth between Lia and me in silence for an uncomfortably long time. Eventually she pushed a lock of pale yellow hair back behind her ear and jotted something down on a scrap of paper. "Of course, sir. A room with dinner will be 7 crowns for the two of you."

I pulled up my purse and fished through the contents for the required payment. *The money from the dungeons won't last us much longer,* I thought with a grimace. *I'll have to look through what Marten gave us before we left.* I slid the coppers across the counter one by one.

"Very good, sir. You'll be in room..." Fishing around underneath the desk, she pulled up an oversized key and slid it to me. "Room 14. That's up the stairs in the back corner." The woman made another note on her paper as she gestured lazily to the right. "Help yourself to some stew whenever you're hungry."

Taking the key with a curt nod, I turned and headed towards the staircase. "Thank you!" Lia said politely before jogging to catch up to me. When we had put some distance between us and the attendant, she chastised me in a low voice. "You know, it wouldn't kill you to be polite sometimes."

"Oh really? I'll have to try that someday." I frowned. "Come to think of it, aside from you, everybody I've met since I got here has tried to screw me somehow. I'm not sure my attitude has been the deciding factor in all that."

Lia pouted. "Well...even so. Maybe if you put out some positive energy, you'll get some in return."

I shook my head with a low chuckle. "You're all the positive energy I need, Lia. Maybe I should let you handle the talking from now on." Having reached the door with a matching symbol to our key I unlocked the room and pushed the door open. Although it wasn't as lavishly furnished as the entryway to the inn, our accommodations looked comfortable enough for a single night's stay; a table with three chairs, one chest of drawers, and a generously sized bed fit snugly within the room's relatively small confines.

"With that in mind, how would you like to head out and replenish our road supplies? I'd like to stay behind and try to get a little extra rest in." Sitting down at the small table in the room I pulled out another handful of copper coins from the pouch at my belt. "This should be more than enough, so try not to spend it all, okay?"

Lia nodded vigorously. "Can do!" I handed her the money and the room key, which she slipped into a pocket in her tunic. "I'll be back soon," She said, turning to leave.

"Lia, wait," I called out, standing to go after her. She spun in the doorway, looking back at me with worry. "Just...uhm, be safe, okay?" After spending the entirety of the past week with her I had a strange sensation of discomfort when I thought of her going out on her own.

Her face reddened as she nodded. "O-of course. I won't be gone long." With that, she turned and left, closing the door behind her. I quickly crossed the room to lock the door, then took the opportunity to finally remove my boots and armor for the first time since we left Lia's home. Stripped down to my comfortable clothes I laid back against the headboard of the bed and sank into the mattress as my body began to relax.

My exhaustion caught up with me all at once. I let out a deep sigh and stretched, worming my way down into a comfortable sleeping position. *All things considered, this trip has been going pretty well so far. I'll feel better once we're out of the country, but two days between us and the capitol helps quite a bit.* As much as I wanted to wait for Lia to return before sleeping, I quickly lost the fight against my descending eyelids and drifted off to sleep.

A soft knocking at the door woke me from my nap. It felt as though I had just dozed off, but the orange light filtering in from the window told me that I had been asleep for at least an hour. A dull thud of metal clattered out from the handle and Lia quickly pushed her way inside, closing the door behind her. She turned with her face downcast and set the room key and the remaining coppers on the table. Her other hand was held behind her back, seeming to be deliberately out of my view.

Her demeanor tightened a knot in my stomach. "Lia? Is something wrong?" I stood and crossed the room, wiping the sleep from my eyes. "Did somebody give you trouble out there?"

"No, that's not it." Lia's voice was low and monotone. She shifted nervously as she tried to come to a decision, then pulled the hand out from behind her back. There was a crumpled piece of paper in her fist which she handed to me silently. I flattened out the sheet, my face darkening as the contents became clear. The majority of the paper was covered in a close to accurate drawing of my face: unkempt black hair, hard jaw covered in overgrown stubble, and my leather armor and cloak showing on my shoulders near the bottom. I couldn't read the words underneath, but the overall meaning was clear.

Fuck. I pinched the bridge of my nose and let out a long hissing sigh. *Fuck! It was one thing to have guards looking for me, but every asshole in the country looking to get a quick payday? There's no way we can make it to Lybesa without someone recognizing me.* Lia was looking up at me with wide eyes, trying to gauge my reaction to the poster. Her face broke my heart, and I had to look away. *This isn't safe anymore.*

"Lia…" I began, but was interrupted when she reached out and grabbed my wrist. There were tears forming in the corner of her eyes.

"No. Don't say it," she pleaded, pulling on my arm. "You can't send me home now, we just left!"

"I promised that I would keep you safe, and if everybody out there is looking for me it's only a matter of time before—"

"You promised that you would show me the world! You said you would take me wherever I wanted to go!" Lia's voice rose considerably, coming close to breaking with emotion. "I don't care if there are guards after you. You don't get to leave me behind!"

I looked away, unable to meet her intense gaze. "The last thing I want to do is break my promise to you, Lia. But if someone confronts me, it could be dangerous. If you're traveling with me when the guards find me, they're going to go after you too." The thought made my fists clench. "And I won't let them do that."

"But that's just it! I can't leave you all alone if people are hunting you down. If someone attacks you, you might—" Lia put her hands up to her mouth abruptly, cutting off her line of thought. She looked away and muttered under her breath. "Nevermind."

"I might what?" I was curious about where she was going with the topic. *Most likely, she doesn't want me traveling alone in danger. I can't say I blame her...I was uncomfortable with her going out to buy supplies, and she doesn't have wanted posters plastered all over town.*

"It's nothing." Her voice sounded defeated as she sniffled softly.

I put a hand on her shoulder. "It's not nothing, Lia. Tell me what you're thinking."

"It's just..." Lia trailed off, wringing her hands as she tried to find the right words. "You're such a good person, Lux. You saved me when I was a total stranger, and you're always so nice to me...I know that's who you really are." She stopped fidgeting and looked me in the eyes, her face awash with...*Is that fear? What is she afraid of?* The knot in my stomach constricted as she continued.

"When I first saw you in that prison cell, you looked mean. I was afraid that you were like the men that took me. But after we talked and I got to know you better, you looked happier. You weren't scowling all the time." A tear ran down Lia's cheek as she spoke. "I thought that, maybe...I was making you happy."

My throat began to tighten as I tried to hold back tears. "You're an amazing person, Lia. Of course you make me happy."

A single sob escaped Lia's lips before she caught herself. "I don't want you to be alone out there. If you're by yourself, and people keep attacking you, you m-might..." She took a deep rasping breath before she continued, her voice trembling. "You might turn back into that person from the prison. The one who killed all the guards. It was so scary the way everything happened with the fire, and that black smoke, and the s-screaming..."

Lia broke down all at once, collapsing forward hard into my chest with a wail. I stood in stunned silence as she cried; her words had hit me harder than any weapon ever had. *She's been worried about me this whole time. Not her adventures, or her safety, but my...soul?* I ran my hand through her hair softly to give her what little comfort I could. Leaning down, I rested more forehead lightly against the top of her head and whispered, "It's okay...It's okay."

The light in the room had dimmed significantly when Lia finally pulled away. I sat down on the edge of the bed and patted the spot next to me. She sat down slowly, purposely avoiding any eye contact as she looked straight down at the floor. Placing my hand on top of hers, I gave it a gentle squeeze. "That's been bothering you for a while now, hasn't it?" She gave a small nod. I leaned back and sighed, closing my eyes.

"It's been bothering me, too. I don't know what that magic was; I've never seen anything like it in all my lives." A shiver ran down my spine. "I've been having nightmares about it lately. About what I did to Jack. Whatever he did, or was going to do, it didn't justify that torture." I let the words sit in silence for a while. "I don't regret killing those men. The world is better off without people like them walking the streets. But how it happened..."

I put an arm around Lia's waist and pulled her into a hug. My chin rested on her shoulder and the smell of her perfume filled my nostrils as I spoke softly into her ear. "You do make me happy, Lia. Before I came to your world, I hadn't truly smiled in years. And the people I met on my arrival here didn't help with that either. But you..." I trailed off for a moment, a smile coming to my face. "From our first conversation, I knew you were a good person. And being around you makes me a better person, too."

Lia wrapped her arms around my chest and embraced me, squeezing hard enough to pop a few of my joints. She buried her face in my neck and I felt the heat of fresh tears against my skin. "That's why I want to keep you safe, Lia. No matter where I go, bad things seem to follow me. I thought maybe if I could get us out of the country, things would be different, but...it doesn't seem like it'll be that easy."

"I'm staying with you. No matter what." Lia's voice was muffled as she spoke into my shoulder. "You're a good person too, Lux. No matter what you've done, or how you feel, I see the good in you. I'm not leaving you alone just because things could get dangerous later." She pulled away from the embrace and placed her hands on my chest, her face just a few inches from mine. "I'm here because I want to be."

The look of pure love on her face was clear, which sent a sharp pang of guilt through my mind. I tipped my head forward to rest my forehead against hers and closed my eyes. "Lia...thank you." Struggling to find the right words to express how I felt, I spoke unsteadily. "I'm sorry that I can't...give you everything you want from me. If things were different, it would be an easy decision, but I...I can't forget my old life, and—"

"It's okay, Elden." The whisper sent chills down my spine. "Amaya is still out there somewhere, waiting for you. I know you're still waiting for her too." A tear dripped down my nose as Lia spoke. "You give me everything I could ever want just by being with me. Please, don't beat yourself up over it. Just let me stay with you."

"Of course...of course you can stay." I nodded weakly. We sat together for a long time, until the sun had fallen well below the horizon outside to leave us in the near darkness of night. I took a deep breath and sat up straight, giving Lia's hands a quick squeeze against my chest before I stood and crossed to the table. Turning the small crank at the base of our lantern, a spark flicked the oil lamp to life and filled the room with orange light and dancing shadows.

"We'll have to do some things differently now, given this new information," I remarked, motioning to the crumpled wanted poster on the table. "I'll have to rely on you to handle any sort of face-to-face interactions, at least until we make it to Lybesa. Do you think you can do that?"

Lia hopped to her feet and hurried over to me, giving a large nod. "You can count on me!" Her eyes were still bloodshot from crying, but she gave me a radiant smile. "I'll go down to the common room and get us some stew. Hopefully there's still some left."

I rubbed my stomach as a hunger pang shot through it at the idea of a substantial dinner. "That's a great idea. It's already paid for, so we might as well take advantage of it." I sat down at the table and pulled out my coin purse. "I've got some things to look over here anyways. Hurry back, okay?"

"Will do!" Lia headed out into the hallway, locking the door behind her as she left. Once I heard her footsteps fade away, I pulled out the second purse that Marten had given me before we left. I winced as I imagined him laughing at how uncomfortable the gift had made me.

He just called it a dowry to mess with me. It's fine. I tugged on the drawstrings and upended the pouch on the table. To my great surprise, the entire bag had been filled with silver steins. Shifting them methodically into piles I counted out forty silvers in total, all shining up at me with a flickering orange smile. *Two full Imperiums...just how much money do you make with that trading business, Marten?* A wry grin crept across my face as all my concerns about money faded away.

The sound of footsteps approaching from the hallway brought me back from my daydreams. I quickly scooped the stacks of silver into my coin purse before moving to the door. The footsteps stopped just outside the room and followed up with a few dull thuds against the wood. Opening the door, I found Lia holding two full bowls of a thick stew, swinging her foot in an attempt to knock. "Dinner is served!" She announced happily, heading inside to set the meal on the table.

"Dinner," I echoed, entranced by the smell of the food. I followed Lia to the table and sat down across from her. The meal in front of me looked about standard for a perpetual stew at a traveller's inn, but having eaten nothing but apples, hardtack and jerky for the past few days, it was the most delicious looking meal I could imagine.

Lia and I ate in silence. After the emotional exchange earlier, it was comforting to be able to enjoy each other's company without the need for words. Although nothing had changed between us, I felt an overwhelming sense of relief from a long-lingering anxiety I hadn't been able to pin down. *Was it guilt over not being able to reciprocate Lia's feelings towards me? Was I really looking for absolution of any obligations I might have to her?* Whatever the reason, I was in much higher spirits than I had been in a while, despite the knowledge that I was indeed a wanted man in Kaldan.

When we finished our meal, we began our preparations for sleep. The bed was much larger than the one in Lia's bedroom at home and afforded us our own distinct sleeping spaces, complete with extra pillows for the both of us. We crawled into bed on our respective sides and laid facing each other in the darkness. The night sky was heavily overcast, providing me with just enough light to make out the general outline of her head and shoulders only an arm's length away from me.

Reaching out with great care as to not miss my mark, I found one of Lia's hands and laced my fingers with hers. "Lia, thank you," I sighed softly, closing my eyes.

"For what?" Her voice floated out of the darkness sweetly.

I smiled, feeling content. "Just for being...you."

"O-oh." Lia stammered awkwardly. As I started to drift off to sleep, she squeezed my hand and pulled it closer to her chest, holding it with both hands. The warmth of her body and breath were the last thing on my mind before it faded to black.

I sat down beside the giant ash tree and rested my head against its trunk with my eyes closed. The wind was blowing gently along the grassy hill, cooling the air to the perfect temperature. Sun shone intermittently down on my face as the leaves shifted in the wind. It was another beautiful summer day in Alderea. And I hated it.

"Nothing like nice weather to ruin a bad mood." Amaya's dulcet voice called out from down the hill. My eyes snapped open in surprise. "Just makes you want to be angry even more, doesn't it?" She stood with her hands clasped behind her back, leaning towards me with a slight smirk.

"Amaya! How did you—"

"I told them I had some last-minute preparations to make before the officials arrived. Technically, it isn't a lie." She looked down at the grass with her head tilted and started to make her way up the hill, slowly and methodically picking each step. "All the time in the world wouldn't prepare me for today."

I swallowed hard. The thought of being away from Amaya for any length of time left an acrid taste in my mouth. "We could still run." Standing, I looked off beyond the ash tree and pointed out towards the distant forest. "We could run straight through Leaning Forest, meet up with the main road beyond there, and be out of the country in a week. We'd have a good head start on them, and they wouldn't know where we were going."

Amaya continued up the hill towards me. "I can't imagine Dad would be very happy with that plan."

It was my turn to smirk now. "It was his idea." She looked up to me, eyebrows askew with surprise, and we both broke out in laughter. We knew how ludicrous the idea was, but it was a small comfort to entertain it for a moment. Unfortunately, the moment faded, and we fell into a sad silence. "It's almost time, isn't it?"

She nodded. "They'll be here soon." Amaya stopped as she finally reached the base of the tree. When I looked at her face, I saw the same strength and resolution as always, but her eyes told a different story. They shone like dappled pools of lilac in the afternoon sun, reflecting the same emotions I was feeling: Sadness, fear, and longing. She reached out and took my hand in hers. "I'm sorry, Elden. You shouldn't have to do this for my sake."

The shame behind her words struck me hard in the gut. Pulling on her hands, I wrapped her into a tight embrace. "This was my decision, Amaya. Your father told me not to go to the keep, and I went anyway. I made the deal with Eadric myself. None of this is your fault." I rubbed her back as I took a deep breath, trying to keep my emotions in check. "You'll always come first for me. If I had to go back and make the decisions again, I would do it in a heartbeat if it meant keeping you safe."

I felt her nod into my shoulder. "I know. It was upsetting at first, but I would do the same thing for you. And you would be feeling the same way I'm feeling now. I guess it's silly to be upset about it." Amaya pulled back to look up at me with a reassuring smile. "Have they given you any more information on what you're doing?"

My eyes rolled involuntarily as I shrugged. "You know how they are. 'Royal secrets, we can't tell you that,'" I mocked. "I doubt they know anything more than I do. My escort will take me north to the capitol, and from there I'll join the military caravan on their way to the eastern border. The whole trip will take just under a fortnight. That's where I'll meet the others who have been...'specially requisitioned' like me. After that, it's still a mystery."

In the distance a lone trumpet sounded, heralding the arrival of royal envoys. Amaya closed her eyes and sighed. "I suppose that means it's time." We both stood statue still, neither of us wanting our last moments alone together for the foreseeable future to end. The trumpet sounded again, echoing with a tinny ring over the rolling hills. "Will you write to me?"

"Of course. Whenever I'm able." I caressed her back, doing my best to comfort her and myself. *"I'll tell you about all the people I meet and the places I go."*

More trumpets sounded now, blasting a dissonant chord. *"I'll be waiting for you, right here. Every day, until you come back to me."*

I tried to blink away the tears forming in my eyes. *"There's nothing in this world that can stop me from coming home to you, Amaya. No matter what happens."*

"I know." She pulled away from the embrace, taking my hands in hers. *"If you stay true to who you are, I know you'll come back to me."*

My brain shifted its sole focus to crystallizing the beautiful woman before me into one perfect memory. *"I love you, Amaya."*

"And I love you, Elden." She pulled me in for a kiss full of passion, and longing, and heartache. *"Forever,"* she whispered as our lips separated. A single tear dropped from my eye and landed on her cheek. Amaya smiled and patted my chest softly. *"Time to put on your brave face, love. The hero always has to look brave."*

I nodded and wiped my eyes in silence, not trusting myself to speak. *"Go on ahead, I'll catch up with you. They'll be waiting for you to start the royal address."* She gave me a light push down the hill.

As I walked away, I absentmindedly spun the thin gold band around my finger. It was a habit I had picked up in the past few weeks, a tick that came out whenever I was feeling particularly overwhelmed. With a heavy sigh, I stood a little straighter and quickened my pace. *"Forever,"* I whispered under my breath with a small smile.

***

18. THE FRUITS OF OUR LABORS

Lia and I left the inn before sunrise. My distrust of strangers had grown exponentially at the discovery of my wanted posters, and I felt it was best to get out of civilization before first light. *Did the clerk at the inn recognize me? Is that why she stared at us so long? Does that mean they might be looking for Lia now, too?* The thoughts plagued me as we walked along the well traveled dirt road out of town. Despite knowing the best way to blend in was to act naturally, I couldn't help but check behind us every few minutes to make sure we weren't being followed.

My worry proved fruitless as the day of travel passed by uneventfully. By midday we had put enough distance between us and the previous town that I could relax enough to hold pleasant conversation with Lia. Our nightly ritual of "a truth for a truth" had evolved into sharing stories while on the road.

A story Lia told me as we ate our late afternoon trail rations had particularly piqued my interest. When she was seven, her parents had taken her on a trip to a town in eastern Kaldan called Malt. It was a three-day trip by wagon, which Lia had spent sitting on the front bench with the wagon driver, presumably talking his ear off. When they finally reached the city, she recounted being amazed by the streetlights lining the main thoroughfare that night. Each lamp was a tall metal rod with a glass orb floating above the top, completely disconnected from the structure. Each one glowed a different color, illuminating the streets in a dazzling rainbow. The sight was so exciting for her that it was the only clear memory she had from the trip, much to her parents' chagrin.

In turn, I told her a story of my early days training in Alderea under the hedge knight Brusch. Although I never learned where he lived or why he was traveling through our village, he always seemed to show up once or twice a season to get his armor and weapons touched up at the forge. The first time he returned after teaching me how to use combat enhancements, I had been so excited to fight him again to show him how much I had improved in his time away. I pulled out all the stops using every enhancement I knew, straining my mana to the max.

It was truly a shock to me when he repeatedly knocked me on my ass without a single enhancement. He always seemed to see how I would approach and had a new step or flourish to counter every time. Brusch laughed the whole fight, mocking me for "knowing ten fancy enhancements while not knowing how to move my feet without falling." I was so embarrassed at my showing that I focused on my footwork and movement for a whole month after that day. When Brusch showed up again after the winter I challenged him again and was summarily defeated when he threw mud in my eyes. The taunt that time was "How can you move so quickly when you don't know what you're looking at?" Lia found that part of the story particularly amusing.

As much as we learned from each other about our pasts, we also learned a great deal in our training. I made the decision to severely accelerate Lia's training routine, aiming to bring her up to a rough competence in all the fields I felt were essential instead of focusing on mastery of a single technique. Every night we camped out in the field was spent learning a new skill: proper footwork, two weapon fighting, using a shield, unarmed fighting, and fighting with enhancements were all on the table.

Lia continued to exceed my expectations at every turn. It was immediately clear that she wasn't any sort of hidden martial prodigy; everything she learned took hours of hard work and intense focus until I felt confident she could perform the skill reliably. Through all of my critiques and the various bumps and bruises, she never once complained. There would be over-exaggerated whines and moans during the next day's travel, but Lia always remained serious and focused during her training.

She particularly struggled the first night I started hand to hand combat lessons. I noticed quickly that she was pulling her punches out of concern for my wellbeing. No matter how many times I reassured her that she wouldn't hurt me, and that at worst I would suffer a broken nose, Lia never threw a punch at full force. It took two nights worth of practice and some particularly relentless attacks to draw out her full power in her attacks, but once that switch was flipped it was never an issue again.

On the few nights that we stayed at a roadside inn we spent the bulk of our time in magic training. Although there was no physical exertion involved, my practice regimen for magic and mana manipulation always left Lia far more exhausted than the combat training ever did. Her first goal was successfully using the most important combat enhancements: Sharpening, Agility, Heighten Senses, and Combat Acceleration. I would demonstrate the ability first and describe what it felt like when cast correctly, and then try to help her replicate the effects. Aside from Combat Acceleration, which was a notably more complicated enhancement, she quickly grasped the concept of the other abilities.

After she felt comfortable with the basics, my entire training plan for her was solely focused on repetition. How many times can you evoke a combat enhancement? How long can you sustain a single ability? How well can you maintain control over multiple enhancements at once? Although the training was simple and somewhat boring, it proved to be extremely effective. The progress Lia made was quite astounding; in less than a fortnight, she had gone from not knowing what mana was to channeling three different abilities at the same time for over five minutes. In comparison, within my first two weeks of practicing magic with Brusch I was proud to have maintained Lesser Agility for three minutes without blacking out.

With our days spent walking from sunrise to sunset and our nights packed full of physical exertion, time passed us by without a second thought. We had little reason to keep track of the days when our traveling directions were so simple: Follow the main road to the west. Without any sort of schedule to keep Lia and I were content to travel as fast or slow as we pleased, depending entirely on how we felt in the moment. As such, we were both taken by surprise when, after emerging from a thicket of trees, a large city was looming on the horizon.

Lia was walking a few paces in front of me and was the first to spot civilization. She gasped loudly and turned to me excitedly. "Lux! We're almost to Atsal!"

I caught up to her and looked through the break in the tree line; off in the distance, I could see a large walled city. We were too far away to make out any details, but it had one distinctive feature: Two ivory white towers stood parallel to one another within the walls, casting menacing shadows over the battlements in the late afternoon sun. The enormous columns looked featureless from my vantage point, glowing immaculately in the clear day's light.

"I guess we traveled faster than I thought," I remarked cheerfully. The idea peeled another layer of stress from my psyche. *At this rate, making it to Lybesa unharassed doesn't seem like such an impossible task.* "Lia, what do you know about Atsal?"

We resumed our travels as she spoke, moving much more quickly than moments before. "Well, I know it's the second biggest city in Kaldan behind Yoria. I think it used to be an important military fort, but we haven't needed those for so long that it's just another city now." Lia had a lightness to her gait as we walked, as though she were just barely suppressing the urge to skip. "I've heard the whole city is made from perfect white marble, and it has the largest garden in all of Kaldan. Oh, and because it's so close to the border, you can find lots of exotic things in the markets!"

Lia's positivity was irresistible, bringing a large smile to my face. "It sounds lovely." Caught up in her excitement Lia broke into a full skip, moving even faster towards the large city. I had a quick internal debate as we continued down the road. *One extra day in Kaldan can't hurt, right? I mean, it COULD hurt, but it won't. Besides, I told her I'd take her wherever she wanted to go, not just out of the country.* "Lia," I started with a smirk, "How would you like to stay a day in Atsal before we head to Lybesa? We could explore the garden, check out the exotic markets, do a little exploring of—"

My offer was interrupted by a leaping hug that threatened to knock me head over heels. Lia hung her arms around my neck and looked up at me, her amber eyes shining brilliantly. "You really mean it?!"

Giving her head a quick pat, I laughed. "Of course I mean it! We'll still have to be cautious of course, but I think you deserve a reward for all the hard work you've been putting in on the trip so far."

She jumped back and placed her hands on her hips, puffing out her chest with pride. "That's right! We can't just work all the time, can we?"

I shook my head with a smile. "No, we can't. Now, let's get going so we can find a room before nightfall." Lia nodded enthusiastically, spinning in place before she took off down the road in a near sprint. "Hey now, let's not be too conspicuous here!" I shouted as I began to jog after her.

At our quickened pace, we reached the city a few hours before dark. Up close, the wall around the city was a much more impressive sight. It looked to be created from one massive piece of marble, stretching up over two stories without any lines indicating where individual slabs were laid together. The main road led to a large iron gate which currently stood open, allowing a large crowd of people to filter in and out of the city at will.

Drawing my hood further down over my eyes, I led Lia by the hand through the increasingly dense throng. As we passed under the heavy portcullis, we were able to get our first true look at the city of Atsal. Lia's stories turned out to be true; every building was indeed made of the same perfect white marble as the walls, as were the roads and streetlamps. The method of construction also looked to be the same, with every structure appearing as if it were carved from a single enormous mountain of white rock. It gave me a sense of vertigo as we passed down the main thoroughfare, which appeared to lead straight to the heart of the city where the two massive towers stood their watch.

Lia tugged at my arm from somewhere behind me, pulling my head down to her level. "The building up ahead on our right is an inn. It's the one with the purple awning, called Ivory Halls," She spoke quietly into my ear. It was a hard building to miss; a sprawling canopy spread around the entire front entrance all the way to the roadside, covering a patio full of tables and massive planters filled with vibrant flowers flanking the doorway. The decor was much the same inside the building as well, with lavish vases of flowers and lush purple carpets covering most of the marble interior.

I pulled out a silver coin from my pouch and handed it to Lia. "One room, two nights." She nodded back to me, well used to handling our lodging arrangements by this point. I did my best to lean inconspicuously against a wall by the entrance as she had a cheerful conversation with the man at the front desk, eventually returning with a set of room keys and a smile.

When we entered our room, I let out an impressed whistle. "This is quite the upgrade from our previous accommodations, wouldn't you say?" All of the fancy trappings from the lobby were present in our room as well. The bed looked particularly posh, with a heavy purple quilt laid over frilled undersheets. Lia and I grinned at each other for a moment as we took in the luxury of the chamber.

With the daylight filtering in through our double paned window fading quickly, we set about preparing for our night's work. I stripped off my armor for the first time in days while Lia changed into a sleeping gown. Once we were comfortable, we each grabbed our weapons and sat down on the bed facing each other, swords rested in our laps. "I don't know about you, but I'm pretty beat tonight. We'll make this a short session," I said softly, closing my eyes.

While I gave Lia various tasks to practice during her meditation, I worked on training my mana detection ability. Once I had discovered the technique on the first night of our travels it had become my sole obsession to study it during our meditations. Reaching out in a pulsing circle my mana traced around our small room, illuminating our immediate surroundings in great detail in my head.

The technique had become particularly helpful in monitoring Lia's progress in regard to magic. Being able to see how she was channeling her mana and the strength of her enhancements made it so much easier to give her instruction on how to improve. Sitting across from her now I watched the warm amber glow of her mana flowing throughout her body. At measured intervals her sword would flash brilliantly as she channeled a new enhancement, outlining her body with a sharp new color. The small world I could see within the darkness of my mind was full of vibrant lights as she practiced various techniques.

As time went on, I could see the intensity of Lia's mana fading, dimming from a bright amber to a dull yellow. I could hear her breath coming with more difficulty as well, but to her credit she showed no signs of quitting. "Alright, let's call it a night." I opened my eyes, grinning when I saw the flush in her cheeks and a bead of sweat running down her forehead. "You're making fantastic progress, Lia."

She flopped backwards onto a pillow with a smile. "You really think so?"

"Of course! Can't you feel it?" I carefully took the sword from her lap and crossed to the table where the scabbard sat, placing the blade inside. "Just think of how far you've come in the past two weeks. You've gone from passing out after just channeling mana to using multiple enhancements at the same time." Returning to the bed I laid back against the headboard, looking down at Lia with a playful grin. "It won't be too long before you're better than me!"

"Oh, sure." She rolled her eyes as she flopped over, snaking her way underneath the velvety sheets. Her face took on a thoughtful look when she finally got comfortable. "Now that you mention it, I guess I do feel a bit more confident. I don't even have to think about moving the mana around anymore, it just sort of...happens."

I nodded. "You know what they say. Practice makes perfect." Following her lead, I crawled under the blankets as well. "Now, we should get some well-deserved rest. We've got a busy day ahead of us tomorrow, right?"

"That's right! I'm making a list of everything we have to see while we're in Atsal, and it's VERY extensive!" Lia giggled to herself as she turned over. I could make out the edge of a warm smile as she looked over her shoulder at me. "Goodnight, Lux." With that, she settled herself into a comfortable position and went to sleep.

Lying back in bed, I closed my eyes and tapped into my mana reserves one more time. Shooting out in a quick pulse, the energy raced in all directions, scanning under the door to our room and into the hallway. Once I had realized the possible uses for the new "detection magic", as I had come to think of it, I had quickly incorporated it into my watch routine. *Although technically it isn't magic. It's just mana manipulation on a wider scale. The energy isn't expended or changed in any way.* I shook my head to dismiss the pedantic thoughts, renewing my focus. With the range of the magic increasing bit by bit from my constant practice, I was able to reach all the way down into the foyer of the inn and out the front doors before I found the ability too taxing to continue.

The information surging through my mind was overwhelming at first, but I was getting better at visualizing the data as a whole without getting inundated with fine details. I could see the desk clerk sitting where we had left him, staring blankly into space. Three figures sat at a small table in the common room eating, their mouths giving shape to a conversation I couldn't hear. Otherwise, the hallways and patio outside were devoid of life aside from various plants.

My mana came rushing back when I was satisfied with my scan. The returning energy always made my spine tingle and raised goose bumps on my arms. I let out a contented sigh and rolled into a comfortable sleeping position. My arm stretched out across the mattress, reaching just far enough for my fingertips to rest against Lia's back. Although the physical closeness I shared with Lia often made me feel guilty of leading her on emotionally, I found the contact to be extremely comforting on a deep primal level. The unconscious tension I had been carrying in my jaw and shoulders relaxed at the touch, and I quickly drifted off to sleep.

"So, we actually have one errand to run before we get to our day of sightseeing." I gave Lia a repentant smile as we stood on the patio of the inn under a bright pink and orange morning sky. "Well, don't think of it as an errand. Think of it as a surprise adventure."

Lia watched me suspiciously. "I'm listening."

I chuckled, drawing my hood further down over my eyes through force of habit. "I need you to find us an armorer; A good armorer, unlike that man from the Tolamar market. It'll just be a short visit and then we can work our way through your list of activities."

"What do you need an armorer for?"

"What do WE need an armorer for," I corrected her with a wry grin, "And I said it's a surprise, remember?"

Lia looked me over with a mix of curiosity, annoyance, and amusement. Eventually the corner of her mouth turned up into a smile as she laughed. "Okay, Lux. I'll play your game." She turned to leave but stopped short and whirled on me with unexpected energy. "But if we miss anything on my list because of this, I'll never forgive you!" With my scolding out of the way she hopped up the steps and back into the inn, leaving me to blend in with the early morning traffic.

She returned a few minutes later with a bounce to her step which I took to mean good news. "The clerk said he knows the best armorer in town! Three blocks towards the watchtowers, hang a right, and it'll be two blocks ahead on the left, too big to miss. It's called the Marble Forge." Lia hopped out into the street and looked back at me with impatience. "Let's go!"

I followed Lia through the early morning crowd, keeping my face downturned as much as possible. It wasn't a long walk until I spotted our destination. Even without reading the lettering, a suit of armor and crossed swords above a roaring fire, painted onto a massive sign above a set of double doors was indeed too big to miss. Pushing through the doors we found ourselves in a relatively small entryway which appeared to be empty aside from a door on either side of us and a large wooden desk near the opposite end of the room. A tiny bell chimed above us as we entered, piercing the silence much louder than I would have expected for its size.

We stood awkwardly in the center of the room for a few moments until the door to our right opened to reveal a stout, burly man with bright red hair. He was wearing a heavy leather apron and thick gloves, and a large utility belt hung with dozens of tools encircled his bulging waist. "Welcome to the Marble Forge, folks. How can I be of service? If you're looking to browse our inventory, you can head through the door to your left to our display room. I can help you with any repair orders you might have."

"Actually, I was hoping I could commission you to do some custom work." I stepped forward and offered out a hand. "Rastor Ashedown, pleased to make your acquaintance. I've heard great things about your establishment, Mr...?"

The man's face lit up at the mention of commission work and he shook my hand eagerly. "The pleasure is all mine Mr. Ashedown. You can call me Hark. I do hope that our work can live up to our reputation." Hark examined me closely, intrigued. "I can work with you to design anything your heart desires, but I must say, you seem to be quite well equipped already."

I smiled graciously. "Oh, the work wouldn't be for me." Taking a step to the side, I gestured to Lia. "It's for her. A full set of leather armor, in the same style as my own. Also, weapons to replace these." I pulled the shortsword and dagger from my belt and presented them to Hark. "Around the same size and weight, but less...poorly made."

The man's eyes gleamed with excitement as he looked over Lia and the offered weapons. In contrast, Lia looked more like a startled deer as she stared at me with her mouth agape. "Of course, sir, of course! We can take her measurements today, and then I'll meet with my men to begin planning—"

"Unfortunately, I have to also request that the work is finished by tomorrow morning," I said, cutting off his train of thought. Hark's expression changed to one very similar to Lia's.

"Mr. Ashedown, that just isn't possible. The amount of work that goes into making custom armor can't be rushed, especially at the level of quality we produce." He rubbed his hands together nervously. "We can accelerate the process, of course, if you're willing to pay the fees, but that deadline, it just, well, we can't..." Hark trailed off as I fished through the coin pouch at my belt. My fingers fished for a distinctive item as we both stood in silence.

With a self-satisfied grin I pulled out a brilliant ruby about the diameter of a silver coin. Rolling the royal cut gem between my fingers, I looked back to Hark. "I'm well acquainted with the process of making leather armor, Hark. If you're as highly regarded as I've heard, I'm sure my deadline won't be an issue...for the right price, of course."

Hark eyed the gem hungrily, looking from my face to the ruby several times. "Could I...?" He reached out timidly. I nodded silently and handed over the stone. Hark produced a small jeweler's lens from one of the pouches on his belt and inspected the gem closely, turning it delicately in his stubby fingers. After a thorough investigation, he returned the lens to his belt and held out to ruby to me with a defeated look on his face. "Sir, this is too valuable for me to accept as payment for your request."

I held up a hand dismissively. "No, I feel that it's an even trade. A rush job for a custom set of armor along with two high quality weapons. And, of course, your discretion." I leaned in and spoke more quietly. "I'm a man who values his privacy, you see. If you could keep this order just between us, I think we'll have a settled deal."

Hark took my hand and shook it vigorously. "Of course, sir! I'll get to work right away. We'll need measurement from the lady, and also from your armor, for reference. My men will start preparing the materials now, and then I'll—" He stopped short, interrupting his frenetic train of thought. "Will you be coming by tomorrow to pick up your gear? What time should we expect you?"

"Have it delivered to the Ivory Halls, care of Ms. Lia. They'll be expecting you," I said casually. Out of the corner of my eye I saw that Lia's expression had hardly changed over the course of the exchange, still frozen in disbelief.

"I'll deliver it myself as soon as the work is finished!" Hark said, nodding his head excitedly. "Thank you for choosing the Marble Forge, Mr. Ashedown. I promise you won't be disappointed!" He took off quickly back through the door he had arrived from, shouting and banging around quite loudly from somewhere inside.

I turned back to Lia with a cheeky smile. "Surprise!" I said, barely containing a laugh.

She looked up at me, blinking quietly for a moment. "Why?" Lia eventually managed to say, her voice sounding genuinely confused. "How?"

"Well, you've been doing such a great job with all your training that I thought you deserved some proper gear. You work so hard and never complain, and I just wanted to show you my appreciation for that." I gave her a pat on the head. "As for the how, I'll just say that I have quite an assortment of trinkets and coins in this pouch. Remind me to tell you about it later." Before she had a chance to respond Hark came bustling back through the door, now adorned with a multitude of measuring tapes that streamed out behind him as he moved.

The fitting process went by quickly with Hark taking precise measurements and accurate notes at a practiced pace. After many profuse thanks we exited back out to the main street, having spent only a half hour total within the shop. I clapped my hands together excitedly. "Okay Lia, where to? The day is yours." She responded with a tight hug, burying her face in my chest. I tousled her hair gently as a smile spread wide across my face. After a moment she withdrew, beaming happily up at me before she took my hand and led me down the busy street.

Lia made good on her promise from the night before over the course of the day, taking us to over a half dozen interesting locations within the city. We explored the gardens that she had mentioned before, marveling at how massive it was; from certain angles it would have been easy to forget we were inside city walls with how dense the foliage was. At one point, an entrepreneuring cart owner pegged us as tourists and convinced Lia to get a chain of flowers braided into her hair, costing me a staggering five crowns. Her joy in posing with the braid displayed proudly in front of her made the price well worth it.

On our way to find lunch we stumbled across a trained animal exhibit. The signage promised performing dogs, talking birds, and a few acts containing animals whose names I was unfamiliar with. When we entered the pavilion, it became overwhelmingly clear that instead of entering the advertised circus, we had found a glorified petting zoo. Judging by the young age of most of the patrons it was clearly intended for children, but it didn't dissuade Lia from playing with the animals for a half hour before we moved on.

Our last stop of the day was the exotic market. True to Lia's word, it was full of strange items and foreign foods neither of us had ever tasted before. She quickly fell in love with a small square fruit that a dark-skinned shop owner let her sample. It had a delicate yellow skin with a bright orange interior, and a flavor so sour it immediately made her lips pucker. My tastes were much more in line with a pepper vendor from the south who introduced me to a curious bifurcated chili; connected by a thin membrane at the top, it had one red lobe and one blue lobe side by side. Eating the red side brought an intense sheen of sweat to my brow, but eating the blue side instantly soothed my palette with a sweet, oozing paste held inside. When we left the market, Lia and I each held a large bag of our respective treats.

By the time we returned to the inn the sun had already set on Atsal. The peculiar streetlamps lit our way with a soft white glow that unwaveringly shone from the marble cages on top. Even though night had fully arrived the streets were still full of people and carriages, bustling to and fro just as they had in the morning. I was relieved when we finally entered the Ivory Halls, giving a break to my constant anxiety about being noticed. Lia quickly told the front desk that she was expecting a package in the morning and then we both headed up to our room for the night.

"It feels like it was yesterday that we were saying goodbye to your parents, and now we're almost to the border. It's the end of an adventure," I commented as we changed into our bedclothes.

"And the beginning of a new one," Lia chimed in. "A bigger one."

"That's right!" I smiled. "Once we're in Lybesa, we'll truly be able to do whatever we want. No directions, no obligations, no worries."

"I'm looking forward to it," Lia said as we climbed into bed. I snuffed out the lamp on the small bedside table and curled up under the blankets.

"Time to get some sleep. You've got some excitement to look forward to in the morning." I grinned and closed my eyes. After a clean sweep of mana detection magic, I began to reflect on the day's events as I drifted off to sleep. *I never thought it could happen again after Hedaat, but...I think I might actually be happy.*

***

19. FINAL EXAM

    The heavy iron door swung open with a grating screech. "Last door on the right," the gruff man stated, handing me a ring of keys. I walked into the dark cell block, stepping down cautiously onto the damp stone floor. The guard closed the door behind me and walked back to his post at the dungeon entrance, clearly uninterested in whatever I was here for.

    The only light source in the cell block was a single sputtering torch hung on the far wall. It took my eyes a few moments to adjust to the low light and I still had to squint in order to make out the details of my surroundings. Each side of the hallway had four cells secured with thick barred doors, although their level of rust and disrepair gave me doubts they could hold back a determined prisoner for more than a day. The sounds of running water and pouring rain echoed throughout the block; The storm that I had walked through to reach the keep was still raging outside the small barred windows in each cell.

    I felt an increasing sense of dread as I walked down the hallway, checking each cell as I passed by. A thick layer of dust and grime coated the floor and benches of each room which further reinforced the idea that this particular cell block was rarely used. I paused before reaching the final two cells and took a deep breath in preparation for what I might find. My mind raced with all sorts of horrible possibilities. I swear, if they've hurt her, nobody is leaving this keep alive.

    "I knew you'd come for me," a beautiful voice called out to me from the near darkness. Amaya was seated on a bench at the back wall of the cell with her hands folded neatly in her lap. She was still wearing her favorite violet sundress from the day she was taken, now sporting rips and stains it hadn't before. Somehow, through it all, she still sat with all the composure of a noble at court and a smile on her face. "I'm sure Dad kept you away for as long as he could."

    "Oh, Amaya..." I managed to choke out before my throat closed up completely. Tears pooled in my eyes as I rested my forehead against the bars of her cell. All of the things I wanted to say to her were gone, washed away in the tidal wave of emotions crashing through me. "I'm so sorry." With a jolt, I regained enough sense to remember the keys in my hand and unlocked the door with a heavy thud.

"It isn't your fault, love." Amaya rose from her seat and crossed the cell carefully. Water was pouring in through the window from the vicious storm outside, making the stone floor a dangerously slick surface to traverse barefoot. I yanked open the door and took her hand to lead her safely to the hall. She placed her soft hands gently on my cheeks and twirled a lock of hair around her finger. "You've been blaming yourself for this the whole time, haven't you?"

"Of course I have," My voice cracked as I spoke. "If I hadn't refused the summons, they would never have taken you." I pulled her into a tight embrace, squeezing her with a resolve to never let her go again. "Are you hurt? Have they been mistreating you?"

Amaya shook her head. "Not at all. The guard who brought me my meals was quite sympathetic, actually. He stole extra dinner rolls for me, so I didn't go hungry." She chuckled faintly. "I don't think any of the men here took any pleasure in imprisoning me. Even Lord Eadric. He's following orders too." Leaning back to look up at my face, she frowned. "Elden, please don't torture yourself over this. I'm fine, truly. It's nothing a hot bath and a long night's rest in our bed can't fix."

I tried to put on a smile for her which freed the tears in my eyes to roll down my cheeks. "Of course, love." Offering out my hand, I nodded towards the far door. "Now, how about we get you home to that bath?"

She nodded and took my hand. "Yes, let's." Amaya turned to survey her cell one last time. "I can't say I'll miss this place."

The lump in my throat turned my laugh into a cough as I began to lead her down the hall. "Well, I'll make you a promise now: This is the last time you'll ever see these cells. I promise this will never happen to you again."

"...will never happen to me again..." Amaya murmured under her breath. I felt her tug on my arm as she stopped in the middle of the hallway. "That's not what I'm worried about."

Puzzled, I turned to her. "What was that, love?"

Her look grew markedly more serious. "I wasn't worried for myself while I was down here. I knew that you would find a way to get me out." Amaya's eyes softened as she paused, looking at me lovingly. "I was worried that this would happen to someone else. Someone who doesn't have...you."

I grimaced. "Your father had similar concerns." Doing my best to avoid specific details, I continued. *"I spoke with Lord Eadric, and we've reached an understanding of sorts. This won't be happening again, to anybody."*

Amaya shook her head. *"Maybe so, but...it just makes me so angry to know that this can happen. That it DOES happen..."* She trailed off as her hands balled into fists. *"I don't understand how people in power can use that power to hurt the people they're supposed to protect. Innocent people like us. What are we supposed to do?"* There were tears in her eyes as she looked up to me.

Gently, I wrapped my arms around her and held the back of her head as she cried into my shoulder. *"It's okay, Amaya."* The depth of her compassion never ceased to amaze me. Even in a situation like this, she's still thinking of other people before herself. *"It must have been hard for you, down here by yourself with all these thoughts."* Amaya nodded weakly into my chest.

I leaned down to her ear. *"I'll make you a better promise. I promise that I will do everything I can to protect the people who can't protect themselves. I promise that I'll stop those injustices wherever I find them. I promise it, no matter the cost I have to pay. I'll do it for you, Amaya."* I planted a kiss on her forehead. *"I'll do anything for you if it will make you happy."*

Amaya gave me a hard squeeze before pulling away. *"Thank you, Elden."* She sniffled and wiped her face with the back of her hand. *"Sorry for...all of this."*

I couldn't help but laugh. *"You're the strongest person I know, Amaya. Now, of all times, is the most reasonable time to be upset. You don't have to apologize."* Taking her hand once again, I started towards the exit. *"I couldn't hold it together for three seconds after seeing you down here."*

A small laugh came from behind me accompanied by a few more sniffles. I knocked on the door to alert the guard I was finished with my business. While we stood waiting, I felt another tug at my arm. When I turned to check on Amaya, she caught me with a kiss, her lips soft and warm against my own. Even after years of being with her, it still woke butterflies in my stomach. *"I love you, Elden. Forever."*

"I love you too, Amaya." The hall door opened before us, and I led her into the warm well-lit guard room. *"Now, let's go home."*

I awoke to a faint ray of light from the far window. The sun hadn't quite crested the top of the walls, but the sky was beginning to brighten, currently a cloudless violet backdrop over the city. Groggily rolling away from the morning light I came face to face with Lia, who had apparently shifted over onto my pillow at some point during the night. She was curled into a tight ball with most of the silky blankets pulled up snugly under her arm. Smiling, I pushed a rogue strand of hair from her face before standing to start my day.

After sliding back into my armor and effects I sat down at the table to enjoy a small breakfast. As I forgot to inquire about the name of the new delicacy I discovered in the markets, I had decided to call them twinpeppers. I pulled one from the large bag in the chair next to me and bit into both halves at once, creating a sweet and spicy combination on my tongue. Doing my best to conserve the bulk of my stock for the road I followed it up with an apple, casually munching on it as I reflected on my plans for the day.

I wonder if Hark delivered my order yet. Lia's equipment order was the only thing keeping us in Atsal at this point and I was eager to leave as soon as possible. The wait had been necessary, though; My experience working on rush orders in Ashedown's forge had given me a good idea of what would be possible for an experienced armorer, and a single afternoon wouldn't have sufficed. I was about to walk down to the front desk to inquire about the package when I remembered another more convenient option: detection magic.

With a quick centering breath, I reached inwards and pulled on my mana reserves, sending the energy shooting off under the door and down the hallway. By not taking the time and effort to scan in an even circle around me I was able to reach the main lobby of the inn without feeling any strain. Scanning around the room I noticed two men in heavy armor sitting together in the common room by the fire, both quietly watching the stairs. Sweeping towards the reception desk, I was pleased to detect a large wooden crate sitting behind the counter next to the attendant.

Satisfied with my findings, I decided to test my abilities and see how far I could extend my mana. Pushing out the door I was surprised to find the street completely empty of foot traffic. The hair on the back of my neck stood up as I slowly scanned outward, revealing in my mind a small display of the surrounding area.

Nine more men clad in the same armor as the two sitting in the lobby were spaced out evenly outside the building. One stood leaning against the wall next to the door, with two sitting at a patio table underneath the inn's canopy. Three men were stationed on the opposite side of the street directly across from the entrance to our building. The last three patrolled up and down the road, never getting too far from the inn before turning around to walk in the other direction. I scanned out as far as I could in either direction down the street, but I reached my limit before encountering anybody else, armored or otherwise.

They found me, I thought solemnly. *Who tipped them off? The receptionist? Hark? Some random passer-by on the street?* Shaking my head, I let out a long, aggravated sigh. *I guess it doesn't matter. They're here, and they know I'm here. That's the most important thing right now.* My eyes fell upon Lia, still buried comfortably beneath the sheets of our bed. *No. She's the most important thing right now.*

I stood slowly and moved to the bedside, sitting down on the corner. "Lia," I said softly, gently shaking her shoulder, "It's time to wake up." One amber eye cracked open just enough to see me before she rolled onto her back and stretched, letting out a small squeak.

"G'morning Lux," She said groggily with a small smile. "Is it time to leave already?"

"Almost," I replied, doing my best to present a calm and neutral face. "I think you might have something waiting for you down at the front desk."

Lia's face gradually lit up with excitement as she remembered the delivery. "You think it's here already?" She launched out of bed, throwing her nightgown over her head as she rushed to get dressed. "I'm going to go check now!" As she yanked her tunic on and ran for the door, I stood to follow her, concerned.

"Lia, wait," I called out, maybe too harshly. She stopped in place with her hand on the door latch and turned to look at me. "Be careful, okay?" Lia looked confused for a moment, but she quickly regained her excited smile and gave me a nod before heading out into the hallway. I reached out with my mana to follow her, worried as to whether the guards downstairs knew she was with me or not.

I watched her bound down the stairs, slowing down only when she rounded the last turn to the lobby. The two armored men still sat by the fire, casually watching as she skipped out to the front desk. To my great relief, they quickly dismissed her and went back to watching the staircase. Lia said something to the clerk at the front desk that caused him to nod and turn around. He retrieved the wooden crate from the floor and slid it across the counter to her, smiling pleasantly.

With her prize in tow Lia returned to the room unharassed. She pushed through the door and triumphantly called out, "It's here!" Moving quickly to the table she sat the box down and unclasped the large latch on the front. She looked at me excitedly before flipping the lid open, gasping when she saw the contents. I stood and rounded the table to admire Hark's work as well.

A full set of leather armor was stacked neatly at the top of the box. Each piece was dyed a beautiful deep forest green color and chased with delicate silver patterns similar to mine. Lia reached into the box and removed the heavy leather gloves, handling them with an over-cautious reverence. She laid them out gently beside her on the table and returned to the box to withdraw the next piece. When she was finished, a pristine set of gloves, vambraces, pauldrons, and greaves were spread out before us with an elegant chestpiece set up on a chair.

Reaching back into the crate one last time, Lia retrieved two matching leather sheaths dyed the same dark green as her armor. Setting the smaller of the two down on the table, she admired the longsword in awe. "Go on," I said, barely above a whisper, "let's see it." Lia pulled the blade from the scabbard, filling the room with an echoing metal-against-metal ring.

The blade was polished to a mirror-like finish which shone beautifully in the morning sun. It had a wide crossguard that swirled upwards like the petals of a water lily and a simple knuckle-bow running down along the leather wrapped grip. As she turned the weapon in her hand, I could tell the balance was impeccable. *Hark certainly lived up to his reputation.* Lia looked over her bounty with a dumbfounded expression and misty eyes. As much as I wanted to let her savor the moment, I knew we had more pressing matters at hand. "Let's see if it fits you."

I showed Lia how to strap on all of her new gear while trying to teach her the tricks she would need to equip it by herself should the need arise. As I expected, the set fit her perfectly; every piece sat sturdy in its proper place when I ran her through a quick range of motion test. Once her armor was on and her new weapons belted to her hip, I stepped back to give her a final appraisal. I let out a low whistle. "It really suits you, Lia. Now you look like a real adventurer, just like me."

Lia's face flushed as she looked away. "Thank you, Lux. This is all so...amazing."

The knot in my stomach tightened with a pang of guilt. "I'm glad you like it." I paused, cringing for a moment before continuing "Lia, I'm sorry to have to do this now, but I have some bad news." I pulled out a chair and took a seat, motioning for her to do the same. She sat down across from me with a solemn look, watching me in silence.

"I don't know how it happened, but the guards have finally caught up to me. You might have noticed two of them in the common room when you went to retrieve your package." Lia's eyes lit up with recognition as she nodded. "There are eleven of them in total. Judging by the size of the deployment and the fact that they cleared the street, they've already decided this is going to end in a fight."

Lia cocked her head to one side. "How do you know all of that?"

Although I knew the question was coming, I still didn't have a great answer. "I know that this isn't a satisfying answer, but I don't have time to explain. You'll just have to trust me." She nodded quietly. "Now that you have that armor, they'll know you're with me as soon as they see you. If you wanted out of this...now's your last chance." I knew what Lia's answer would be, but I felt obligated to give her the option regardless.

"I told you before, I'm not leaving you. No matter what," Lia said, her expression serious. She reached across the table and took my hand. "I made you a promise, and I'm not going to break it now because things are getting scary." Even though I expected the response, it was still comforting to know I wouldn't be alone in the coming trials.

"Thank you, Lia." I gave her hand a squeeze before standing to begin my preparations. "In that case, you're about to have your first real combat test. I don't imagine the guards will allow us to leave, even if we ask nicely." Pulling my sword from the ether I sheathed it on my hip opposite my dull sparring longsword. "Once we go downstairs, the two inside will follow us outside, meeting up with the man by the door to cut off any retreat. I'm going to leave those three to you."

Lia's eyes widened. "Three? You want me to fight three of them, at the same time?" She shook her head as she scanned the room vacantly. "You really think I can do it?"

I remember that feeling...the pre-battle nerves when you start doubting everything you've ever done. Shoving Lia's old dagger down into the back of my belt, I turned and gave her a reassuring smile. "I'm sure you could handle more than that, but we'll start there. They'll never expect you to be trained in combat, so you'll be underestimated the whole time. You'll be at a major advantage in that regard. Just remember what you've learned these past few weeks."

I crossed to where she sat at the table and put my hands on her shoulders. "I know that it's scary, Lia. The last thing I ever wanted to do was put you in any sort of danger, but danger has a habit of following me around. I'm truly sorry for that." Taking a deep breath, I let out one final sigh as I began to transition into a tactical mindset. "I swear that I'll do whatever it takes to keep you safe. I have promises to keep, too."

Lia nodded with determination as she blinked away the tears in her eyes. "Okay. I'll do my best to keep you safe too!"

I smiled and gave her a quick hug. "Alright. Stay close to me and don't draw your sword until you need it. We don't want to kill them, so make sure you dull the blade before you use it. Otherwise just stay alert, and don't be afraid to call for help. I'll be right beside you." With that, I opened the door and headed into the hallway with Lia following close behind.

My breathing quickly fell into a deep, measured rhythm as we made our way down to the lobby. *I can't lose control in this fight like I did in the prison. A level head and measured response is infinitely more effective than rage and instinct.* My hand rested comfortably on the pommel of my manasteel sword with my thumb absentmindedly circling the small golden band at its base. Mana was flowing freely throughout my entire body as a result of my breathing technique, some of which I sent down to the runes carved into my blade.

Heighten Senses. Combat Acceleration. I felt the familiar lag of time somewhere in my inner ear as the world slowed and sharpened around me. My mind processed the increased information from my enhanced perception in stride, operating far beyond normal capacity due to the thought acceleration enhancement. I could hear Lia's heartbeat three steps behind me drumming out of control from adrenaline, and the scent of her mint perfume mixed with a fresh layer of sweat. Nothing escaped my notice as we moved; I heard the creak of a floorboard two doors down to our left, smelled the burned bacon wafting up from the stairwell ahead of us, and saw the slight warping due to age of wooden floorboards beneath my feet.

When we rounded the final corner to the common room I quickly scanned over the guards in the corner. I could tell immediately that my suspicions were correct; Both men tensed up when they recognized me, looking at each other with sideways glances. Keeping my face neutral to not alert the guards I continued through the lobby, slowing my pace to allow Lia to walk next to me. I reached down and laced my fingers into hers and pulled her close, trying to offer her some small comfort as we walked out the front door.

The cool morning air was refreshing against my face as we exited the building. A lone guard standing only a few paces to our left did a double take as we walked by, taken off guard by our sudden appearance. My count from before proved accurate as I recounted the soldiers outside: Two to our right on the patio, three grouped together across the street, and a final three patrolling towards us from the left. Looking down the marbled street I could see wagons pulled up to block traffic, two blocks away on either side. *Eleven on two...not the worst odds.*

As we continued down the stairs to the street, a man with slightly more ornate armor than the rest approached from the group opposite us. Whereas the rest of the men wore unadorned steel armor, this presumed captain had a breastplate etched and painted with a crest I had seen multiple times around the city of Yoria: an ornate golden throne superimposed atop a crescent moon shaped stained glass window. He stood a full head taller than me with close cropped salt-and-pepper hair and silvery grey eyes, wielding a spiked mace and a tower shield emblazoned with the same Yorian emblem.

"You there!" He barked out, his voice thick with gravel. "Stop where you are!"

I took one final step off the curb into the street and stopped. My battlefield bravado was fully upon me now as I presented a friendly, confident smile. "Good morning! How can I help you, good sir?" The clinking of metal and soft scuffing of boots told me that the two guards from the lobby had joined the door lookout, and the three had approached within five paces. The two men from the patio had stood from their chairs as we passed and were now moving up as well, circling to my right.

"By order of the Golden Throne, you are to immediately accompany us to the capitol city Yoria to await judgement!" The man spoke slowly with a voice that seemed accustomed to command.

With an overexaggerated grimace I sharply inhaled. "Oooh, that's going to be an issue. You see, I have plans to travel to Lybesa. I've heard it's lovely this time of year, and I don't want to miss out on the sightseeing." Pulling Lia closer behind me, I casually turned to observe the men to our rear. They each stood with a hand on their military standard longswords, eyeing us cautiously. The rest of the men in front of us were armed the same way, save for the two guards flanking the captain who held large crossbows. "Perhaps I can come visit the throne later?"

The captain glowered as his eyes flicked down to look at Lia. "Girl, step away from this man, or you'll be charged with obstructing the will of the Throne!"

"No! He hasn't done anything wrong!" Lia's voice was loud but shaky as she hollered back at the captain. He looked surprised by the response.

"We have orders to bring this man in alive. That same courtesy does not extend to conspirators," the captain bristled. Lia refused to move, staring out at him defiantly from behind my shoulder. After an uncomfortable moment of silence, he grunted. "Have it your way." Motioning to the men positioned behind us the captain hollered, "Take her to the wagons. She'll stand trial after this one."

Turning calmly to Lia, I placed my free hand on her shoulder. "It's time," I whispered softly into her ear. "Just do your best, Lia. I believe in you." She nodded, her face changing from one of fear to hard determination. One of the three guards positioned behind us approached slowly.

"Come with me, girl," The man called out to her, extending a hand to grab her shoulder. Lia lunged towards him, grabbing his arm as she twirled to face me. In one swift movement she curled forward and yanked down hard on his trapped limb, which sent him flipping over her back to land stunned on his side against the hard marble. I heard the breath get knocked from his chest and the faint crunch of bone as one of his ribs fractured. Without missing a beat, Lia sent a vicious kick at his head, knocking him onto his side where he landed in an unmoving pile.

A grin spread across my face as I watched the scene unfold in slow motion. Taking one final centering breath, I exhaled hard and snapped around to survey the field. *Two to the right, close to flanking Lia. Three more, fifteen paces to the left. Two at range with lever crossbows, behind the commander.* As my adrenaline kicked in time slowed to a crawl as I analyzed my options. *Disable the flanking group. Run wide to draw the crossbow fire, opening a fifteen second reload window to engage the left group. Ground the commander, deal with the bowman, and then engage the commander head on.*

Windstep. Greater Agility. Blunted Blade. A beautifully synchronized ring echoed across the empty street as Lia and I drew our swords in unison. *She can do this.* I gave her one last look over my shoulder, watching as she lowered into her practiced combat stance with her sword held out at the ready. Even in the midst of a battle, I felt a great surge of pride in how far Lia had come in such a short time. *She can do this.*

I spun to face the two men on my right, rushing them with unnatural speed. Both of the guards had begun to draw their weapons when Lia kicked her first target unconscious, but I closed the gap between us before the blades had left their sheaths. I took the first man in the side of the head with the flat of my blade, sending him careening towards his partner. The force of the impact threatened to topple them both, but the second man was able to disentangle himself from his injured comrade and fully draw his weapon as I advanced.

Unfortunately for him his stance was sloppy, with his feet far too close together for efficient movement. His first easily dodged swing set him off balance, leaving me a perfect window to slide into close range and loop my sword arm up under his armpit. My free hand flew up to his forehead as I kicked out the back of his knees, sending him cartwheeling past me. The torque on his pinned shoulder dislocated the joint with a sickening pop as he fell. He screamed as he crashed hard onto his face and toppled head over heels into a crumpled heap.

My mind raced as hundreds of important bits of information accosted me from all sides. My first target was unconscious, and the second wouldn't be rising in time to see the end of battle. Swords clashed from where Lia engaged her two targets, but her steady breathing and the sliding of her feet across the marble informed me she was in control for now. Three pairs of heavy footfalls headed my direction from the street, and the captain was shouting at his bowmen to open fire.

I heard the two small clicks followed by the whir of bowstrings as I dove forward, rolling in a tight arc on my shoulder. The bolts whizzed past me to clatter angrily against the wall of the inn far to my rear. *They're reloading. Window open.* With the ranged threat momentarily out of play I took to my feet and sprinted to meet the approaching group head on. The two in front both sent overhead blows at my face while the man behind them stumbled, unsure of how to leverage a clean blow at me without hitting his friends.

Supporting the flat of my blade with my free hand I caught both swings above my head simultaneously. I leaned hard to the right, letting both blows slide off the end of my weapon, using the momentum from the deflected strikes to spin past my attackers to the man behind them. My blade whirled in a horizontal arc as I spun, catching the third man by surprise. It completely crushed the side of his breastplate as the full weight of the blunted weapon connected, sending him to the ground with a ragged gasp.

The men turned to catch me, lashing out with their longswords. I narrowly avoided the blows with a quick backstep, watching a blade hiss by my face deadly fast. I could hear the bowmen scrambling to reload their crossbows, wrenching against the heavy draw levers. *Eleven seconds.* Lashing out in a wide arc, I opened enough distance between myself and my current attackers to draw the practice sword in my offhand. "Is five on one not good enough odds for you?" I taunted cockily. "Why don't you try actually hitting me this time?"

My goading proved successful as both men roared out a frustrated battle cry and doubled their assault. I parried each blow in turn, waiting for an exploitable mistake. *Six seconds.* Finally, the error came: The guard to my right overextended himself with a brutal two-handed strike that sent him stumbling past me. Catching the other man's attack on my training blade, I dropped my bastard sword into a reverse grip and punched him hard in the face with the crossguard. A brilliant red spray painted the flawless marble behind him as his nose and mouth exploded with blood.

Capitalizing on my advantage, I turned and slashed down with both weapons at the unbloodied guard. He tried to catch the attack on his sword but was instantly overpowered, which sent his own sword smashing down onto his forehead. I saw his eyes roll into the back of his head as the blow knocked him out cold. *Three seconds.* The bowmen were throwing their levers to the ground and attempting to load a bolt into the weapons. *Not enough time. New plan.*

I could hear Lia fighting somewhere behind me, now in a one on one match with the last remaining guard. The captain was closing in on me now, apparently tired of watching his men fail in their efforts to put me down. In the back of my mind I heard an odd scraping sound coming from near the inn that I couldn't place, but I didn't have time to look back, so I filed it away to process with the less important sensory input. With a flying leap I punched the last standing guard a second time just as he regained enough composure to face me again. A wet squelch came from his ruined face as he fell still onto the bloody marble.

Sheathing the practice blade quickly I gripped my manasteel sword in both hands. The captain beat his mace against the side of his shield as he approached, most likely an attempt to intimidate me. *Time's up.* I took cover from the archers behind the one available option I had in the middle of the street: the commander. Standing side face, I placed myself in cover behind his tower shield, out of a safe firing line from the bowmen. Somewhere the scraping sound continued, a faint scratch of metal against stone. Part of me knew the sound should worry me, although I didn't know why.

The heavy bang of the mace renewed my focus. *As long as I keep him between me and the archers, they'll never risk shooting him to hit me.* To my dismay, the captain sneered and began to circle around me with his shield raised, clearly understanding my strategy and using it against me. It put me at a disadvantage to move towards his protected side, but I was intimately familiar with the damage a crossbow bolt could do and had no plans to experience it again.

Scrape. Scrape. The soft grating was still present, barely loud enough to reach my ears with my enhanced senses. I stepped in with a two-handed strike leveled at the captain's head, which connected hard against his raised shield. With a low growl he pushed back against my blade, separating us again. *This is going to be a battle of endurance. If I can keep the pressure on, he'll tire out and make a mistake soon enough.*

Scrape. Scrape. He followed up with a rising swing of his mace, forcing me to dodge towards his shielded side again. My forced position was maddening; I knew I could end the fight in mere moments if I could just circle to his weak side, but he knew how to work his advantage effectively. I planted a firm kick center mass on his shield which sent him skidding back a few paces. Chasing him in, I swung another heavy blow upwards to clip the edge of his shield.

The captain grimaced in response to the intense pressure on his defending arm. His eyes flicked back and forth from me to a point in the distance behind me. *Lia.* I could hear her grunting from exertion, sending powerful blows at the final standing guard who was clearly outclassed. From just beside their skirmish I heard the continual scraping sound moving towards them. My stomach dropped as I finally pieced together what my brain had been trying to tell me.

I turned just in time to watch as the first guard Lia had knocked down reached her, having dragged himself slowly across the patio in near silence aside from the soft scraping of his armor on the marble. He sprang at Lia in a tackle, knocking her legs out from underneath her which sent her tumbling forward. The guard she had been fighting kicked her sword away and reached down roughly to pull her up by her hair. She cried out in pain and kicked violently, catching the man on the ground in the face for a second time.

"That's enough!" The captain shouted at his men. With a quick hand signal, he sent his archers ahead to take up two positions with clear shots at Lia, who was now held in a tight headlock. "Surrender now, or the girl dies." His eyes were hard as ice, fully convincing me that he would give the command should I refuse.

"Lux, run!" Lia screamed, struggling against the guard fruitlessly. "Just run!"

An alarming sense of calm washed over me. I knew the consequences that would come from continuing to resist. If I wanted to, I could kill the captain with a deadly quick blow to the neck while his guard was down. It would be easy to clean up the rest of the guards as well, but I wouldn't be able to save Lia. In turn, I knew what would happen if I surrendered. Lia and I would be put in chains and shipped back to Yoria. There, I would be sent before whoever sat on the Golden Throne to face judgement for my crimes.

It would all be a farce, of course. The real reason I was being summoned, and the reason I was kept in the dungeons, was to be recruited to aid in whatever devastating conflict the country of Kaldan was currently embroiled in. For the third time in as many lives, the world was sending me down the path of bloodshed and loss without giving me a choice. The memory of those injustices I had suffered usually evoked a burning rage inside me, but my head was clear.

"I promise that I will do everything I can to protect the people who can't protect themselves." My own words came back to me as a crystal-clear memory, filling my heart with resolve. *"I promise that I'll stop those injustices wherever I find them."* My decision was already made, but my mind hadn't caught up to realize it yet.

Why should I play along again? This world has done nothing but attack and harass me at every opportunity. The faster it burns down, the better. I tried to convince myself I didn't care, but deep down I knew it wasn't true. Relenting to the inevitable pull of the world now would only bring me grief, pain, and hardship. There was something worth saving here, and it depended entirely upon my next actions. Lia was staring across the patio at me with tears streaming down her face, shaking her head.

"*I promise it, no matter the cost I have to pay.*" My arms relaxed to my sides as I let my sword drop to the ground. Slowly, I unhooked my belt and threw it forward into a pile, relinquishing the last of my weapons. I gently knelt to the marble street and looked up to the captain towering over me. "Don't hurt her. Please."

He gave me a curt nod and motioned to his men. The two bowmen came to his sides and patted me down, placing me in manacles when they were satisfied I wasn't concealing any additional weapons. At the sight of my surrender Lia stopped fighting as well, falling limp in the arms of the guard who restrained her. He locked her in chains and led her across the street to where I was knelt. Surveying the scene one last time, the captain nodded and led the way down the marble street to the wagon barricades.

As the guards led me down the street, a dumb grin spread across my face. For the first time since I arrived outside the walls of Yoria, I had a clear purpose. Even though I was walking towards a fate certain to be full of suffering and turmoil, I had a goal now. *There is one thing in this world worth protecting.* I watched Lia shuffling along meekly in front of me, half obscured by a guard. *No matter what happens, I'm going to protect her. I pulled Lia into this alongside me, and I'm going to bring her out. No matter the cost.*

"I'll do it for you, Amaya."

***

Author's Note

    I never in a million years would have thought I would be sitting here writing an author's note for the end of a book I wrote, but here we are. If you're reading this, I'd like to sincerely thank you for reading this novel. Writing has always been a hobby of mine, but it was something I kept to myself or shared with a few close friends. It's a bit frightening to be putting the finishing touches on this project that'll soon be released for anyone and everyone to read and criticize, but I had a lot of fun writing this, so I think it's time I put myself out there a bit!

    With that being said, I hope you enjoyed the preceding pages. If you're wondering what's next for Lia and Lux, don't worry! Book two is already well under way. Things are just getting started, and I plan on writing this story out to the very end. Whether you stick around or not is up to you, but I hope you'll stay along on this journey with me. As I'm just a hobbyist with a full-time job, I can't promise that the books will come at any sort of reasonable pace, but believe me when I say I'm always working on it in one way or another.

    I'd like to indulge myself for a moment and thank a few people who were instrumental to this whole project happening. Sam, thanks for keeping me going when the book was still in its infancy, and a full book was just a ridiculous dream. Maria, thank you for taking the time to edit my work, and for teaching me how to be a semi-competent writer (I hope!). Don and Trevor, the feedback you gave helped to encourage me to pursue actually publishing my work. Kyle, thanks for lending me your artistic talents to make everything look presentable and book-like. This one's for all of you!

    Anyways, I'll put a cap on the rambling for now. If you liked what you read, keep your eyes peeled for Volume Two, coming out just as soon as it's finished! Thanks again for reading.

    ~Adam

Made in the USA
Middletown, DE
11 April 2020